My Cousin Jane

By the same author

A Pressing Engagement

My Cousin Jane

Barbara Bell

ROBERT HALE · LONDON

First published in Great Britain 2008

ISBN 978-0-7090-8371-9

Robert Hale Limited
Clerkenwell House
Clerkenwell Green
London EC1R 0HT

www.halebooks.com

2 4 6 8 10 9 7 5 3 1

Typeset in 10½/13pt Sabon
Printed and bound in Great Britain by
Biddles Limited, King's Lynn

For Theresa Yirka Crow,
sister-in-law *par excellence* and good friend—
a rare and precious combination

Cast, in order of appearance

* Lord Simon Talent
* Marcus Crowne, the Viscount Stedford, Simon's friend
Jane Burch, cousin to
Winifred Timburton
Gerard Burch, Jane's brother
Harry Bridgeworth, Gerard's friend
Charles Drummond, the Earl of Wye, Simon's friend
* Lady Felicity Talent, Simon's sister
* Annabelle, Lady Teague, Simon's aunt
Sir James Beemish, Harry's uncle
Lady Hermione Stickleford, a visitor at Selworth
Gertrude, Lady Wimpole, Lady Hermione's mother
* Jared Talent, the Marquess of Chamford, Simon's brother
* Diana, Lady Talent, Jared's wife

* appeared in an earlier novel, entitled *A Pressing Engagement*

Prologue

Paris, The Palais Royale
October, 1817

It was coming up on three o'clock in the morning, and the usual tumult reigned in *Le Cochon d'Or*. Card games were underway in dark corners, some boisterous and contentious, others silent and intense. The gleam of dice flashed in other shadowy nooks, and throughout the premises, painted denizens of the *demimonde* circled for prey, their shopworn charms lavishly exposed in cheap satins and grimy lace. The noisy clink of tankards and glasses provided a background for their peregrinations, as waiters scurried to ply their already sodden patrons with various potent beverages.

The clientele of the Gold Pig was a mixed lot. The nobility of several countries rubbed shoulders with the dregs of Parisian society, for the establishments of the Palais Royale catered to all, the only requirement being a taste for the sordid and the money to pay for it. Thus, the gentleman who entered at that moment, seemed oddly out of place.

He was tall and slender and impeccably garbed in correct evening wear, but it was not his appearance that set him apart from those already availing themselves of the Gold Pig's dubious hospitality. It was, perhaps, the clean line of his jaw and the quiet but undeniable air of strength in his gaze that distinguished him from the bleary-eyed habitués seated at the sticky tables scattered about the room.

Two thickset men dressed in workmen's garb eyed him speculatively as he strode into the room, but settled back immediately into their chairs, recalled to prudence by the tautly muscled frame evident beneath the gentleman's elegant exterior.

He remained for a moment in the doorway, surveying the crowd, before his attention was caught by a small altercation at a table in a far corner.

'Lord,' he whispered. 'I might have known. There he is.'

Pausing only to murmur a courteous, softly spoken refusal to the hopeful tart who approached him upon his entrance, he moved toward the disturbance, at the center of which was a thin, foppish young man, more than somewhat the worse for drink. His shrill voice was raised in whining uncertainty to a burly fellow who loomed over him menacingly.

'I tell you, Villedon, I paid!' the fop squealed in execrable French. 'I paid her full price and then some, and if she told you any different, the slut is lying! Forty sous I gave her – and I bought her dinner and wine, too.'

'You mewling little weasel,' growled the other man. 'Lisette is one of my best girls, and to me she does not lie. It is you who speak false.' He raised a boulderlike fist, and the fop cringed.

The gentleman sighed, and having reached the perimeter of the dispute, placed his hand on the young man's sleeve.

'Wilfred—' he began, and the young man swung about.

'Simon! Good God, what are you doing here?' he cried. 'By all that's holy, I'm glad you've come.' He jerked a thumb toward the other combatant. 'This *merde de tête* is trying to chouse me out of ten louis.' He straightened with a pitiful assumption of authority and turned to face his accuser. 'You had best be on your way, Villedon. Your little charade has been amusing, but unproductive,' he concluded with a cocky smile.

Enraged, the huge man advanced with both fists upraised, and Wilfred dodged behind his protector. 'Simon!' he shrieked. 'Do something! He's going to kill me!'

Unperturbed, the gentleman faced the man named Villedon, also called *Le Sanglier* – the Wild Boar. 'Monsieur, we seem to be party to a misunderstanding here, but I'm sure—'

'There is no misunderstanding,' snarled Le Sanglier, his broad face black with anger. 'This sniveling *belette* has cheated me for the last time. He will pay what he owes me or I will separate his ugly head from his scrawny neck.'

Emboldened, Wilfred waved a finger in Villedon's face. 'I owe you nothing, you fat pig!'

The folly of this course of action was proved almost immediately as Villedon drew a murderous-looking knife from beneath his coat.

Undaunted, Wilfred sneered at his foe. 'If I were you, you slimy toad, I'd be very careful how you go about threatening honest citizens.'

As Villedon gestured meaningfully with the knife, Wilfred once more leaped to safety. 'Do you have any idea who you're dealing with?'

Exasperated, the gentleman turned to glare at the fop. 'Wilfred, for God's sake, this is not the time to—'

'I do not care if your grand friend is the King of Prussia,' Villedon growled. 'No one speaks to me thus, particularly you English, who are of a stupidity unbelievable.'

In rapid, fluent idiomatic French, the gentleman spoke to Villedon. 'Monsieur, you must see that battling with this *canaille* is beneath your dignity. I do not doubt that you are in the right, and that poor Wilfred does indeed owe you. As he says, however, he is my friend, and I shall pay his debt.'

At this, Villedon subsided somewhat, and although he retained the knife in his hand, his expression lightened minimally.

'Fifty sous,' he said, 'and the little English weasel does not go near Lisette again.'

'You are being more than reasonable, monsieur,' replied the gentleman smoothly. 'It shall be as you say.'

He withdrew his purse from his waistcoat, only to be stayed by an indignant Wilfred.

'Simon! You can't mean to pay the fellow off.' Once more, he moved drunkenly in front of Simon to wave his fingers in Villedon's face. 'How dare the likes of you demand money from my friend. We shall have you up on charges. We'll—'

'Wilfred, shut up,' said the gentleman harshly. To Villedon, he said quickly, 'Please pay him no mind, he is not himself tonight. As you have observed, he is not very bright, and—'

'*I* am not very bright! Hah!' Wilfred waggled his fingers again. 'It is you who is of a stupidity *incroyable*, you great ape. I've been tupping Lisette for weeks on the sly with you none the wiser. What do you think about that?'

Instantly, Le Sanglier lunged forward with an unintelligible howl. In that moment, it seemed to Simon that time halted, and seconds passed with interminable slowness. He grasped Villedon's arm and with surprising strength, began to force the assailant backward. At the same time, Wilfred uttered a piercing scream and tried to scurry once more behind his friend. Stumbling, he fell against Simon, breaking his grip on Villedon's arm, which swept forward in a murderous arc, directly toward Simon's breast. Wilfred, still struggling to retain his balance, fell forward into its path. The next moment the knife found its mark in Wilfred's brandy-soaked shirtfront.

In the frozen instant that followed, Wilfred gazed down in astonishment at the brightly blossoming stain, before collapsing in his friend's arms. Villedon's eyes widened in realization of what he had done, and after only a moment's hesitation, he bowled his way to the door through the paralyzed crowd, vanishing into the night.

'Wilfred,' whispered the gentleman in horror, cradling the younger man in his arms. 'My God! Wilfred!'

Wilfred's face rapidly took on the unmistakably grayish hue of death but, oddly, a faint smile curved his weak mouth.

'I think I'm for it, Simon,' he gasped faintly.

'No,' said Simon soothingly. 'Look, someone has gone for a doctor, and in—'

Wilfred raised his hand in a trembling gesture of negation.

'No, I've done it this time, and it's probably all to the good, considering.' He shifted in an effort to look into Simon's face, and a groan escaped his bloodless lips. 'You'll take care of ... of everything, won't you, old boy?'

Simon nodded, at a loss for words, and with an obvious effort, Wilfred continued. 'You're the best friend a man ever had, Simon. Y'saved my bacon for me – before. I'll never forget that.' He grimaced, but in the next moment, the smile had returned, widening as a thought struck him. 'By God, I saved your life tonight, didn't I?'

'Yes,' answered Simon softly. 'Yes, you did, Wilf. You put yourself in between Villedon and me.' If Simon recalled that the younger man had stumbled into the path of the knife through his own clumsiness, none of this showed on his impassive features.

'So now ...' Wilfred's voice was growing weaker, '... you are in debt to me, are you not?'

'Of course, Wilfred, but try not to talk. The doctor—'

'Bother the doctor. By the time he gets here, I'll have cocked up my toes. Listen, Simon,' he grated, brushing ineffectually at the trickle of blood that appeared at the corner of his mouth, 'do you remember the matter we were speaking of?'

'The...? Oh. Oh yes, of course, but—'

'I know you don't like the idea, but now that you're in my debt, you have no choice. Do you?' he added, feebly clutching at Simon's coat. 'Promise me you'll do as I ask.'

'Wilfred, I can't. You must see that.'

'Yes, you can.' The young man coughed weakly. 'Simon, I'm dying here – swimming in my life's blood, for God's sake! You can't deny a man his last wish! I ... I'm your friend!'

Simon hesitated as Wilfred's eyes closed, his lashes a dirty smear against his white face. They fluttered open again, gazing with bleary anguish into Simon's countenance.

'Simon, I beg you. I know I did not do right by her, and you – you must make it up. You *must*.'

Wilfred's head lolled back and his breathing subsided into harsh gasps of pain. Simon placed his hand beneath the young man's head, his own gaze falling beneath the agony in the other's.

There was a moment's silence as Wilfred held his friend's gaze, until at last Simon whispered, 'All right, Wilfred. I'll do it.'

Wilfred was panting now with the effort it took to breathe, but at this, he started eagerly. His fingers plucked at Simon's waistcoat. 'You promise?' he whispered.

Simon bent his head toward his young friend. 'I promise, Wilf. Word of honor. I'll do all that you asked.'

Satisfied, Wilfred turned a radiant smile on Simon. 'Thank you, old fellow.' The smile fell from his lips suddenly, to be replaced by another painful spasm. His blood, which had been spilling with ghastly steadiness, soaked Simon's coat and pooled on to the floor.

'Looks like it's time, then.' A rasping laugh shuddered through him, causing a froth of blood to bubble around his mouth. 'Must say I prefer going this way than the other. If you—'

But the sentence was never finished. Wilfred jerked in one last spasm. His hand clutched Simon's, and his tortured breathing stilled.

Oblivious to the shocked exclamations of the onlookers that surrounded him, Simon knelt on the filthy floor for a long moment, the young man's still form cradled in his arm. At last, he uttered a long, shuddering sigh, and with infinite tenderness, laid his burden on the floor. He reached with gentle fingers to tousle Wilfred's mouse-colored hair.

'Dear Lord, Wilfred,' he murmured softly. 'You unconscionable little bounder, you've really landed me in the suds this time.'

One

'Full of vexation come I, with complaint ...'
—A Midsummer Night's Dream, I, i.

I *don't want to be here. I do not want to be here. I do* not, *by God, want to be here!*

The words trooped wearily through Lord Simon Talent's mind in a litany that had repeated itself endlessly over the last day and a half. He gazed out through the window of his elegant traveling coach, but the beautiful landscape of Hampshire, with its rolling green downs and grassy valleys failed to soothe. His fingers raked through hair the color of mahogany, and his chocolate-brown eyes sparked as he dwelled on the injustice that had been done him.

'For Lord's sake, Simon, that's the hundredth time you've said that in the last hour.'

Simon started, not realizing that he had spoken aloud, and he gazed sourly at the young man who sprawled across the seat opposite him in the elegant carriage. Marcus Crowne, the Viscount Stedford, provided a startling contrast to Simon's compact elegance, being very tall and composed mostly of angles. His curling, light blond hair and snub-nosed features were counted part of his charm, putting most observers in mind of a mischievous schoolboy, despite the fact that he was three and twenty. At the moment, however, the young man's insouciant grin produced nothing more than a surge of irritation in Simon.

'Oh, put a sock in it, Marc,' he growled. 'You're not the one being sent on a fool's errand.'

Marcus lifted his brows. 'Good God, you're on your way to claim an estate that was virtually handed to you. I'd hardly call that a fool's errand.'

'You're forgetting Winifred,' Simon replied balefully, immediately experiencing a twinge of compunction. He could hardly expect Marc to understand his dilemma, for they'd been acquainted for less than a week, despite the fact that they were in-laws of a sort. His brother, Jared, had married Marcus's sister, Diana. They had only become acquainted after Simon's recent return home after a three-year absence.

'Ah, yes,' said Marcus with a grin, 'your benefactor's little sister. Your ward.'

'My ward,' echoed Simon gloomily.

'What is she like?'

'Who? Oh – Winifred? I have no idea – never met her, you know. If she's anything like her big brother, however, the briefer my dealings with her the better.'

'Come now, Simon. The man left you what was probably his most cherished possession – to say nothing of the guardianship of one who must have been dear to him. Being a little harsh, ain't you?'

Simon uttered a muffled snort. 'If only you'd known the fellow. Just why the Creator saw fit to inflict Wilfred Timburton on an already beleaguered planet is a mystery to me. He was a stupid, pompous, whining ass, and a coward to boot.' Observing Marc's startled expression, he added, 'And I haven't got started on his really serious flaws.'

'But, how is it you became friends with this – specimen?' asked Marc, chuckling.

'We served together in the Peninsula. I lost my head one day and saved his life.' Simon frowned furiously at the sound of Marc's ill-contained laughter. 'It was during the battle of Vitoria,' he continued. 'I merely happened to be near him when he stood up when he shouldn't have. I pulled him off his feet just as someone was firing on him. After that, the fellow attached himself to me like a snail to a petunia. Somehow, he survived Waterloo, after which I thought he'd retreat to hearth and home and I'd be rid of him. But no. When I was taken on by Lord Symington to work on Castlereagh's staff in Paris, young Wilf decided that life on the Continent would suit him right down to the ground. There he was my best friend in the world – or so he told everyone – and his intimations that I did not so much as choose my waistcoat without his approval almost ruined my fledgling career in world diplomacy. The fellow was an absolute laughingstock.'

'Why didn't you simply tell him to go away?' asked Marc carelessly.

Simon shrugged. 'I suppose it's because he would have been devastated. There was no real evil in him, after all. He wanted so desperately to be thought a prime go – top o' the trees, and all that.'

'I see your point. Still, you must have gone out of your way to encourage him, if he made you the beneficiary of his will.'

'I swear to God, Marc, I merely remained civil to him – which many did not. When he told me of his idiotic plan to leave me all his worldly goods – and his blasted sister, to boot – I argued and pleaded till my tongue shriveled, all to no avail.'

'Mmm. I see now what Diana meant when she told me of your, er, pronounced sense of duty. She said Jared told her you were always bringing home strays, and that you could always be depended on to dance with all the wallflowers at the ball.'

'Your sister is too kind,' returned Simon stiffly.

'You told me how Wilfred died – the disgruntled pimp and all that. Lord, did he not know enough to take his pleasures elsewhere than the Palais Royale?' Marcus, who had been born and raised in Paris, grimaced.

'No,' replied Simon. 'Wilfred had no sense at all. Which was, perhaps, how he happened to contract the French disease.'

'How fortunate,' said Marcus unsteadily, 'that he was knifed to death before parts of him began falling off. But never mind that. Tell me, how did the sister come into it?'

Simon groaned. 'Wilfred's mother died when the children were small. His father remarried about ten years ago and turned up his toes five years after that. When Wilfred went away from Selworth, Winifred was left—'

'My God,' Marc interjected in an awed tone, 'Wilfred and Winifred. Timburton *père* has a great deal to answer for, doesn't he?'

'In more ways than one,' was Simon's heartfelt reply. 'As I was saying, Winifred was left on her own with the stepmother, a woman named Millicent. Wilfred warned me about Millicent, who is a former stage actress, and according to Wilf, a wicked, scheming harpy who inveigled their father into marrying her. When the old man died, Wilfred became concerned about his sister. He considered Millicent the last person in the world to be entrusted with the rearing of an innocent young maid. In fact,' added Simon with a visible shudder, 'it was Wilf's dearest wish that I marry Winifred, thus solving his problems.'

'If he was so concerned,' asked Marc, 'why did he join the army instead of staying home to protect the damsel's virtue?'

Simon laughed shortly. 'Good question. Apparently, his concern did not extend to inconveniencing himself. You see, our Wilfie quite fancied himself in a uniform.'

Marc threw up his hands. 'Good God,' he murmured.

'Quite. In any event, Millicent is no longer a threat to Winifred's virtue. When I visited the family agent, George Soapes, in London a couple of weeks ago, he informed me that the woman ran off with a raffish baronet from Bath not a month ago, and is currently residing with him in Italy.'

At this, Marc succumbed once more to laughter. 'Lord,' he gasped, 'this just gets better and better. "A raffish baronet from Bath" – it sounds like the first line of a particularly racy limerick.'

'I'm pleased to have provided you with amusement,' Simon returned frigidly.

Marcus, unfazed, flung up his hand. 'I don't understand why you're in the dismals over all this. It sounds like a marvelous lark. I should think it would be just what you're looking for after rusticating at Stonefield with Jared and Diana since you returned from Paris. I mean, your brother is a fine fellow as marquesses go, but Lord!' Marc's blue eyes sparkled. 'Don't you miss the excitement on the Continent?'

'No, I do not,' Simon said wearily. 'I have had enough excitement to last me a lifetime, and all I want in the world is to settle into the life of a country squire.'

'Ah, well,' said Marc, 'perhaps it will not be as bad as you foresee. In fact, you might enjoy yourself.' He waved a hand toward the view to be seen through the window. 'The countryside is beautiful, and you'll have plenty of time to find a husband for your heiress, and – what?' he asked, as Simon closed his eyes, apparently in pain.

'That's just it, I have precious little time. I have not told you the worst part. Just before Wilfred died, I – I promised that if I did not get her wed within six months, I would marry her myself.'

'What?' Marc leaned forward in astonishment.

'Either that, or Selworth and all the rest of Wilfred's estate will go to charity.'

'But – but—' Marc stuttered in puzzlement. 'If you don't want the place yourself, what difference would that make to you?'

'Good God, what kind of a monster do you take me for? It would mean leaving Winifred destitute and without protection. She has very little money of her own, you see, her father assuming that Wilfred would take care of her. I may wish to strangle the chit, but I can't very well throw her out into the snow.'

'Well – you say that her inheritance from Wilfred is sizeable. Surely you can dragoon someone into marrying her within that time.'

'Yes, I suppose I could, but I cannot in all conscience see her wed to someone who is completely unsuitable.'

Marc chuckled. 'Wilfred certainly knew his man. He chose the one person among his acquaintances whom he knew to be so honorable that he could be suborned with impunity.'

Simon flushed. 'That may be,' he said stiffly, 'but look where it's got me.'

'Still,' said Marcus, 'you have six months. Surely within that time you should be able to dredge up a suitable *parti*. Perhaps the fair Winifred is already smitten with one of the local sprigs.'

'I fervently hope so,' replied Simon, 'for I haven't got six months. You see, I thought the period was to start after I took up residence at Selworth, but I was informed by Soapes, the family man of affairs, that the clock started as soon as Wilfred passed on to his dubious reward.' He threw up his hands. 'My good fellow, I now have precisely five weeks to get Winifred down the center aisle.'

'Oh, my God,' said Marc, digesting this information. 'Does Winifred know of all this?'

'No. She knows that I am her guardian, of course, and that I have control of all the money she will supposedly inherit from Wilfred. But she thinks she will automatically receive that sum in total when she reaches the age of six and twenty – which is as it was originally stipulated, before Wilfred got this maggot in his brain about my taking her on as my life's work.'

'Do you mean to tell her?' asked Marc, fascinated.

'Good God, no. I plan to keep my relationship with her as businesslike as possible. I don't want to muddy the waters by introducing myself to her as a possible *parti*.'

'Lord, yes,' said Marc, with a barely suppressed chuckle, 'why would she want to look elsewhere for a lifemate when she has handsome, wealthy Lord Simon Talent on the horizon?'

'You really find this whole situation little more than a three-act farce, don't you?' exclaimed Simon indignantly.

'I'm sorry, old man.' Marcus chuckled. 'It's just that it all seems so – bizarre.'

'Yes,' Simon said with a despairing sigh, 'I suppose that's precisely the word.' He leaned forward and allowed his head to sink into his hands. 'I keep wondering just what it is I've done to deserve all this.'

When Marc said nothing, Simon, weary of the subject, straightened. 'And how about you, my Lord Stedford? Your decision to join me on my travels was rather sudden – not that your company has not been welcome.'

The laughter fled suddenly from Marc's face and he flushed. 'Oh. Well. That is to say – I have been staying close to home since I acceded to the title – and ... I have an estate north of here that I have never visited. When I learned of your journey in that direction, it seemed like a good opportunity to, uh, to do a little traveling myself.' He shot an oddly speculative glance at Simon.

'Ah,' said Simon noncommittally, 'I was wondering if your sudden wanderlust had anything to do with Lissa.'

Marc jerked upright. 'Lissa?' The word emerged in a strained squeak. 'Why, no, that is ...' His jaw squared pugnaciously. 'If you don't mind, I'd rather not talk about Lissa.'

Startled, Simon lifted his hand in a gesture of withdrawal. 'Certainly, old man – no wish to pry.'

'No-no, of course not,' replied Marc hastily. 'It's just that – Lissa is enough to drive a man to Bedlam – if you don't mind my saying so. Don't wish to speak ill of a man's sister.'

'No, indeed.' Simon laughed. 'You're not telling me anything I don't already know. I'm fully aware of her shortcomings.'

Curious as to the source of Marc's displeasure, Simon would have said more, but was forestalled as Marc said hastily, 'Look! Up ahead. Those stone pillars must mark the beginning of the Selworth property. If the directions we received at the posting house are accurate, we should be – ah. Here we are,' he finished, as the carriage turned off the road to wheel through a massive stone gate.

'Mmph,' grunted Simon. 'Left wide open for just anybody. Not a soul in the lodge house. Soapes told me the estate was in the hands of a competent manager, but it doesn't look like—'

'Oh, stubble it. Are you going to begin finding fault before we're even inside the house?'

Disgruntled, Simon leaned back and allowed his gaze to wander over the green manicured parkland that formed a welcoming vista. In the distance, a young boy could be seen racing over the hills on a sleek bay. Simon frowned. Wilfred had not mentioned a boy. Could the youngster be a stablehand? If so, it seemed a talk with the head groom would be in order regarding the manner in which the hands exercised the horses. A full-out gallop was hardly— He caught himself. Marc was right. There was no point in looking for things to criticize. Hopefully Soapes had been correct – the place was well run and could be put up for sale as soon as he could get Winifred off his hands.

There was the house at last. Marc must have caught sight of it, too, for he echoed Simon's, 'Good God!' It was an extraordinarily beautiful dwelling, lying in a fold of earth. Like a lovely woman awaiting her lover, it spread arms of glowing Cotswold stone on either side of a serenely graceful portico. Unwillingly, Simon experienced a stir of anticipation as they approached the building.

From atop her massive bay gelding, Jane Burch watched the carriage as it approached the house. Leaning into the wind, she urged her mount to even greater speed, and an unladylike epithet slipped from her generously curved lips.

It had to be him in that carriage – Lord Simon Talent, even though they had not expected him until much later in the day. Hell and damnation!

The carriage disappeared from view, hidden by the spreading wings of the manor house, and Jane wheeled the horse about toward the back of the building. Galloping into the stable yard, she barely waited for the animal to come to a halt before leaping to the ground. Tossing the reins to the groom who hastened to meet her, she said breathlessly, 'Please, Musgrove, I'm in a fearful hurry. Will you rub Talavera down for me?' A quick, grateful smile lit her wide gray eyes before she turned away, her fingers working at her shirt buttons as she ran into the house.

'Winifred!' she called, savoring the shadowed coolness inside the house as she raced through the service passageways and into the great hall. 'Winifred!'

By the time she had negotiated the wide staircase that rose from the hall, Jane had finished with the shirt buttons, and when she slammed the door of her bedchamber behind her, she had begun on the fastenings of her breeches.

'Oh! Hannah!' she gasped in greeting to the comfortably plump woman who appeared from another chamber. 'Where the devil is Winifred?'

'Language, Miss Jane!' replied the woman austerely. 'Miss Winifred went to the village this morning with Mrs Mycombe and Miss Emily. She said she'd be back before luncheon.'

Breathing more unladylike epithets, Jane shrugged from the shirt and breeches and, delving into a nearby wardrobe, emerged some moments later with an odd contraption that resembled a cross between a tailor's dummy and a full set of horse tack. With the assistance of Hannah, her maid of some fifteen years, she slid into the apparatus and commenced arranging and buckling until by the time she whirled with lifted brows for the older woman's inspection, she had been transformed from a lithe, slender young woman to a flat-chested, thick-waisted frump. Reaching once more into the wardrobe, she produced a gown of plain, gray muslin, which she hastily slipped over her shoulders.

'There,' she said a little breathlessly. 'Am I put together?'

'I suppose,' said the maid in a tone of vast disapproval, 'you could say that. You are a complete dowd. Except, you forgot the cap.' With an exaggerated flourish, she plucked the article in question from a hook on the wardrobe door. It was much the same size and shape as a generously fashioned sofa cushion, and when Jane pulled it ruthlessly over her head, her feathery blond curls disappeared, as well as most of her face. In profile, all that could be seen was the tip of a small, sharp, red nose. From the front, it looked as though she were peering out from under a bed ruffle.

Hannah sniffed in exasperation. 'Lord, Miss Jane, just look at you. With your eyebrows plucked to nothing and your lashes bleached out and a nose like a raspberry, you look like a skinned rabbit. I cannot believe you mean to greet his lordship in this fashion. Whatever will the man think?'

'He will think,' retorted Jane, tucking a pale tendril into the confines of the cap, 'that Miss Winifred Timburton is thoroughly and properly chaperoned by her thoroughly proper spinster cousin, Miss Jane Burch.' She bobbed an impudent curtsy and put out a hand for the serviceable shoes proffered by Hannah.

'And why,' continued the maid, grumbling, 'you found it necessary to drop everything and leave your papa's house to travel all the way from Suffolk at Miss Winifred's summons, I'll never understand. It's not as though the little minx – begging your pardon – could not have dredged up a real companion, and it's not as though you're beholden to her. If you ask me—'

'You're making me feel guilty, Hannah. I'm not doing this out of the goodness of my heart, you know. After Millicent scarpered with her baronet, Winifred couldn't stay here alone – although it took the Reverend Arthur Mycombe and his wife weeks to persuade her otherwise. She didn't want some prunes-and-prisms old maid living with her – even if she knows one, which she probably doesn't. Anyway, when she told me of her scheme, it suited me right down to the ground.'

'That's the part I don't understand. You should be out and about in the world, finding yourself a husband, not doddering around in this backwater disguised as an elderly, maiden relative.'

'I've told you,' responded Jane patiently, 'I need Winifred. At least, I need her patronage in London after she marries. For Patience and Jessica, you know.'

Hannah made no reply, merely fixing a long-suffering gaze at a point out the window.

'Oh, Hannah, please try to understand. Sometimes I think you are my only friend in the world and I need you on my side.' She glanced at the maid, noting with satisfaction the softening of her rigid features. 'I had my opportunity, you know,' she continued in a low voice. 'Both of my Seasons were disasters. I told Papa it would be no good, and I told Aunt Dimstowe the same thing, but she insisted on sponsoring me. At any rate, I have no desire for a husband. Patience and Jessica are different. They're pretty and biddable and don't say uncomfortable things. I know that given half a chance they will each make excellent *partis*. They're my sisters, after all,' she added defiantly, 'and I owe it to them. After that, I can get on with my own life. I've always wanted to travel, you know.'

Hannah grimaced. 'That's no kind of a life for a gently bred female. What you want is a husband,' she said again, but Jane merely waved her hand in negation.

'In fact,' she continued, completely ignoring Hannah's strictures, 'I've been wondering if this Lord Simon wouldn't do for Winifred. Mister Soapes – the family agent in London – told me when he visited here that Lord Simon's brother is a marquess. That is not as good as if he had a title himself, of course, but with any luck, he's swimming in gravy. From what Soapes said, he's certainly not too old. He might even be reasonably presentable.'

'Miss Jane!' gasped Hannah, her fingers busy with Jane's cap, trying without noticeable success to turn it to a becoming angle. 'You sound like a vulgar, grasping harpy. What would your sainted mama say?'

Jane's luminous gray eyes clouded, but in a moment she said briskly, 'Needs must when the devil drives, Hannah. I know I'm manipulating Winifred – putting her under an obligation to me – but it's not as though I'm doing her any real harm, after all. Lord knows she needs a strong hand, which so far neither Mister Soapes nor the vicar has been able to supply.'

Hannah rolled her eyes ceilingward. 'You have that right, Miss Jane, but what about this crazy idea of hers?'

Jane frowned. 'Yes, that is a problem. Drat Millicent for putting such notions into her stepdaughter's head. Her muse calls? To London, for heaven's sake. I don't know what—'

She was interrupted by a diffident scratch on the door, which was opened to admit a housemaid with the information that Lord Simon Talent had arrived – with another gentleman – and they were waiting below to see Miss Winifred.

Jane paused, arrested. 'Another gentleman? Soapes did not say anything about another gentleman. Well, his lordship will just have to settle for Miss Winifred Timburton's companion.' She turned to the mirror once more and pulled the cap even farther over her face and drew a handkerchief from the sleeve of her gown, with which she rubbed her nose furiously, thus providing additional lustre to its already virulent hue. She drew her eyes into an unattractive squint and, with another wave to Hannah, swept from the room.

A few moments later, a small, vague form flitted into the drawing room, only to be brought up short by the sight of the gentleman standing before the fireplace. He was tall and lean and impeccably garbed in cream-colored pantaloons, a dark coat, and brilliantly polished Hessian boots. His arm was flung negligently against the mantel, but the lithe strength in his tautly muscled form was more than evident. Brown hair curled modishly over his collar, but it was his eyes that caused a peculiar flutter in Jane's interior. They were brown, too, but of a deep, velvety chocolate, flecked with gold, and in their depths lurked something unsettling. A faint air of danger, she thought dazedly, certainly one of authority. Lord

Simon Talent was most assuredly used to command – and probably used to being obeyed. He did not look the sort of man to be easily deceived.

With some trepidation, she moved forward into the room and put forth her hand.

Two

'... I do repent
The tedious moments I with her have spent.'
—A Midsummer Night's Dream, II, ii.

Simon turned to view the woman who had entered the room and his heart sank in resigned dismay. 'Miss Timburton?' he asked grimly.

'Miss Tim...?' she responded with a fluttery gesture. 'Oh, my, no! Oh, no, indeed. I'm afraid you are under a sad misapprehension, sir. Yes, a sad misapprehension.' She fell silent then, gazing dreamily before her.

Good God, thought Simon, was the woman feebleminded? Catching his glance, she started.

'Oh! Yes. That is, no, I am not Winifred, for the dear girl is gone. That is, she is not here.' She uttered a dissonant tinkle of laughter and Simon felt an urge to clap his hands over his ears. 'I' – She pressed a hand to her meager bosom – 'am Jane Burch. I am dear Winifred's cousin. Although,' she went on with another vague waggle of her fingers, 'that is not strictly correct. Dear Winifred and I are actually second cousins.'

Simon gritted his teeth. 'How nice for you. Might I ask, where is Miss Timburton?'

'Winifred?' Miss Burch glanced about abstractedly as though expecting to find the girl crouched behind a settee. 'Oh, she's – why, we have another gentleman present!' she cried in girlish delight, apparently noticing Marcus for the first time. She lifted brows so pale as to be almost invisible. Altogether, thought Simon, viewing her with distaste, with her pale eyes, her fringe of bristly, colorless lashes and her pink-tipped nose, she resembled nothing so much as a middle-aged, tame white rat.

'The Viscount Stedford,' he said brusquely, nodding in Marc's direction and back. 'Miss, er, Burch. Now then,' he continued in some haste as the lady opened her mouth again. 'Where is Miss Timburton?'

'Why the dear girl went to the village with one of the neighbors and her daughter, that would be Mrs Mycombe and Miss Mycombe. Miss Emily Mycombe, that is. She and Winifred are such good friends. Just the other day we were saying—'

'When,' interrupted Simon in a controlled voice, 'might we expect Miss Timburton to return?'

'Oh.' Miss Burch glanced toward the young viscount. 'Well, I'm not sure what time she left, or what she expected to accomplish in the village, but I do think,' she concluded with the air of one promising a special treat, 'that she will return in time for luncheon.' She rose from the chair upon which she had been perching. 'But where are my manners?' A faint neigh of laughter escaped her lips which, noted Simon in surprise, were full and well-shaped. She crossed to the bellpull. 'We must have tea.'

Simon observed with interest the butler's prompt response to the summons. Apparently there was someone in the place with some knowledge of running a polite house. The steward, no doubt, or perhaps the housekeeper.

'I trust you had a pleasant journey, my lord.' Miss Burch negotiated her way back to her chair with an exaggerated air of delicacy. 'How fortunate that you chose such an agreeable time of year to travel. Though, of course the weather in June can become frightfully warm. When we went into Basingstoke last week, I positively thought we'd expire. But lately—'

Simon lifted his hand in a desperate attempt to stem the flow. 'The timing of my visit was not of my own choosing,' he said irritably. 'I came because of Miss Timburton's brother. His last request—'

He was interrupted by a sound like steam escaping from a ruptured pipe. He glanced up to see that Miss Burch had flung a large handkerchief over her face and had begun to gasp in small, sibilant sobs.

'Oh, poor, dear Wilfred,' she hiccupped, dabbing ostentatiously with the handkerchief. In the next moment, however, she appeared to make a remarkable recovery. The hissing sounds ceased abruptly, and she tucked her handkerchief into the hem of her long sleeve. She continued prosaically, 'That is, I only met him once or twice, but Winifred was, of course, quite prostrate with grief.'

Since this statement differed markedly from the information he had received from Soapes, Simon said nothing, merely lifting a sardonic eyebrow.

'Yes,' continued Miss Burch hastily, turning to face Marcus. 'Tell me, Lord Stedford, how is it you chanced to accompany Lord Simon on his journey?'

For an instant, Simon thought he beheld a spark of intense, intelligent interest in the spinster's eyes. It was so quickly replaced, however, by a placid stare that he felt he must have been mistaken. He and Marcus launched on a condensed explanation of the viscount's decision to go a-traveling.

'Your estate marches with that of Lord Simon's family?' Miss Burch asked interestedly. 'A large estate, one assumes?'

Startled, Marcus nodded a brief assent.

'Splendid! I'm sure Wini— That is, everyone hereabouts will be anxious to make your acquaintance. How lovely that you have come!' Miss Burch clapped her hands in a singularly inappropriate gesture of girlish delight. 'I know dear Winifred will be delighted to welcome you, as well. Perhaps a dinner party will be in order to introduce you – both of you, of course – to the neighborhood.'

She prattled on in this vein for some minutes until Simon was forced to conclude in some puzzlement that Miss Burch was inordinately pleased at Marc's appearance at Selworth.

'Tell me about Miss Timburton,' Simon said determinedly. 'You spoke of her friendship with Miss, er. Does she have any other particular friends in the neighborhood?'

'Oh, my, yes.' Miss Burch's words were accompanied by a wide smile that, to Simon's astonishment imparted a certain charm to her sharp features. 'There's Squire Bridge's daughter, Susan, and Maria Dillon. Sweet girls, both of them. Winifred is also quite fond of Lady Ann Brace, although her family – her papa is the Earl of Granbrook – lives some distance away. When they are in the area, of course—'

'What about male friends?' interjected Simon, immediately cursing his own bluntness. Oh, well, he thought, in for a penny ... 'That is, I was wondering, frankly, if she has formed any attachments among the local sprigs.'

'Oh, that.' Miss Burch's face fell and Simon's heart sank as well. Was Winifred an antidote then, as he had feared?

'As to that ...' Miss Burch fiddled with the fringe of her shawl.

'Dear Winifred's heart appears to be untouched – not that she is not greatly sought after,' she finished in a rush.

Suspicions confirmed, thought Simon grimly, fancying he could hear a clock ticking loudly in the background. The girl was obviously planted on the shelf like a begonia and it would take every bit of ingenuity at his command to uproot her. Surely, though, with her dowry ...

'What?' he asked, startled, in response to a sharp nudge.

'May I offer you a sandwich?' Miss Burch hovered above him, gesturing to a refreshment tray that had just been brought into the room by Fellowes. 'We have cucumber and potted ham. Although, perhaps you should not indulge, since luncheon is only an hour away. Of course, we could put luncheon back – or rather' – she threw her head back in another unattractive bray of laughter – '*you* could put it back – for you are master here now.'

God, was there no end to the woman's tactless inanity? Swallowing a scathing retort, he selected a sandwich, which he placed with rigid fingers on his plate. Miss Burch moved to Marcus who, with his usual insouciant aplomb, accepted a cucumber sandwich and one of ham.

'Speaking of which,' said Miss Burch, sipping her tea primly, 'I am sure you will wish to confer with the staff at the earliest possible – oh!' she squeaked, as the door opened suddenly. 'Here is dear Winifred now!'

Simon swung about in his seat. His mouth, full of ham sandwich, fell open as he faced the most beautiful girl he had ever seen. It was as though a goddess had stepped from the heights of Mount Olympus. To state that Winifred Timburton was tall and well-formed scarcely did justice to her willowy, perfectly proportioned figure. A scented cloud of dark hair swung tantalizingly about her exquisite face, which featured a pair of huge eyes, the color of hyacinths in full bloom, thickly fringed with long, sweeping lashes. Her classically formed nose was perfection itself, and her mouth was a sweetly curved, eminently kissable, pink bow. With a surprised glance at those assembled, she moved forward with the lithe grace of a young queen.

'Fellowes told me we have visitors,' she said, and in her voice, thought Simon dazedly, could be heard the melodious chime of distant bells. Advancing into the room, she extended her hand. 'You must be Lord Simon,' she murmured. Her celestial gaze traveled about the room to come to rest with mild curiosity on Marcus, who stared in frank appreciation. He hesitated for a moment, then stepped forward with an outstretched hand.

'Allow me to introduce myself. Miss Timburton. I am Marcus Crowne, Simon's friend.'

'Oh, my,' chirped Miss Burch. 'How silly of me. Lord Simon, may I present Miss Winifred Timburton? And this' – she turned a meaningful gaze on Winifred before gesturing to Marcus – 'is the Viscount Stedford.'

The emphasis placed on the latter phrase was unmistakable, and Marcus blushed. Winifred blinked. 'How very pleased I am to make your acquaintance, my lord.' Her smile was nothing short of incandescent, and now it was Marcus who blinked. 'Tell me,' she asked Marcus, 'do you reside in London?'

'N-no,' was Marcus's stammered response. 'I live in Kent.'

'Oh.' Winifred dropped the young man's hand and turned away from him to Simon. 'We were not expecting you so early, my lord. I am sure my cousin Jane has made you comfortable, though.' Her attention strayed, coming to rest finally on the table where the trays rested. 'Oh, good, food. I'm simply famished.' In a fluid motion, she hurried to the table and in a moment, with a sandwich in each hand, she turned to survey the little group.

'Did you have a pleasant journey?' she asked. And without waiting for an answer, continued somewhat irritably to Simon, 'Mister Soapes says that you do not live in London, either.'

As Simon uttered a startled assent, she turned again to Marcus. 'Will you be staying long, Lord, er, Steward?'

'That's Stedford, ma'am,' replied Marcus somewhat stiffly, 'and no, I do not plan to stay but a week or so.'

'Oh, no,' said Winifred calmly, her incredible blue eyes wide and ingenious. 'Now that you are here, we'll need you for much longer than that.'

'I beg your pardon?' Marcus asked blankly.

'What the devil...?' began Simon.

Winifred swung about to face her companion, her eyes sparkling. 'Isn't this famous, Jane? Now we have Lysander and Demetrius!'

'Oh,' said Miss Burch. 'Ah. Yes, well, perhaps, but—'

'Who?' asked Marcus.

'What?' echoed Simon.

'Lysander and Demetrius,' replied Winifred with a brilliant smile.

'You two will be perfect, I should think. That is ...' She paused, then asked anxiously, 'Have you ever acted before?'

Marcus and Simon shot each other a wary glance as two people might who find themselves stranded in a lunatic asylum. Miss Burch stepped forward.

'Lysander and Demetrius are the two main male characters in *A Midsummer Night's Dream*.' She tittered. 'Dear Winifred plans to mount a production of the Bard's play here at Selworth.'

'*Does* she?' asked Marcus, fascinated.

'Yes,' said Winifred with pretty enthusiasm. 'It's a delicious comedy, and so popular. With the lovers' mix-ups and the fairies and the magic in the forest, I think it a perfect choice for country entertainment. But I am having such trouble putting a cast together. Mr Mycombe, the vicar, and his wife have promised – well, almost promised – to be Theseus and Hippolyta. I shall play both Titania and Helena, and I am still searching for Hermia. I had almost decided I'd have to have Jack Bridges and Tom Dillon for the male leads, but they are really quite unsuitable. Perhaps I can still use them as Bottom and Oberon.'

As she spoke, Winifred fairly glowed, and a becoming tinge of pink spread over her beautifully modeled cheeks. 'And, of course, I chose my cousin Jane to play Puck because she is so sm—'

Miss Burch coughed convulsively. 'Winifred, dear, perhaps the gentlemen do not wish to participate in the play.' She directed an apologetic look at Simon.

Simon, still immersed in the vision of dumpy Miss Burch in the role of the mischievous fairy Puck, at first made no response to this statement, but coming to himself with a jerk, said hurriedly, 'No! That is, I have no inclination for theatrics, and Marcus must be on his—'

'I'd be delighted to be in your play!' exclaimed Marcus, and Simon, whirling to face his friend, noted with dismay that Winifred's glow of anticipation was plainly reflected in Marc's light blue eyes. 'I have never acted, precisely,' continued the young man, 'but I have been a professional entertainer. You see,' he stated with becoming modesty, 'I used to be something of an acrobat.'

'No!' Winifred was almost breathless with awe, and under her admiring stare, Marcus bloomed like a thirsty weed in a spring rain. 'Oh, how marvelous!' she continued. 'But, you would be wasted on Demetrius. You must be Oberon! Imagine, you'll be able to leap and tumble just like a real fairy king! Oh! Do but think …' She rushed to grasp Marcus's hand in both her own. 'If I can play both Titania and Helena, you could play both Oberon and Demetrius!'

Marcus said nothing, but nodded and beamed in fatuous agreement.

Simon experienced an unpleasant chill in the pit of his stomach. Good God, was Marc already smitten with the exquisite Winifred? He felt perspiration break out on his brow. Lord, Diana would kill him. Jared would dismember him bone by bone, and Lissa … He groaned. Lissa was all but formally betrothed to Marcus. She was a very good sort of girl as sisters went, but she was volatile as flash powder. When she discovered that her older brother had introduced her intended to a siren of Winifred's blinding attributes, there would be hell to pay. He groaned again.

'I beg your pardon?' asked Miss Burch brightly, her squint more pronounced than ever.

'What? Oh, nothing.' Simon chewed the sandwich, which had turned to ashes in his mouth.

Jane smiled. She had also been watching the interplay between Marcus and Winifred and she was well pleased. The Viscount Stedford, with his property in Kent and probable wealth, was a much better prospect for Winifred than Lord Simon, the perhaps even wealthier but titleless second son. To add to her satisfaction, it was obvious that the viscount was already more than half in love with Winifred. Certainly it wasn't his passion for the theater that had prompted him to extend his stay at Selworth. True, he did not reside in London, which apparently meant a great deal to Winifred, but he no doubt possessed a town house there. With luck and a little encouragement, he and Winifred would be betrothed inside a month. Jane had no doubt of Winifred's ability to winkle the viscount out of his country estate and into his city residence.

She shot a glance at Lord Simon. Why, the man was positively livid. Was he jealous of Winifred's seeming attraction to his friend? A small twinge snaked through her. Unwilling to consider the reason for this momentary discomfort, she rose hastily and moved toward the bellpull.

'If you have finished your tea…?' she announced briskly. Turning to Winifred, she continued. 'The gentlemen have not yet been shown to their rooms, dearest.'

Winifred did not so much as turn her head to acknowledge this statement. 'But I wish to discuss the play. And I wish to hear more about Lord Stebbins's acrobatics.' She began propelling Marcus toward a brocade settee, but was stayed by Jane's hand coming to rest firmly on her arm.

'Later, dearest. The gentlemen wish to freshen up before luncheon.' She grasped Marcus's arm and accompanied her words with a gentle push toward the door, which was opened at that moment to admit Fellowes again. Marcus, capitulating to a superior force, merely murmured, 'That's Stedford,' once more and, bestowing another dazzling smile on Winifred, followed the butler from the room. Simon bowed stiffly to the ladies and moved toward the door, pausing there to turn once again to Winifred.

'You are not truly serious about mounting a production of a Shakespearian comedy in your – my – our home?' he asked, with the air of a drowning man grasping at the last floating remains of a sinking ship.

'But, of course,' Winifred replied with a musical laugh. 'I am planning to make the stage my career, after all.'

'W-what?' stammered Simon, and Jane could swear she saw the hair on the back of his neck rising.

'Oh, yes. I was planning to go to London this summer, but Jane persuaded me to wait until next year when I am a little older.'

'But, you can't be serious!' he said explosively. 'What about marriage? You will be ruined if you pursue such a mad idea. I – I forbid it!'

Winifred's smile remained undiminished. 'Oh, I hope you will not. I should hate to have to run away. For I am quite determined, you know. I have no interest in marriage right now. Perhaps in a few years, when I am established as a – a prima actress, or whatever they're called, I shall consider taking a husband – one who can keep me in the luxury I will have become used to. In the meantime, I shall pursue my art.'

This last was uttered with a hand to her forehead in a dramatic gesture as she wafted out of the room. Lord Simon whirled on Jane, but possessed of a strong instinct for survival, she scuttled through the door in Winifred's wake, pretending she did not hear the muttered curse flung after them.

Three

'Run when you will, the story shall be changed.'
—A Midsummer Night's Dream, II, ii.

Night had fallen on Hampshire, and not a moment too soon, thought Simon morosely. He and Marcus were relaxing in the master's suite, where Simon had been ensconced earlier with due ceremony by Fellowes, the butler. The chamber in which they sat was suitably furnished in the first style of elegance. Large, comfortable chairs were scattered pleasingly about the room, and a small, efficiently designed writing desk was placed below the window. In the chamber beyond lay an enormous tester bed, hung with rich damask and embellished with old-fashioned carvings of dragons and mandarins.

Simon sat at the desk, with Marcus sprawled nearby in a satin-covered wing chair, eagerly perusing the copy of *A Midsummer Night's Dream* given to him earlier by Winifred.

Simon's earlier admiration of that young lady had rapidly given way to an urgent desire to wrap his fingers around her lovely throat. All through luncheon she regaled her increasingly uninterested audience with tales told by her stepmother about the delights of life on the London stage. Despite his best efforts, he had not been able to sway her in her determination to follow in Millicent's footsteps. The beautiful widgeon could find no flaw in her ridiculous scheme. The fact that she would be ruined socially, particularly in the unlikely event that she became a success in the theater, meant nothing to her. 'For,' she concluded ingeniously, 'my stepmama was the toast of the London stage for years, and she married Papa in the end. She was received everywhere.'

'Well, not quite everywhere,' intoned Miss Burch repressively.

'The Duchess of Bentwater gave her the cut direct when they were both visiting at Maybridge. The Earl of Granbrook's seat,' she explained to Simon. 'Of course, everyone knows the duchess is extremely high in the instep, but there it is.'

'Oh, pooh!' was Winifred's response. 'As though anyone would care what that old gargoyle thinks.'

Simon had nearly cried out in his despair. With such an attitude, Winifred would be lucky to receive a proposal from the local tinker.

Returning to the present, he bent an accusing glare at Marcus, who was still perusing the play manuscript. 'I wish you would put that damned thing down. You cannot be serious, after all, about appearing in Winifred's production.'

Marcus lifted startled eyes. 'Of course, I am. It sounds like great fun and I wouldn't miss it for the world.'

Simon snorted. 'Since when did you develop such a consuming interest in the Bard?'

Marcus gazed blankly at him for a moment, then started up indignantly.

'You don't think I'm sniffing around Winifred, do you?'

'Oh, no,' came the sarcastic response. 'Why would I think that, when you spent the entire afternoon practically glued to her pink little fingers? Good God, Mark. I never saw anyone make such a cake of himself.'

'I was not glued to her fingers. I may have taken her hand a few times ...'

Simon snorted again.

'But it was only in courtesy, I assure you. As for making a cake of myself, you merely mistook my enthusiasm for ... for—'

'For an absolutely nauseating display of adolescent infatuation.'

Marc leaped to his feet. 'Now see here, Simon, I do not intend to take this from you. Are you forgetting Lissa?'

'No, but it's apparent that you have.'

'*What*?' Marcus swelled with indignation. 'That's just – just nonsense! I love Lissa. I have from the first moment I saw her.'

'That's what I was told.'

'Well, it's true.'

Simon was unmoved. 'Then, how could you behave in that revolting manner to Winifred this afternoon?' he snapped.

'I told you,' the young man replied with wounded dignity, 'I am interested in this project of hers. Can't you get it through your head that I am looking forward to acting in that play?' When Simon made no response beyond hardening an already belligerent stare, Marc dropped the book on a nearby table and leaned forward. 'Simon, I was not raised to be a peer. I spent most of my life in the streets of Paris, scrabbling for a living, never knowing of my background. I discovered that I had a talent for acrobatics, and that I could earn a living at it. I did a little acting, too, and I discovered something else about myself. Performing is food and drink to me.'

'Mmm,' said Simon warily. 'I recall Diana saying something about your incorrigible tendency to make every situation into a melodrama.'

Marcus grinned. 'Guilty as charged.' His face grew serious again as he turned to pace before the fireplace. 'I have an itch that has remained unscratched for three years now – ever since I assumed my title, for the duties of viscount do not ordinarily include tumbling in a ring or posturing on stage.' He turned again to face his friend. 'I've worked hard at being a good landlord. I've studied land management and I pay attention to the needs of my tenants. But, I've missed the actor's life, Simon. I've missed the posturing and the camaraderie – and the adventure of it all.' He shuffled his feet. 'You know, when I asked to come with you to Hampshire, it wasn't just a desire to visit another of my estates. I thought it might be a chance for a lark – and that's what it's turning into. An opportunity has fallen from the sky to let me live the life of an actor again for a little while – at least, part of it. Winifred's little theatrical won't be the same as professional theater, but it will be a taste. And,' he concluded with a pugnacious thrust of his jaw, 'I intend to enjoy every minute of it.'

Simon heaved a disgruntled sigh. 'I suppose there's no more to be said, then. As long as you stop nibbling on Winifred's pretty fingers.'

Marcus grunted. 'For Lord's sake, Simon, why would I look at Winifred, when I have Lissa? Although,' he added, his brow darkening, 'sometimes I'm not so sure I do. She says she loves me, but she seems stuck in London with Charlotte her older sister like a pig in mud. All I ever hear from her is all the balls she goes to and how many odes have been written to her fine eyes.' He flung himself into a chair. 'All that aside, Winifred is a beautiful girl, but she can't hold a candle to Lissa.'

'I'm pleased to hear you say that,' said Simon, keeping his skeptical reflections to himself. 'Oddly, it seems to me there is a certain resemblance between the two.'

'Umm,' Marcus replied thoughtfully, 'I don't see that at all. They're both slim and dark-haired, but Winifred is taller and more – substantial than Lissa, and doesn't have her – her inner spirit. They both chatter rather a lot—'

'And they're both autocratic and self-centered,' finished Simon. 'To my mind, Lissa is basically a much nicer person – I see a lot of Wilfred in Winifred – but that might be my brotherly prejudice talking.'

Marcus laughed. 'Perhaps, but I agree with you wholeheartedly. Lissa has her faults, but she's loving and giving and – and altogether a darling.' He halted suddenly and blushed. He gestured abruptly toward the desk at which Simon was sitting. 'What's all that?'

'Ah,' said Simon, picking up the quill he had laid before him, and drawing to him paper and ink. 'I am writing to an old friend, to invite him here for a visit.'

'An old friend? Here? Do I know him?'

'I doubt it. We served together briefly in the Peninsula. He sold out right after Toulouse. His wife had just passed away, leaving him with two small daughters. We have corresponded sporadically since he left Spain, and ...'

'And, if he hasn't remarried, he must be in need of a wife?'

Simon smiled crookedly. 'Very astute of you. Yes, I believe my friend, Charles, the Earl of Wye is looking for someone to take charge of his motherless children, and he is extraordinarily susceptible to a pretty face.'

'But, you heard what Winifred said about getting married.'

'Nonsense,' said Simon, attempting to infuse his tone with authority. 'All she needs is to be presented with the right opportunity. What female in her right mind is going to turn down a title and ninety thousand pounds a year?'

Marc whistled softly. 'Ninety thousand? How has he escaped being leg-shackled for so long?'

'Well, as I said, he has an eye for the ladies. I hear he's been cutting quite a swath in his corner of Huntingdonshire, driving the mamas of eligible daughters distracted. He may be ready to make a commitment at last, but he's highly selective.'

'And,' finished Marcus sardonically, 'what man in his right mind could resist the fair Winifred?'

'Precisely.'

'You'd better keep her companion out of the way. That woman is enough to make a man run screaming for cover.'

Simon grunted. 'If I thought I could confine the insufferable Miss Burch to her room until I get Winifred down the aisle, or better yet, send her packing to wherever she came from, I'd do it in a minute. Although,' he added musingly, 'there's something dashed odd about her, don't you think?'

'Odd is scarcely the word.'

'No – I mean – did you notice the creaking?' In response to Marcus's blank stare, Simon continued. 'Almost every time she moved, I heard it plainly – as though she were encased in barrel staves. In addition, her expression sometimes—' He laughed shortly. 'I must be all about in my head. Go back to the Bard, Marc, so I can get on with my letter.' Picking up quill and paper, he waved dismissively and turned to his task.

In another wing of the house, Winifred sat at her dressing table, her hand lifted in unconscious grace as she brushed her hair. She glanced at her cousin, who stood behind her, reflected in the mirror.

'Really, Jane.' Winifred's laugh was a tinkling arpeggio. 'Just because he's attractive and bears a title doesn't mean I wish to encourage him.'

Jane had shed her padding and tack and stood small and straight and slender in a demure cotton dressing gown. She gave Winifred's hair a small tug in exasperation before turning to seat herself, her feet tucked beneath her, on a straw satin chair nearby.

'Be serious, Win. Marcus Crowne is a viscount, for heaven's sake, and he's very good looking. He's apparently quite wealthy, and even though he doesn't actually live in London, he's bound to have a town house there.'

'Mmm, that's true – and he is interested in the theater. I suppose he might do. I'll think about it.'

Jane gazed at her cousin in irritation. 'Winifred, you *must* give up this insane idea of becoming an actress.'

Winifred's hyacinth eyes were limpid and wide. 'Why?'

Jane threw up her hands 'Well, because – because respectable women just don't do that sort of thing. Actresses are considered almost on the same level as – as Cyprians, and you'd be putting yourself completely beyond the pale.'

'I've told you, I think you're wrong about that, and even if you're not, I simply don't care.' She rose and flung her arms wide. 'I want to take London by storm. I want my name on everyone's lips as the most exciting performer that ever graced the boards. I want—'

'Yes,' interposed Jane dryly. 'I know what you want. But,' she asked earnestly, 'what if you go to London and no one will hire you?'

Winifred blinked incredulously. 'Not hire me? But I am beautiful!'

'My dear,' sighed Jane, 'there are thousands of beautiful women in London. I would wager that ninety-nine percent of them cannot act. What makes you think you are among the blessed?'

Winifred stared at her. 'Because I can *feel* it just here.'

Jane gazed at her cousin in consternation, considering the faint possibility that Winifred's dream might come to pass. She shook herself. No – it simply was not to be contemplated. She could not let Winifred make a complete fool of herself. More to the point, her own scheme for her sisters would come wholly unraveled without the presence of a respectably married Winifred established in a town house – with a large ball room – in the metropolis.

'Somehow,' Winifred continued, gazing thoughtfully at her reflection, 'we must work on Lord Simon. We simply must persuade him to take me to London.'

At the sound of his lordship's name, Jane's heart gave an odd little lurch. 'We? Please,' she said curtly, 'don't include me in your machinations, Winifred. I shall have my hands full maintaining my own little pretense with him.'

'Pooh!' Winifred's perfect brows lifted incredulously. 'Lord Simon has fallen completely for your middle-aged spinster faraddidle.' She giggled engagingly.

Jane smiled, but she remained troubled as she recalled those perceptive, chocolate-colored eyes. 'I shouldn't play any of your tricks off on him, just the same.'

'Pooh,' said Winifred again. Then, as though weary of the subject, she added, 'Did I hear you say you received a letter from Gerard today?'

Jane brightened. 'Yes, he says he has been studying for the Little Go – and it's almost killing him. By next year at this time, he will be studying for the bar. If,' she amended, 'he doesn't get sent down first. He says he and Harry – his friend, Harry Bridgeworth, you know – he and Harry played such a trick on the dean last month. I don't remember all the details, but it involved one of the fellows' wife's pet pug and a ventriloquist from the fair.'

Winifred smiled distantly. 'Your brother is such an infant.'

'He sent you his love.'

'Mmm, yes. I suppose.'

Jane rose in some irritation and moved to the door. Bidding her cousin a rather stiff good night, she walked the short distance to her own chambers. Once in bed, her thoughts returned to the arrival of Lord Simon and what it might portend for her grand plans.

At any rate, she thought complacently, his friend, the viscount, is a godsend. He'll be perfect for Winifred. Firmly banning the unsettling brown eyes from her thoughts, she fell asleep making hopeful plans for her sisters' comeouts in the elegant London home of Lord and Lady Stedford.

Simon was awakened early the next morning by the sound of birdsong and the rays of sunlight slanting between heavy, crimson-velvet window hangings. He stretched, considering the day ahead of him. Before Miss Burch had retired at a blessedly early hour the evening before, she had informed him that Harold Minster, the estate manager, would be available to Lord Simon at his lordship's convenience. Good. He was anxious to get down to business here.

He rose, and declining to ring for his valet, shucked his nightshirt and donned britches and a shirt. Shrugging into a serviceable coat, he made his way to the stables, where he found an elderly personage supervising the exercise of a prancing filly. When he observed Simon's approach, the man hurried toward him.

'Ye must be Lord Simon,' he said, pulling respectfully at his forelock. 'I'm Musgrove, the head groom. We didn't expect ye out so early, me lord, but I'm pleased t'welcome ye.' An odd expression of unease crossed his wrinkled features. 'Be ye wishin' fer an early mornin' ride?'

Simon glanced about with approval at the tidy yard. The stables themselves appeared neat and well-maintained as well. He smiled.

'Thank you, Musgrove. Yes, I was hoping for a good gallop before breakfast. Unfortunately, my own cattle will not arrive for a day or two, but I was hoping you would be able to mount me.'

To Simon's puzzlement, the expression of unease on Musgrove's face deepened, but the old man said heartily, 'Why, of course, me lord. We have Argo, a well-ribbed gray, or Tuppence. He's a two-year-old. Not quite up to weight yet, but a sweet goer nonetheless.'

As the two walked toward the stable, a thought struck Simon. 'I saw a young boy on a bay yesterday. Big fellow, he was. The bay, that is. Is he available?'

To Simon's astonishment, the older man stopped stock-still. When he turned, Simon could perceive only blank puzzlement in his eyes, but he could have sworn that the man had been unpleasantly startled. 'A boy on a horse, yer lordship? Dunno who that could be. We got no boys around here. Leastways not young'uns. There's the stable lads, o'course, but—'

'No, this one cannot be in his teens yet – slight, with pale blond hair.'

'Nope,' said Musgrove stolidly. 'Nobody around here like that.'

They had by now reached the stable and as they entered its cool, dark interior, Musgrove propelled Simon toward one of the stalls. 'Here ye go, me lord,' He said hastily. 'Argo'll do ye just fine. Jemmie!' he called, and in answer, a youth scurried from the rear of the stable. 'Here, saddle up Argo fer 'is lordship.' The older man swung again to Simon. 'There now, we'll have ye on yer way before the cat can lick her ear. In the meantime, ye'd like to be shown about a bit, I expect.'

Simon, every instinct aroused, opened his mouth to protest. The next moment, he resolved to let the mystery rest for the time being, and allowed himself to be led around the stable area, murmuring suitable expressions of admiration.

It was not long before he was mounted on the mettlesome gray, and waving a hand to Musgrove and his young helper, cantered out of the stable yard.

He breathed a sigh of satisfaction as he topped a small hillock a mile or so distant from the manor house. It was, he thought for the hundredth time since he had returned from the Continent, good to be back in England. He paused to gaze over the sweep of green, rolling land that was the manor's home farm. All seemed in order. Ripening grain waved in silky profusion in the field nearest him, while farther away could be seen a burgeoning orchard. Altogether, he mused, this was not a bad place to spend some time – if only, he thought in sudden, sour recollection, the place did not include the troublesome Winifred, whose very existence was like a noose swaying above his head. And that was to say nothing of Winifred's ghastly cousin.

For another hour he allowed Argo to wander in a heedless pattern before an insistent grumbling in his interior brought home to him that it was long past time for his breakfast. Wheeling about, he started at a placid pace for home. He had covered perhaps half the distance to the house when his attention was caught by the sight of another rider, flying across the fields on – yes, a huge bay gelding. By God, it was the same lad he'd seen yesterday. According to Musgrove, the boy did not belong on Selworth land, but damned if that wasn't where he was.

He urged his mount to greater speed, following a path that would intercept that of the unknown rider. It was not until he was a hundred yards or so from his quarry that the boy glanced over his shoulder, apparently observing his pursuer. The bay was already galloping almost flat out, but the lad slapped his reins and crouched low over the saddle. Rider and horse became a blur against the landscape.

With a muttered oath, Simon attempted to draw more speed from Argo, but it soon became apparent that the bay was the stronger of the two animals. Lord, the boy must be part centaur. Slight though he was, he clung to the back of the huge animal like a small burr, moving as one with his mount.

Boy and horse vaulted over a hedge and Simon followed suit, only to observe an even greater obstacle ahead. Another hedge lay in the boy's path, thick and tall and wild. Beneath it lay a wide, water-filled ditch. Ah, good – he had his trespasser now. Surely, he would not try— Good God, the little idiot was going for it! Simon's heart caught in his throat as the huge bay soared in its attempt to clear the hedge.

The sound of the horse falling came clearly, followed by an anguished neigh. Within seconds, Simon had reached the hedge, and without thought spurred Argo on. He held his breath as the gray became airborne, coming to earth neatly on the other side. Simon brought the horse to a shuddering standstill. Leaping to the ground, he saw the boy sprawled awkwardly on his back, his eyes blinking in mute astonishment.

'My God!' Simon cried. Kneeling, he lifted the still form in his arms, cradling the boy against him. It was then he discovered that the boy was not a boy at all.

Four

'Now I but chide; but I should use thee worse,
For thou, I fear, hast given me cause to curse.'
—A Midsummer Night's Dream, III, ii.

Simon stared down, openmouthed, into wide, gray eyes which gazed back without comprehension. Without thinking, he placed his hand on her shirtfront, conscious immediately of the curving softness of her breast. To his relief, he felt a heartbeat beneath his fingers, at first febrile and fluttering, but then growing strong and steady. At the same time, the girl began to stir, first blinking up at him like some creature of the wild disturbed in its nest, and then struggling to free herself from his embrace.

'Are you all right?' asked Simon, hastily removing his hand to safer territory.

The girl drew in great, gasping lungfuls of air. 'Yuh – yes – I'm fine.' She thrust herself to a sitting position, falling immediately back against Simon in a half swoon.

'Gently, now.' He laid her carefully upon the ground and hurriedly removed his coat to place beneath her head. In a moment, having caught her breath once more, she sat up again.

'That was an insane thing to do,' he said severely.

'It was not!' retorted the girl. 'Talavera has taken me over that hedge a hundred times. I don't know what happened this time. He landed a little shorter than I expected, I think.' She struggled to her feet and ran to where the horse stood a few feet away, placidly cropping at the lush grass that surrounded them. She examined the animal briefly, running expert hands over head, legs, shoulders, and flanks. 'Thank God, you're all right, old fellow.' She turned to address Simon. 'At any rate, it was all my fault.'

'I daresay,' replied Simon dryly, collecting his own mount and returning to where she stood. Who the devil was she? he wondered, glancing in unwilling admiration at the lithe curves in evidence beneath the cotton shirt. Short, blond hair, so pale as to be almost silver, cupped her head like a sleek, silken cap, curling about her cheeks in feathery wisps. Her eyes were deep and luminous as mountain pools touched by moonlight, fringed with – white, scraggly lashes that clumped together unevenly.

He drew back suddenly, a horrid suspicion creeping into his mind. 'Who—?' he demanded hoarsely. His gaze traveled down over her pink-tipped nose and firm little chin. 'My God, you can't be—'

He noted abstractedly the blush that started in the slender 'V' of her throat, exposed by the shirt, and flooded upward until her cheeks and then her whole face matched her nose.

Simon stood abruptly. 'Well, well,' he said unpleasantly. 'If it isn't "my cousin Jane." '

Jane stared at him for a long moment, and Simon fancied he could see the thoughts scrambling behind those polished pewter eyes. She drew a long breath, and said finally, 'Yes.' She continued hastily. 'I thank you for coming to my rescue, Lord Simon, although it was not really necessary, after all. That is, I suffered no serious damage, and neither did Talavera.'

She flashed him a wide, brilliant smile, and turned to remount her horse.

'One moment, if you please, Miss Burch.'

Jane hesitated, with one foot in the stirrup then, sighing, she straightened and turned to face him.

'Might one ask,' began Simon, in the tone he had often used on recalcitrant ensigns, 'what you are doing in – male garments, riding astride an animal that is obviously not a lady's mount?'

The tone, which had reduced many a junior officer to stammering incoherence, had no noticeable effect on Miss Burch. She merely stiffened her shoulders and reissued the smile.

'I am forced to agree that the shirt and breeches are not acceptable,' she said, 'but I was not expecting to meet anyone. One cannot ride with any degree of freedom hampered by a skirt, and I do love to gallop.'

'So I noticed.'

'If it really oversets you,' she said with a martyred air, 'I promise not to do it anymore. At least,' she added ingeniously, 'not when you're likely to be about.'

'I see. And what about the neighbors?' snapped Simon. 'Or the staff, for that matter?'

'Oh, I am careful to remain unobserved by anyone who might be visiting, and as for the staff, they are quite used to my oddities.'

'Which brings me to another point.'

Jane's heart plummeted into her worn, scuffed boots. She glanced at Lord Simon from beneath her sparse lashes and her heart gave an uncomfortable lurch. His expression was forbidding, to say the least. He looked very different from the impeccable gentleman who had made his appearance in the Selworth drawing room the day before. His mahogany-colored hair, ruffled by wind and exertion, glinted with golden highlights in the early morning sun. He had rolled up his shirt sleeves, and the expanse of tanned forearm, as well as the muscled frame visible beneath the snowy lawn, created a queer, prickly sensation in the bottom of Jane's stomach.

'I beg your pardon?' she asked distractedly.

'We were discussing your oddities. And I must say, Miss Burch, the marked difference between your appearance this morning and that of yesterday seems extremely odd.'

Jane turned swiftly and mounted Talavera. Once seated, she faced him straightly.

'Yes,' she said in a low voice, 'I suppose I do owe you an explanation. It was—'

'But not now,' interrupted Simon, swinging into his own saddle. 'I want my breakfast. I shall speak with you later in the study.'

Incensed at his peremptory tone of voice, the apology she had been about to utter shriveled on her lips. Tossing her head, she spurred her horse into motion. 'Clod!' she murmured to Talavera as the wind whipped tears to her eyes. 'Idiot! Arrogant boor!'

Some ten minutes later, however, as she guided her mount into the stable yard, her indignation spent, cold reality seeped in to replace her anger. It was an understatement to say that she had not handled the situation well. Dismounting, she chastised herself. She should not have indulged herself by galloping off in a huff. She should have remained to explain – logically and rationally – to Lord Simon why she had chosen to present herself to him in the guise of a middle-aged spinster. She should have ... Her shoulders slumped. What on earth could she possibly have said to assuage the man's understandable wrath? He must think her either a complete idiot or the worst kind of schemer. Dear God, what if he sent her away?

That would mean the ruin of all her grandiose plans for Jessica and Patience.

She trudged despondently into the house. She would just have to try to repair the damage when she met with Lord Simon later. In the meantime, there was breakfast to get through. Perhaps, by the time she had changed from her breeches, he might have departed the dining room.

She spent some time pacing in front of her wardrobe. Deciding to abandon her padding and tack, she chose one of her own gowns and, having completed her ensemble to her satisfaction, she paused before the mirror. After a moment of indecision, she artificially darkened her brows and lashes to their normal color, a shade of charcoal in startling variance to her silver blond hair. She applied a little salve to her raw, reddened nose, but was forced to admit that only time would heal her abused appendage.

As she entered the breakfast room, her hope that Lord Simon would have finished his breakfast was shattered. He sat at his ease among the remains of a repast of sirloin, eggs and ale, reading *The Times*. Feeling remarkably foolish, she snatched toast and coffee from the sideboard and slid into a place at the table as far away from his lordship as possible. She lifted her eyes with great reluctance, to discover that he sat motionless, a forkful of eggs halfway to his mouth, staring as though he had never seen her before. Which, in point of fact, she thought, he hadn't really.

'G-good morning,' she said hesitantly, a flood of heat surging over her cheeks. When Winifred entered the room a moment later, Jane sighed with relief.

'Good morning,' caroled Winifred hurrying to the sideboard, where she helped herself to a substantial portion of eggs and York ham. 'I hope no one has made any plans for the day because I want to get started on rehearsals for the play. I already have Act One, Scene One, blocked out in my mind, but – oh, my goodness! Jane! You're not—' She darted a glance at Simon. 'That is – you forgot—'

Jane cast an anguished glance at Simon, who said nothing, merely sending a sardonic glance to each of the young women before returning to his paper. Jane cleared her throat.

'Ah,' she began. Her usually quick mind, however, had deserted her and she trailed off into a despairing silence. Once more, Winifred spoke, this time, in a voice pregnant with meaning.

'Jane, dear, I wonder if I might have a word with you.' She jerked her head toward the corridor.

At this, Jane forced herself to attention.

'I have just come in from outside, Winifred,' she said, her voice brittle in her attempt to keep it steady.

A blank, 'What?' was Winifred's immediate response.

'Yes,' continued Jane, picking up momentum, 'I went out for a gallop before breakfast, and I wore the – the clothes I usually wear to go out, er, galloping, and I met Lord Simon out on the greensward.'

'Oh?' said Winifred, her expression still uncomprehending. 'Oh,' she said again. 'O-o-oh,' she concluded, her eyes now wide with horror. She glanced at Lord Simon, who was still immersed in *The Times*, apparently oblivious. She lifted her brows in agonized query to Jane, who merely closed her eyes and nodded. The newspaper rustled, and both women jumped.

'Ah, good morning, Miss Timburton,' said Simon frigidly. 'I wonder, would you take it amiss if I were to call you Winifred? It seems so much simpler, considering our present relationship.' Winifred nodded in numb acquiescence. 'Good. As for the play, I'm afraid you will have to exclude me from your plans. I will, however, wish to speak with you later in the day regarding your future.' With a tight smile he laid *The Times* down on the table and moved toward the door. 'I shall bid you ladies good day, then.' He bent a look of chilly propriety on Jane. 'Miss Burch, I shall see you shortly.'

Without waiting for an answer, he closed the door firmly behind him. Winifred immediately swung to her cousin. 'Jane!' she shrieked. 'What happened? Does he Know All?'

'Of course, he knows,' replied Jane tiredly. 'I all but fell into his lap, wearing my shirt and breeches.'

'Well, what are you going to do?' Winifred's voice lowered only minimally.

'What am *I* going to do? I rather thought you might ask what *we* are going to do, since this whole charade was your idea. However' – Jane lifted a hand against Winifred's incipient protest – 'I cannot see where this is anything either one of us can do at the present. Lord Simon will, in all probability, send me packing.' She paused suddenly, an arrested expression in her eyes. 'Unless—'

'Unless what? Unless what, Jane?'

'Unless I can talk him around, of course. I only hope—'

Her words were cut off by the entrance of the Viscount Stedford.

'Ah, ladies. I thought I would be first down, but I ...' He trailed off uncertainly, staring at Jane, who nodded in a genteel fashion.

'Good morning, my lord,' she said demurely. 'I trust you slept well.'

'Ur,' responded the viscount. 'Ah. Oh, yes, very well indeed.' His eyes still on Jane, he moved unsteadily to the sideboard and paused for a long moment, still gaping, before turning to procure kippers and eggs.

'Well,' said Jane, rising, 'do pray excuse me. I'm sure Winifred will keep you well entertained during your meal, my lord. Lord Simon expressed his desire to see me as soon as I finished here. There is something he wishes to discuss with me.'

'Is there, by God?' asked Marcus faintly. He sat down at the table with rather a thump, and when the door closed behind Jane, he turned to Winifred in bafflement.

'Ah, about your cousin ...' he began.

'Enter.' The voice within sounded coldly in response to Jane's soft knock. Throwing her shoulders back and thrusting her chin forward, she did as she was bade. She had determined, on what seemed like the very long journey from the dining room to the study, that she would not stand in trembling fear before Lord Simon Talent. She had not done anything so very wrong, after all. She had not actually lied to the man, had she? She had perhaps nudged him into the wrong conclusion as to the matter of her age and general degree of respectability, but if he had asked her how many years she had on her plate, would she not have told him the truth? Of course, she would have. She moved to the desk behind which his lordship sat in rigid expectancy. Without waiting for permission, she seated herself in a comfortable chair before him. He said nothing, merely subjecting her to a scrutiny that she felt was scouring her very soul. His eyes, she decided, lightened when he was angry, for they were almost the color of cinnamon at the moment. And, suddenly, she felt herself in imminent danger of falling into them. Those golden flecks seemed to envelop her, surrounding her in a dizzying warmth.

She fastened her gaze determinedly on her fingers, which lay in her lap, clenching and unclenching.

Simon found himself unexpectedly at a loss for words. It had not taken him long to deduce the reason for Miss Burch's absurd charade. From what Soapes had told him, Winifred had been extremely reluctant to encumber herself with an elderly companion, and inveigling a young, and equally foolish friend to play the role of one was just the sort of harebrained scheme one would expect from the little widgeon. It had already become apparent that once Winifred decided on a course of action, she tended to pursue it with the tenacity of an army mule. But the Burch female must have windmills in her head to have agreed to the girl's mad plan. Lord, had any of the neighboring gentry been introduced to 'my cousin Jane' in her cumbersome battle garb? Granted, he and Marcus had been completely fooled. Silently, he cursed himself. How could he have been so blind that he did not perceive the delicate features all but hidden by the cap, or discern the enticing curves beneath that ridiculous padding?

Seated behind the imposing desk that was the focal point of the study, he had composed a succinct but eloquent speech on the evils of impropriety in young females, and by the time he heard the faint knocking on the door, he felt he was quite prepared to deliver a stinging indictment of Miss Burch, Winifred Timburton, and their insupportable scheme.

'You wished to see me, my lord?' she asked softly, and instantly every word of his prepared sermon vanished from Simon's brain. If only the irritating wench were not so – so captivating, with her great gray eyes like summer clouds full of rain, and the late morning sun streaming through the window to touch her feathery curls with silver. Even swathed in dark blue muslin, the womanly curves of her body were enticingly delineated. Now that she did not move with deliberate clumsiness, her slender grace was evident. Dazedly, he recalled his disbelief yesterday at the thought of her assuming the role of Puck. Now, he could only wonder that a creature seemingly composed of light and air had managed to transform herself into an unattractive, earthbound lump. With an effort, he pulled himself together.

'Wished,' he replied stiffly, 'is perhaps too strong a word, but it seems it has become necessary to discuss a certain matter. It is beyond my understanding—'

'Of course,' interposed Jane with an ingenuous smile. 'You wish to know about my, um, rather odd manner of dress yesterday.'

'Oh, no, Miss Burch. I know all about your *extremely* odd manner of dress. It is quite obvious that you are endeavoring to present yourself as an elderly spinster in order to give countenance to Winifred's position here. What I want to know is why you chose to lend yourself to such a preposterous plot. Good God, have you any idea of what you have done to Winifred's reputation? For precisely how long do you think this – piece of chicanery could have been carried out – if it is not already blown? Just who are you, anyway?' he concluded, noting with some fury the pettishness in his voice.

Relieved, Jane fastened on the one question she was prepared to answer in all honesty. For she had contrived a carefully edited rationale of her actions for presentation to his lordship.

'Oh, I really am Winifred's cousin. I live with my father, a country squire in Suffolk, and my two sisters, Jessica and Patience. I have a brother, too. His name is Gerard, and he is presently at Oxford.'

Simon lifted his hand impatiently. 'Yes. Thank you, I do not require a complete family history. What I wish to hear, is—'

'About Winifred's and my little, er, deception,' finished Jane. 'Well, you are quite correct, of course. When Winifred was finally persuaded to bring in a companion to live with her, she was most averse to having someone she felt sure would try to thwart her plans to take up a career on the stage. She immediately thought of me, for we have always been fairly close. My mother and hers were first cousins, and when we were small, we visited back and forth a great deal.' Jane glanced into her lap, where she had begun to pleat the folds of her skirt, for it was here that she planned her small divergence from the truth.

'I was at first reluctant to fall in with her plan, for despite what you must think, I am a sensible sort of female, not given to mad starts.' She continued hurriedly, as though she had not heard his snort of derision, 'However, it soon began to be borne on me that if I did not do as she asked, she would simply ask someone else – someone who might not have the ability to – to make her see reason. I do not, you see, see eye to eye with her in the matter of this absurd idea of a career on the London stage.'

'You don't?' asked Simon in some surprise.

'No, I most certainly do not. In fact,' Jane added tartly, 'you might show a little appreciation for the fact that I have so far managed to keep her from peltering down to London on the first available stage.'

'Well, I would not say—'

'As to my pretense, it was necessary, after all. With Wilfred gone to his reward and Millicent heading over the horizon with Sir Clifford, the vicar and his wife, with all their kindness, could do nothing with her. She has no close relatives left, and her guardian was miles away.' She allowed a hint of censure to creep into her voice. If his lordship could be make to feel just the slightest bit guilty, it could do her plan no harm. 'Thus, she had no guardian, nor anyone else to lend her countenance. If we were going to make her charade work, I had no choice but to appear much older than I really am. I am four and twenty, by the by.'

'But, surely—' Simon began again, only to be interrupted once more.

'We did not, after all, plan for the thing to go on forever. We knew you would be coming along, at which point Winifred planned to convince you to let her go to London. I know,' she said as Simon shook his head in disbelief. 'However, Winifred is very headstrong. At any rate, I felt that when you arrived, you would bring a companion for Winifred of your own choosing, and I would fade gracefully back to Suffolk, with no one the wiser.

'And yes, I have played my part in the presence of several of the Timburtons' neighbors, but only once, and I kept well in the background. I assure you, no one suspects that Winifred's cousin is not a thoroughly respectable, if somewhat eccentric, middle-aged spinster.'

Simon sighed, and the frown, which had settled between his brows in what seemed like a permanent cramp, eased somewhat. 'I noticed the eccentric part. I will confess to you that I am relieved to discover that, while I am not convinced that you did the right thing, you are not the addlepated female I met yesterday. Might I ask what possessed you to appear in such a guise? It must have been terribly wearing, if nothing else.'

Jane laughed. 'Well, I am already a spinster, of course, but when Winifred mentioned the words "respectable" and "elderly", I thought immediately of Miss Horatia Binbud, Squire Binbud's older sister. She is a dear old soul, and the very personification of propriety. I decided I could do no better than to model my efforts on her, even though she is, frankly, the silliest woman of my acquaintance. To tell you the truth' – she chuckled engagingly – 'it's been rather fun being a shatter-brained lackwit.'

Simon's lips twitched despite himself. 'Allow me to congratulate you on your masterful portrayal,' he said dryly. 'I cannot tell you how it relieves my mind to know that I shall no longer have to listen to your – or Miss Binbud's – demented twitterings. Oh yes,' he added in response to Jane's quick intake of breath, 'it is time to end your pretense, Miss Burch. I cannot countenance duping the county any further.'

'I see,' said Jane, and Simon was forced to drop his eyes to avoid drowning in the liquid intensity of her gaze. 'Very well, my lord, and how soon do you plan to depart?'

'Depart?'

'If I return to my home, you cannot very well stay here with Winifred unchaperoned. Particularly with the additional presence of your young friend.'

Simon scowled. 'I have no intention of leaving, nor did I intend for you to do so. Unless it is what you wish, of course. You are Winifred's relative as well as her guest. Your future plans must be worked out between the two of you. As for a chaperon ...' He gestured toward a folded paper, sealed and ready to be posted. 'I am writing to my Aunt Amabelle – Lady Teague – to come to my rescue. She is a widow and makes her home with my brother in Kent, and if I know her, she will drop everything to come to my rescue. The distance is not great, so I expect her within the week.'

'But,' said Jane with a confident smile, 'in the meantime, what about visitors?'

'I think,' replied Simon judiciously, 'that we will put it about that both Miss Timburton and her cousin are ill with, er, putrid sore throats and are not receiving visitors at present.'

'What a bouncer!' gasped Jane. 'And you have the gall to reprimand me for my dishonest behavior.'

Simon flushed. 'It is not my wish to deceive anyone, but I do not see how it is to be avoided, at this point. I might add that it is you and Winifred who have made this subterfuge necessary. As I said, it will only be for a week or so. After Aunt Amabelle arrives, you are welcome to remain.' His expression, reflected Jane, was anything but welcoming. 'You may still continue existence as Cousin Jane, I should think. Just mention casually that you've found a new modiste, or some such. Aren't they supposed to wreak magical transformations?'

'Magical, perhaps,' muttered Jane, 'but not supernatural.' She rose from her chair and paced before the desk, and once more Simon marveled that such a lushly formed body could still move with the grace of a young sylph fresh from the forest. Spinster indeed!

'If we—' began Jane, but she was interrupted by a commotion that was taking place in the drive just outside. 'What in the world...?' she murmured, hurrying to the window, Simon close behind her, just in time to behold a smart curricle pulling up to the front door with a great flourish. Two young men, dashingly attired in many-caped greatcoats leaped from the vehicle. One of them, the driver, tossed the reins to a diminutive tiger, who had also exited from the curricle, and they made their way hastily to the house.

'Good God!' cried Jane faintly. 'It is my brother Gerard, and – dear Lord, he has Harry with him!'

Five

'Here's a marvail's convenient place for our rehearsal.'
—A Midsummer Night's Dream, III, i.

Jane, with Simon on her heels, raced from the study and arrived in the entrance hall just in time to be lifted quite off her feet in a tumultuous embrace by a tall, dark-haired young man.

'Janie!' he cried, laughing.

Simon immediately noted the resemblance between brother and sister, despite their difference in coloring. Gerard's gray eyes mirrored his sister's excitement, and their firm chins were remarkably alike. Another young man waited diffidently to one side for Gerard's boisterous greeting to subside. His straw-colored hair seemed to spring up in all directions at once from above a pair of round, blue eyes, giving him an appearance of gentle astonishment.

'Gerard!' cried Jane breathlessly. 'Why did you not tell me you were coming, you wretched boy? Whatever are you doing here? Hello, Harry,' she said to the second visitor, when at last her brother returned her to her feet. 'It's nice to see you again.'

Simon noticed with some amusement that Harry blushed furiously as he planted a chaste kiss on Jane's cheek. She turned as Simon moved forward.

'Oh! Lord Simon, allow me to present my brother, Gerard, who is *supposed* to be at Oxford, and his friend, Harry Bridgeworth of whom I might say the same thing.' She turned back to her brother. 'Lord Simon is Winifred's recently appointed guardian and he has come to take up residence here. Now,' she asked again, 'what in the world are you doing here?'

Gerard flushed slightly, but his confident smile remained undiminished. 'Well, as it happens, we got into a spot of trouble with the bag wig.'

'You've been sent down?' asked Jane in dismay. 'Oh, Gerard, how could you?'

'It's nothing serious,' Gerard assured her hastily. 'We have been ordered to rusticate for a few weeks only – by which time term will be over, anyway. Of course, we must pay up for the damages before we can go back.'

'Damages?' asked Jane in a failing voice.

'Well, yes. There is the organ grinder's equipment – and a new suit for the monkey. And in all probability a new bonnet for Mrs Bishop. Just trifles, I assure you. Nothing you need concern yourself with.'

'But, what are you doing here?' asked Jane with some asperity. 'Why did you not go home?'

'Ah. Well, I didn't wish to cause an upheaval at the old homestead. You know how Father hates having his routine disturbed.'

'In other words,' said Jane, her eyes narrowing, 'Papa knows nothing of this latest contretemps.'

Gerard's eyes dropped and a guilty flush suffused his cheeks. 'Um,' he muttered, 'seemed like the best course of action. Unless ...' He cast a wary eye toward Simon. 'If we're intruding ...'

'No, not at all,' replied Simon in smooth, if somewhat bemused, assurance. 'If Miss Burch wishes you to remain here, you and Mr, er ... are more than welcome.'

'Bridgeworth,' said the young man, flashing a hopeful smile. 'Harry Bridgeworth. From Lincolnshire.'

Simon nodded cordially in return.

'Ah—' said Gerard, whose gaze, Simon noted, had been roaming expectantly about the hall for some minutes, 'where is Winifred?'

A flicker of displeasure sprang to Jane's eyes. 'She's at breakfast, I believe. Or – no, here she is now.'

Gerard whirled in the direction indicated by his sister. Winifred drifted into the hall with Marcus in tow, and Simon watched as Gerard's mouth dropped open in blatant adoration.

'Why Gerard,' said Winifred, blinking, 'whatever are you doing here?'

Another flurry of introductions and explanations flew around the room as the group moved from the hall into the largest of the nearby salons. Tea and scones were brought to nourish the travelers, who admitted that, though they had breakfasted at an inn not far distant, where they had spent the night, they rather fancied they could stand further sustenance.

Gerard had taken a place near Winifred, where he regaled her with his exploits regarding the organ grinder and his monkey. Harry, steadily ingesting the lion's share of the scones, was content merely to gaze worshipfully at her. Simon found himself scrutinizing Jane until, suddenly, he became aware that the conversation between Gerard and Winifred had taken an unwelcome turn.

'Why, yes,' Winifred was saying with the sparkle in her eyes that Simon now knew very well boded no good, 'I think you would do very well as Bottom, and your friend can be one of the other clowns – Flute, perhaps.'

'Oh, I say, Winifred,' breathed Gerard worshipfully, 'it sounds like a splendid idea. Do you really think you can pull it off? Putting on a play, I mean? Do you think anyone will want to come see Shakespeare? Not that he isn't quite popular in some quarters,' he added hastily.

'Oh, yes,' replied Winifred with a serene smile. 'Everyone likes *A Midsummer Night's Dream*, and it will be of particular interest to all hereabouts when it is learned that I am mounting the production. And when everyone hears that I am to play two parts, I am sure our audience will crowd the chamber. I have not decided whether to use the gallery or this room, since—'

'You may ease your mind on that score, Winifred,' Simon's voice sliced through her words. 'You will require neither the gallery nor this room, since the play will not take place.'

'What?' gasped Winifred, her violet eyes wide and astonished.

'I have been forced to reconsider my decision to let you proceed with your plans.' His voice sounded sententious in his own ears as he continued. 'I feel the whole idea of putting on a play is giving your mind an unwholesome tenor, for I am inalterably opposed to your ludicrous idea of a career in the theater.'

'A career in the theater!' echoed Gerard in open admiration. 'Really, Winifred? Do you plan to go to London? Why, you'll take the place by storm!'

Harry, seeming to find no fault in this program, merely nodded his head in vigorous agreement. Simon groaned inwardly.

'Gerard, do try not to be such a booberkin,' said Jane severely. 'If Winifred were to go on the stage, she'd be ruined.'

'Oh,' said Gerard. 'Hadn't thought of that. You sure?'

'Yes, she is sure,' interposed Simon. 'As am I, so could we have no more discussion of the matter?'

Winifred leaped to her feet, her violet eyes glittering darkly. 'But, it is my heart's dearest wish! How can you be so cruel! I cannot believe my brother would set a ward over me who has so little regard for what I want to do!' She stamped a dainty foot. 'I *will* go to London, you just see if I don't, my Lord Tyrant, and I *will* put on *A Midsummer Night's Dream*!'

With a petulant rustle of her skirts, she turned on her heel and flounced from the room.

Simon followed her speculatively with his gaze. Curst, unmanageable chit, he thought. Concealing his anger, he turned to Jane.

'I am sure you will wish to see your brother and his friend to their rooms, Miss Burch. I must leave you now to return to my duties.'

He rose, and with a curt bow, moved swiftly from the room.

Oh, dear, thought Jane. His lordship may have demonstrated his abilities as a leader of men in the Peninsula and at Waterloo, but he had a great deal to learn about managing headstrong young females.

Her mind was busy as she shepherded her brother and Harry upstairs, after suggesting to Lord Stedford that he search out Winifred in an effort to soothe her sensibilities. Pleased with herself at seizing this opportunity to throw Winifred and the eligible viscount together, she made plans for another session with Lord Simon. Really, the man must be taken in hand if he were to come to terms with his obstreperous ward.

It was not until well after luncheon that she was able to beard his lordship in his den, for Simon was closeted for most of the day with Mr Minster, the estate manager. His lordship must have been pleased with the outcome of his conversation, for his voice, when Jane once again scratched for admittance, was cordial as he bade her enter.

'Minster and I have been touring the estate,' he said, beckoning her into the room. 'I have been happily surprised at what I have found so far. Selworth is an extraordinarily pleasant place. The house, in particular, is quite beautiful.'

'Yes,' replied Jane enthusiastically. 'I've always loved it. It was built, I think, early in the last century.'

'By an early Timburton?'

'No, I believe it was built for a Lord Barrington, and it remained in his family until 1770 or so, when it was purchased by Winifred's grandfather. Old Silas Timburton was a nabob, you know.'

'Yes, so Wilfred told me.'

'At any rate, it is said the architect had just returned from Italy, hence the lovely curving wings and the little courtyard beyond the entrance hall. It was Silas who added the north wing and the orangery. He must have been a man of taste, despite his association with the shop, for I think the new part as lovely as the old.'

They discussed the house and its environs for another few minutes, and Jane found herself enjoying the conversation. She concluded that when Lord Simon was not being managerial, he was a most pleasant companion – informed, intelligent, and endowed with a lively wit. He was also, she noted, very good to look at. His dark hair was once more brushed tidily, but the morning sun beaming through the long windows of the study, spackled it with bronze, and slanted across the strong line of his jaw. He had settled back casually in his chair, and she was struck by the utterly masculine assurance displayed in that lean, taut form. As he toyed first with his quizzing glass, and then with the papers stacked before him, she was shocked to discover herself becoming increasingly mesmerized with the lean strength in his fingers, and her thoughts flew back to the moment when they had lain against her breast.

She shook herself. She had come here for a reason, and she'd better get to it.

'It's about Winifred,' she said, shifting in her chair.

'Of course, it is,' Simon replied with a sigh. Leaning back, he eyed her warily.

'As I told you earlier,' Jane began, 'I am in complete agreement with your disapproval of her plans to become an actress.'

'You relieve my mind,' responded Simon dryly.

'However,' continued Jane as though he had not spoken, 'I am not so sure it is wise to forbid her to put on this play.'

Simon frowned. 'Oh?'

'It serves no purpose,' said Jane with some asperity, 'to put her back up for no good reason.'

The frown became more pronounced. 'I thought I had an excellent reason.'

'You mean the tenor of her mind?' Jane shifted in her chair and tapped the desk for emphasis. 'Do you really think forbidding her to put on a play is going to sway her from her purpose? The only thing you will accomplish is to harden her resolve. Believe me, my lord, I know Winifred. She is stubborn as a pig, and unless you plan to barricade yourself here in this room with wads of cotton in your ears, she will make your life a living hell until you give in to her.'

The frown phased into a black scowl. 'Do you really think, Miss Burch, that I will give in to the demands of a featherheaded, spoiled young miss scarcely out of the schoolroom? If she continues to treat me to tirades, I shall simply confine her to her room.'

Jane chuckled. 'And when we have visitors? You cannot claim she is down with a putrid sore throat forever. Sooner or later she will have some contact with the outside world, at which time she will broadcast such an exaggerated tale of your cruel iniquity that there won't be a single member of the county gentry willing to give you the time of day.'

'Good Lord!' exclaimed Simon. 'You can't—'

'I speak from experience,' said Jane calmly. 'That's what happened the one and only time Millicent attempted to restrain her from one of her starts.'

'Good God!' Simon was completely indifferent to the opinion of the neighbors, but what about his expected guest, Charles, the Earl of Wye? Winifred must be taught that she was no longer dealing with a shatter-brained stepmother. However, he most assuredly did not want Charles to arrive to find the household in chaos and himself immersed in a pitched battle with his intransigent ward.

'Very well,' he said stiffly. 'I shall inform her that I have reconsidered my decision. Would you be so good as to find her and ask her to come see me?'

'Certainly,' said Jane, smiling in relief. 'I believe she is with Lord Stedford.'

'Lord Stedford? Marcus?' The cold feeling returned to the pit of Simon's stomach. 'What the devil is she doing with him?'

'Why, ah …' Jane's face was blank with bewilderment. 'When we all left the Crimson Saloon, I suggested to him that he search her out in the rose bower. That's where she usually goes to work off her temper.'

'I see,' returned Simon frigidly. 'You did not think she could manage to work off her temper by herself'?'

Jane was more than a little taken aback, and a small, cold hand closed about her heart. He *was* disturbed by Lord Stedford's attraction to his ward. 'Well – I – that is …'

Simon gestured impatiently. 'Never mind. Forgive my being so abrupt.' He sighed and rubbed the back of his neck. 'To tell you the truth, Miss Burch, I am in the devil of a coil.'

Jane lifted her darkened brows. Were they normally that color?

Simon wondered. They seemed formed of sable tips and were startling beneath the pale silver of her hair. He came to himself with a jerk. Lord, what had made him speak of his problems? He was not in the habit of discussing his personal affairs with strangers. He opened his mouth to utter a dismissal, and in some astonishment heard himself relate the circumstances that had led to his journey to Hampshire. Having been slightly acquainted with Wilfred, his tale of woe concerning Wilfred and his dying wish that he take over the responsibility for Selworth and for Winifred earned Jane's ready sympathy. Simon omitted the ticking-clock aspect of his problem. For some reason he was reluctant to divulge to this engaging but exasperating female his necessity to get Winifred signed on the dotted line within the month, or the consequences of the failure thereof.

'I am a plain man, Miss Burch,' he concluded. 'It is my most urgent wish to get Winifred married off so I can put Selworth on the market and return to my own home. I wish nothing more than to marry and settle down to life as a country squire. I have a great many plans for Ashwood, and I'm anxious to begin.'

'Of course,' said Jane, startled. 'Will you be married soon?' she continued, immediately appalled at her own temerity, 'Do you intend to bring your fiancée to Selworth for a visit?'

'As a matter of fact,' replied Simon stiffly, 'I am not betrothed as yet.'

'Ah,' said Jane, her heart unaccountably lifting. Her glance fell to her lap again until, recalled abruptly to her Grand Design. 'Winifred is a very beautiful girl, do you not think?' she asked innocently.

Lord Simon's expression darkened. 'You have the delicacy of a street thug, Miss Burch. I would like to choose my own wife, if you do not mind, and Winifred is probably the last woman in the world I would consider for such a position.'

'Oh,' said Jane, scarcely breathing.

'No. The woman I marry will be even-tempered and sensible. She will be a comfortable sort of person, and biddable,' Simon continued, warming to his subject, 'yet capable of running a gentleman's home.' *And why I am telling you all this, you beautiful little witch, I have no idea*, he concluded silently.

Ump, thought Jane, feeling an odd heaviness in her heart, he certainly knows what he wants in a wife. If he doesn't fancy Winifred – well – good, then. She felt free to pair Winifred with the viscount.

'I am so happy to hear you say that, my lord – about Winifred,' said Jane enthusiastically. 'For, although I agree it doesn't sound as though she would do for you, I think a good husband is just what Winifred needs.' She gazed at him, all wide-eyed eagerness, and Simon felt a stirring of unease. What was the little minx up to now?

'I wonder, Miss Burch, if we could dispense of "my lord"? And "Miss Burch", as well. Could we not, in the confines of the house, at least, be Simon and Jane?'

Jane stiffened. 'Oh, no, my lord. That would not be proper.'

'You are quite right, of course. I am pleased to see you have an appreciation for the proprieties. Does this mean you plan to cease galloping hell for leather across the fields in shirt and breeches?'

Jane flushed and lifted here chin. 'Touché, my lo – Simon. But only here in the house, of course.'

'Of course.'

The thudding of Jane's heart sounded loud in her ears in the silence of the room. She became aware of a sudden sense of intimacy surrounding them. She rose quickly.

'I – I'll just go and find Winifred,' she said, a little breathlessly.

'Good,' Simon returned, and it seemed to Jane that he must be displeased about something because his voice had become suddenly harsh. 'One other thing, Mi— Jane. I intend to make it plain to Winifred that I do not intend to participate in her little project.'

Jane cast him a skeptical glance and hurried from the room.

A week or so later, Simon stood upon a podium erected at the far end of the Crimson Saloon, manuscript in hand, scowling furiously.

'No, no, Lord Simon,' caroled Winifred. 'This is a lighthearted moment for Lysander. You must try to infuse your tone with joy.'

'Dam – dash it, I don't feel joyous. I feel ridiculous. I cannot think why I am doing this.'

'Because you are so very kind, my lord.'

Like hell, thought Simon. It was that blasted Burch woman again. She had inveigled him into this without so much as drawing a deep breath. Why the devil was it that every time she sought him out, he found himself so lost in the mysterious depths of her moonlit eyes that he agreed to things that he would certainly never consider were he in his right mind? Somehow, he had momentarily lost control of the situation. It was a feeling he was wholly unused to and he did not like it above half. The wretched female must be part witch!

His attention was caught by Marc, who stood next to Winifred, his hand on her shoulder. That was another thing. Marc's continued proximity to Winifred was making him extremely uneasy. They spent hours rehearsing scenes from the play, discussing how it should be produced, and wrangling over the casting. Look at the way she was flapping her lashes at him. In addition to all his other problems, it appeared that he was going to have to spend all his time – when he wasn't making a fool of himself in laurel leaves and a short skirt – keeping Marc safe from that predatory goddess.

Dammit all to hell, anyway.

'Now,' continued Winifred, 'since I have not yet found anyone to play Hermia, Jane will take on the role in this scene.'

Simon glanced at Jane. Dressed in a gown of jonquil muslin whose modest folds did little to conceal the lithe curves beneath them, she perched on the back of a nearby settee, watching the proceedings with barely concealed mirth. At the sound of her name, she hopped to her feet. 'Ready,' she called.

'Good,' said Winifred. 'Shall we start at the top of page five, where Lysander and Hermia speak together? Lord Simon, you are over there – between the chairs I set up. As you speak you will move to Jane. Jane, you are over here, seated on this ottoman.'

Moving in the direction indicated by Winifred's pointed finger, Simon strode into the space cleared of furniture in the Crimson Saloon. Coming to an awkward halt before Jane, he recited stiffly, '"How now, my love! Why is your cheek so pale? How chance the roses there do fade so fast?" '

'No, no,' said Winifred once more. 'You must sound as though you are happy to be with Hermia, although you are sad because of the impediment to your love. Yet, tender, withal.'

With an impatient gesture, Simon read the line once more, his voice lightening only marginally. Jane giggled. Catching his eye, she sobered immediately, but the twinkle lurking in the depths of her gray eyes was not dispelled.

'I'm sorry, Simon, but for an impetuous swain, you sound more as though you are being led to the gallows.'

'I told you, I have no talent for this sort of thing,' he said testily.

'Well, never mind.' Winifred waved her hand. 'Let us go on.'

' "Belike for want of rain, which I could well beteem them from the tempest of mine eyes," ' read Jane, extending a hand to Simon. Gingerly, he seated himself next to her.

'"Ay me!"' he began.

'Oh, you must sit much closer to her,' interposed Winifred. 'You are lovers, after all. Do put your arm about her shoulders. Thus.' She pushed Simon up against Jane and, picking up his arm as though it were a feather boa, draped it across Jane's shoulders.

Turning her head, Jane found herself staring into his eyes. The warmth of his breath on her cheek seemed to spread all the way to her toes, and her composure fled. She felt a tide of heat rise to her cheeks. She could not recall ever being this close to a man before, even in the dance, and she was finding the experience rather shattering.

' "Ay me!" ' Simon repeated in an unsteady voice, and Jane, who felt herself sinking into those chocolate eyes, wrenched her gaze away to her manuscript.

Simon found himself gazing at the soft nape of her neck, where silky ringlets lay in soft profusion. He supposed that was better than drowning in the opalescent pools of her eyes, but he was having a great deal of trouble with his breathing. The scent of her, composed of violets and something else, fresh and indefinable, rose to envelop him, and he was intensely conscious of her pliant warmth pressed against him.

' "O cross! Too high to be enthrall'd to low," ' mumbled Jane, and Simon took the opportunity to rise rather jerkily to his feet.

' "Or else misgraffed in respect of years," ' he proclaimed before Winifred could issue another ukase, and hurried through his sequence of lines, almost gasping in relief when the fledgling directress called for rest and tea.

He glanced at Jane, who had hurried to leave the 'stage', at Winifred's words. In the several days since he had been closeted with her in his study, he had discovered that it was she who kept Selworth on its even keel. Minster had been loud in his praise of her domestic management, pointing out that she had taken it upon herself to make the visits to the tenants, which were so necessary to the well-being of the place. No one felt that she was overstepping her place. Indeed, both the indoor and outdoor staff seemed grateful that someone, at least, was capable of carrying out the responsibilities of the landed gentry.

Simon watched Jane, now in consultation with Marcus over the manuscript, and his lips curved into a reluctant smile. He had seen other evidence of her managerial talent over the last week. Gerard and Harry, when they were not occupied with fawning over Winifred, had been set to assisting the vicar in the placement of the new church organ. Winifred herself had been winkled out of her preoccupation with the Bard on several occasions to help make up baskets for the indigent among the tenants. That was all to the good, Simon thought, a shadow creeping over his features, if only she had not seen fit to haul Marc into the proceedings. Young Marcus, to Simon's mind, was spending entirely too much time in the delectable Winifred's company, a situation that Jane, for some reason, seemed to encourage. Good Lord, she had said something about wishing her cousin to marry. Was Marcus the chosen sacrifice?

He sighed in exasperation. Look at her. Seated next to the window, bathed in morning light, she looked a veritable sunbeam herself. How could someone so ethereal possess the temperament of a field marshal? Well, much as he hated to put a spoke in Miss Jane Burch's arrangements, she would just have to plan around Marcus, for the would-be thespian, by God, was spoken for, and Simon was not about to brave Lissa's wrath for the sake of Jane Burch's grand designs. To say nothing of dealing with Jared and Diana.

A murmur of voices brought him out of his reverie. Apparently, the rest was over, for Winifred was marshalling her forces once more. She had decided to proceed to the end of the play for a scene between Oberon and Titania. Oh, for God's sake! Simon watched, fuming, as Winifred and Marcus glided into the center of the stage area. They stood close together and gazed into each other's eyes in a perfectly nauseating assumption of young love, and when Winifred placed her fingertips delicately on Marc's arm, he lifted them to his lips for a lingering kiss before replacing her hand on his sleeve and covering it with his own. Simon glanced at Jane just in time to intercept what he could only call a fatuous look at satisfaction.

' "Then, my queen, in silence sad, / Trip we after the night's shade, We the globe can compass soon, / Swifter than the wandering moon." '

' "Come, my lord," ' returned Winifred throatily, and Marc bent upon her a look of such feeling that Simon was forced to the conclusion that either Marc was a much better actor than he gave him credit for, or it was high time to step forward and put a stop to this burgeoning display of passion.

Simon cleared his throat, but before he could give utterance to any one of the strictures he had been about to utter, a commotion at the doorway drew his attention.

Gerard and Harry stood at the threshold. Ordinarily, they would have already have been there for hours, an enthralled audience to the rehearsal, but this morning some other task had beckoned.

'Jane!' cried Gerard. 'We have a visitor. The most smashing phaeton is tooling up the driveway.'

'And I think it bears a coat-of-arms!' chimed Harry.

This, naturally, brought the rehearsal to an abrupt end as the entire assemblage hurried from the room into the hall. They arrived as Fellowes, emerging from the rear of the house, sailed majestically to the front door. He flung it open just as the phaeton, whose seat swayed precariously several feet above the ground, swept to a halt.

Simon, in quizzical surmise was the first to reach the vehicle, and thus was in a position to greet its occupant, who placed his whip in its holder with a flourish and leaped to the ground. He was a very tall gentleman, thin to the point of emaciation, but dressed in the first stare of fashion. His traveling coat bore at least sixteen capes, and beneath it could be glimpsed a waistcoat of colorfully embroidered Turkish silk. Buff pantaloons and gleaming Hessians completed the ensemble.

'What ho, Simon,' he said in a nasal drawl as he advanced toward his host. 'Here I am, as summoned. Bring on the heiress.'

'Charlie!' exclaimed Simon. Grasping the gentleman's arm, he turned to the group clustered behind him. 'Ladies and gentlemen, may I present Charles Drummond, the Earl of Wye.'

Six

'... man is but a patch'd fool.'
—A Midsummer Night's Dream, IV, i.

'You made extraordinarily good time, Charlie.'

It was some time later. The guest had been introduced all around and whisked into the Emerald Saloon for refreshments, and now Simon sat with him in the study. Upstairs somewhere, he knew Jane was giving frantic instructions for the readying of a guest room, and soothing the sensibilities of Brummage, Charles's supercilious valet. This personage had descended with great consequence from the huge traveling carriage loaded with luggage, that had lumbered in behind the phaeton.

'I was not expecting you for another week,' Simon continued.

'Mmm,' responded Charles, surveying the room through his quizzing glass. 'Your message came just as I was preparing to set off for m'sister's place in Shropshire. Told her I'd be there for the christening of her latest. So, I was all packed and sails trimmed, so to speak. Sent m'regrets to Hortense and set out for your new demesne at once. Only a couple of days' drive, after all. Must say, old boy, your ward lives up to her billing.' He let out a low whistle. 'What a stunner. Surprised she hasn't been snapped up before now. The sprigs hereabouts must be a parcel of slowtops.'

'Oh, she's been pursued hotly enough, but she's standoffish and there seems to be a dearth of prime candidates in the area. She's not been to London – had no one to sponsor her for a Season.' He paused to divulge the tale of the totty-headed Millicent and her concupiscent baronet. 'I suppose I'll have to get one of my female relatives to take on the duty, but since my real chore is to provide her with a suitable husband, I sent round for you. I'm not trying to push you into anything,' he said soothingly. 'But I thought if you are amenable, I'd present you, and let events take their course.'

Charles shifted in his chair. 'Well, as to that, m'family has been at me ever since Margaret passed away. Rest her soul,' he added as a pious afterthought. 'M'sister in particular – the one who just popped – presented me with a number of choices, each more depressing than the last. At least …' He paused suddenly, and after a moment, delivered himself of a monumental sigh.

'Well then,' Simon said heartily, 'you could do no better than Winifred. She will be an ornament to your house, to say nothing of providing you with a quiverful of children.'

To Simon's surprise, Charles merely heaved another sigh. 'Yes, there is that,' he said noncommittally. He straightened, and a spark of interest crept into his voice. 'Who was the other female? The one with short, fair hair.'

'Jane?' asked Simon in uneasy surprise. 'She is Winifred's cousin – Jane Burch. She has been acting as Winifred's companion.'

'Bit young for a companion, ain't she?'

'Yes, she is, but there was apparently no one else at hand. I have written to my aunt to come fill the position temporarily.'

'Ah. Impoverished relative is she? The Burch female, I mean?'

Simon did not at all like the earl's tone of voice. He was well aware of the penchant of some so-called gentlemen for sniffing after females of a certain class. Gently bred and attractive, but with no tedious male relatives about to interfere in one's pleasure.

'Not wealthy, but hardly impoverished, I think.' He added sharply, 'She is a respectable young woman, Charles, and she is under my protection here.'

'Of course, old boy,' said Charles hastily. 'No need to take a fellow up.'

No, of course there was not, thought Simon. Charlie was not the sort of chap to pursue a wood sprite when there was a dazzlingly beautiful goddess on the premises.

'What,' asked Charles after a moment, 'did Miss Timburton mean about my having a perfect bottom. I must say—?'

Simon's lips twitched. 'No, that's Bottom, from Shakespeare's *A Midsummer Night's Dream*. Winifred is – rather an aficionado of the theater and she is planning a home production of the play. She said that you would be perfect in the part of Bottom.'

'Ah,' said Charles, 'you relieve my mind. Thought for a minute she might be one of those modern females who delight in putting people's backs up. Bottom, eh?' he continued after a moment of judicious thought. 'I participated in a spot of home theatricals last year at Summervale in Bedforshire, the Duke of Capsham's place. The duchess put on one of her do's. Didn't like it much. Felt somewhat of a fool.'

'Well, as Bottom, your head will be covered with a mask most of the time, so you needn't worry on that score,' said Simon, a little unsteadily.

'Oh?' said Charles. 'The play chosen by the duchess was *Love for Love* – by Congreve, I think, and if I do say so, I was much commended for my portrayal of Tattle. Mmm – yes.' His eyes brightened. 'I think I should much enjoy doing Shakespeare.'

'Winifred will be pleased,' Simon said.

Which proved to be very much the case. At rehearsal the next morning, Winifred plunged into Bottom's first scene and, while there was an initial contretemps when Charles discovered that the mask that would cover his head was that of an ass, Winifred soon managed to soothe his wounded *amour proper*.

Gerard and Harry seemed perfectly content in their roles of Snug and Flute. Marcus was pressed into service to take on the parts of Quince and Starveling temporarily, thus rounding out the company of clowns, except for Snout, whom Winifred said she would worry about later.

As might be expected, since the proceedings involved several single gentlemen and a beautiful young woman, the rehearsal soon grew boisterous. Simon, emerging from yet another interminable session with Mr Minster just before luncheon, strode into the Crimson Saloon to find Charles, Gerard, and Harry on stage, gesticulating mightily, while Marcus sat to one side with Winifred, their heads bent close together over the playbook.

'No, no, Winifred,' Marcus was saying. He had removed his coat and neckcloth, and rolled up his sleeves, creating, to Simon's mind a disgraceful atmosphere of casual intimacy. He watched the young man place a hand on Winifred's arm as he ran his fingers over the lines on the page. 'You see – it says that all the clowns enter together. You can't have Bottom enter from stage left and get all the way over to the table in the space of a few seconds. He'll have to come in from the back with the others, as it says.'

'Yes,' replied Winifred, her flowerlike face flushed with determination, 'but if he does, he will cross directly in front of Flute, who will be speaking at the moment.'

Simon glanced in irritation at Charles, who was enthusiastically disputing Gerard's interpretation of the part of Flute, oblivious to the woman he was supposed to be courting.

'Good God,' Simon called loudly as he approached the group. 'Can you people not keep the noise down? It sounds like a public hanging taking place here.'

Marcus laughed unrepentantly and rose to greet Simon. 'Sorry about that, old man. The muse will not be quelled, you know.'

'Would your muse not be better served with a little solitude?' snapped Simon. 'Shouldn't you be studying your lines – or something – elsewhere?' Recovering himself, he took a deep breath and he turned to Winifred. 'Perhaps you should dismiss your ensemble so we may all prepare for luncheon. Then, I would think you'd wish to rehearse the scene between Titania and Bottom.'

'That is an excellent idea, my lord,' replied Winifred. 'The scene is quite pivotal to the plot – oh, dear!' she exclaimed with a lift of her hand. 'I cannot.' Her smiled remained undiminished. 'I promised Jane to go out driving with Lord Stedford this afternoon. She said he has expressed a desire to see the sights of the neighborhood.'

Now, what the devil was the meddlesome chit up to? Simon wondered in exasperation.

'What a splendid idea,' he said, his voice cracking only slightly. 'But, I'm afraid that will not be possible. If you will recall,' he continued firmly as Winifred's mouth set mulishly, 'You are supposed to be sick abed with a putrid sore throat. We can't have you romping about the countryside, the picture of health.'

'What about Winifred's health?' Simon swung about at the sound of Jane's voice. She stood in the doorway of the saloon, a quizzical expression on her delicate features.

Simon, with some relish, repeated his words, and was pleased to note the frown that darkened her forehead.

'That's ridiculous,' she said sharply. 'No one is likely to visit this—'

'We cannot afford to take that chance,' interrupted Simon. 'May I remind you,' he continued, as Jane's eyes flashed angrily, 'that it is only due to your duplicity that such measures have become necessary.'

Jane's mouth snapped shut, and Marcus, to whom Winifred had confided Jane's abortive charade, chuckled. The others present, ignorant of the events that had led to the present contretemps, demanded enlightenment.

'No!' exclaimed Gerard, when all had been explained by a somewhat sheepish Jane. 'And you had the nerve to comb my hair for my little rig at Oxford.'

'I wasn't running a rig,' said Jane stiffly. 'At least, not precisely. It was merely a little subterfuge – and it was necessary.'

'Of course, it was,' chimed in Harry. At Simon's glare, he flushed, but continued stoutly, 'Well, she couldn't leave Miss Timburton in the lurch, could she?'

'By Jove, 'course she couldn't,' said Charles, nodding in approval. 'Although, must say, Miss Burch, I cannot imagine you looking anything other than your winsome self.'

Simon transferred the glare to his friend, who remained oblivious. Instead, he moved to Jane, bending over her to examine her eyelashes. 'They seem to be growing out nicely.'

Jane stepped back hurriedly. 'Well,' she began, 'if the trip to the village is off, Winifred, why don't you take Lord Stedford out to the Roman remains this afternoon?'

'Roman remains?' echoed Marcus blankly.

'Oh, yes,' replied Jane. 'They were discovered some ten years ago here on the estate, just beyond the bluebell wood.'

'Oh, pooh,' interposed Winifred. 'Who wants to go out on a hot afternoon just to look at some old bricks?'

'Nonsense,' said Jane, faint but pursuing. 'They are quite extensive. We think it must have been a villa. I'm sure Lord Stedford would enjoy them immensely.'

Before Marcus could make a response, Simon, who was wishing Jane Burch in the lowest circle of hell, spoke again. 'But why do we not make a party of it? We can take refreshments, and the ladies can sketch if they wish.'

'Oh, but—' began Jane, but she was drowned out in the general chorus of approval with which Simon's proposal was greeted.

'That sounds lovely,' Winifred acceded with a graceful smile. 'We can take Lord Wye's phaeton, and Harry's curricle as well, and the rest of the gentlemen can accompany us on horseback.'

The matter disposed to her satisfaction, she turned away and began directing Gerard and Harry in the placement of chairs and small tables that were to represent rocks and other woodland features necessary for the exchange between Bottom and Titania.

Jane opened her mouth to speak once more, but Simon drew her aside. 'I thought you said,' he hissed, 'that you wished Winifred to marry.'

'I do. And please stop gripping me in that fashion. You're going to leave a bruise. What are you talking about?' she continued, as Simon released her with a muttered apology, only to grasp her again almost immediately to haul her bodily from the Crimson Saloon and into his study, several doors down the corridor. Here he thrust her into a leather wing chair and stood above her.

'Why are you constantly throwing Winifred in Marc's company, when I am trying to get her interested in Charles?'

'Charles?' asked Jane in some surprise. 'You mean the earl?'

'No,' growled Simon, 'Charles the First of England! Of course, I mean the earl.'

Jane stared at him in uneasy surmise. Her only conversation with Charles had occurred the evening before, when she had descended from her room a few minutes early to join family and guests in the Gold Saloon before dinner. The earl had been the room's only occupant, and he had responded to her courteous greeting by sidling over to stand very close to her.

'How fortuitous,' he had said, with a fatuous leer, 'that we have this little opportunity to become better acquainted.'

She backed away, but he followed her, step for step.

'I really do not think—' Jane said in some indignation, but the earl continued as though she had not spoken.

'Yes, indeed, I look forward to rehearsing Miss Timburton's play with you.'

'Since we have only one, very brief scene together,' she snapped, 'the time spent in each other's presence will be negligible.' She felt she had managed to infuse in her tone the impression that she was grateful for this dearth, but to her shocked surprise, he moved even closer, twining one of her curls about his finger. Backing away again, she found herself pressed against a sofa table.

She jerked her head away from his questing fingers, and Charles reached for his quizzing glass, surveying her with insulting familiarity.

'Still ...' His breath was hot on her cheek and Jane thought she would choke from the odor of stale brandy and the overpowering scent of the cologne liberally sprinkled on his weedy person. 'Still, I look forward to seeing you, er, perform. It is seldom once sees Puck portrayed by one so well-endowed' – He allowed his suggestive gaze to rove over the swell of her breasts, modestly covered by her high-necked, muslin gown – 'with talent.'

'Really, my lord,' gasped Jane. 'You go beyond what is pleasing.' She placed her hands on his chest preparatory to thrusting him away from her, but she was stayed by the noisy entrance of Gerard and Harry, who were engrossed in yet another of their friendly brangles. Charles stepped back at once, but not before he had slid a hand around Jane's bottom, cupping it in a lascivious caress. Before she was quite aware of what he was doing, he closed his fingers in a gentle squeeze before withdrawing his hand.

Jane fairly flew to Gerard, but by the time she had crossed the room, she realized that relating the earl's perfidy to her brother would result in an extremely unpleasant scene. Gerard, she supposed would be forced to call Charles out, or would take a horsewhip to him, or something equally disastrous. Therefore, when she reached Gerard's side, she merely held out both hands in welcome to her brother and his friend.

'I hope you two are hungry,' she said, and if the words emerged a little breathlessly, no one seemed to notice. The others drifted in soon afterward, and Jane, after an indignant dialogue with herself, and a resolution not to be caught alone with the earl again, managed to put the incident out of her mind.

Now, recalling the contretemps, she gazed up at Simon from the depths of the wing chair. Briefly, she considered what her reaction would have been if it were he who had taken such liberties, but in the next moment, quelling the odd little flutter the image provoked, she upbraided herself for such a ludicrous fancy. Lord Simon was certainly not among that despicable breed, the pinchers of feminine derrières. He was a model of masculine moral rectitude, she thought with the merest hint of regret.

She shook herself to attention. No, indeed. While, on the face of it, the Earl of Wye would certainly be a far superior *parti* than the Viscount Stedford, a match between Winifred and the lecherous peer was unthinkable. Jane thought not only of Winifred, but of Patience and Jessica, who, if all went as planned, would be spending a great deal of time in the town house of Winifred's wealthy, titled husband.

It was imperative that said husband should be of unimpeachable virtue.

Jane stared with as much equanimity as she could muster into Simon's angry brandy-colored eyes, and smiled primly.

'It is not my intention to push Winifred into marriage with anyone. I merely wish to provide her with an opportunity to get to know a number of eligible young men, in the hope that she will make a wise choice among them.'

'May I remind you,' he said curtly, 'that Winifred is my ward, and it is my responsibility to find her a suitable husband. I will thank you to refrain from meddling.'

Jane's indignation rose. 'And just how do you propose to stop me, my lord? Will you lock me in my room along with Winifred?'

Simon smiled nastily. 'I hardly think that will be necessary. I shall simply pack you off to your father's home, which I wish to God you'd never left.'

Jane wondered at her immediate desire to trace the line of that taut jaw with her fingertips, while at the same time wishing urgently to remove his smile with the back of her hand. 'Leaving Winifred as the lone female in a house presently full as it can hold of bachelors?' she asked silkily.

Simon stared at her.

'As I told you,' he said at last, 'that situation will soon be remedied. I have written to my aunt, and I expect her within the week. In the meantime, you will cease your wretched machinations.'

Jane stood silent for a moment, fuming. 'I fail to see why you are so concerned, my lord. Are you telling me that Lord Stedford would not make a good husband?'

'Of course not,' sputtered Simon, pacing the floor before her. 'That's my point. Marcus will make an excellent husband – for somebody else altogether.'

'I beg your pardon?'

Simon drew a deep breath.

'There is an understanding between Marcus and my sister, Felicity.'

Jane's heart sank. She might have known that such a marital plum would not have remained so long unplucked. 'They are betrothed, then?' she asked, a pall of gloom settling over her.

'Well, no – not precisely.'

The pall lifted just a trifle.

'What do you mean,' she asked, ' "not precisely"?'

'It is just as I said,' replied Simon stiffly. 'They have acknowledged their love for one another, and have declared their intention to wed, but they are not formally, er, betrothed.'

'Why not, if I am not presuming?'

'Because,' he said, a hint of desperation in his voice, 'Felicity – or, Lissa, as we call her – is at present in London, enjoying a hugely successful Season, and she wishes to remain until its conclusion.'

'Oh, is this her first Season?'

Simon cleared his throat. 'Actually, she was presented two years ago. She has, in that time, received a number of eminently suitable offers, but she has refused them all, because of the, ah, the understanding between her and Marcus.'

'But, why,' asked Jane innocently, 'is she still in London? If she and Lord Stedford are so enamored of each other, why were they not wed long ago?'

Simon ran a finger around his collar. 'Really, Miss Burch, none of this is really your concern.'

Jane stood, drawing herself up to her full height, meager though it was. 'I think it is very much my concern. I mean no offense, my lo— Simon, but your sister sounds to me like the veriest flibbertigibbet. It does not seem to me that she loves Lord Stedford at all, or she would not leave him to his own devices while she prances about London. If she chooses to let him slip through her fingers, I see no reason why Winifred should not be at hand to scoop him up on the first bounce.'

Simon had swollen visibly during this speech. 'Good God!' he exclaimed in some dudgeon. 'We are not discussing a horse to be brought to stud!' He flinched at his own words. 'I beg your pardon. That is not at all what I meant to say. What I meant to say was ...' He found himself unable to complete his sentence to his satisfaction, and Jane stepped into the breach.

'That's perfectly all right, my lord,' she said kindly. 'We females are used to being discussed as though we were breeding stock. If truth be told, it is rather refreshing to hear a man discussed in such terms.'

Simon moved to stand directly in front of her. 'Have you no sense of decorum, you detestable wench?'

Jane flushed scarlet. 'At least,' she said angrily, 'I have enough decorum not to offer gratuitous insults to persons who have done nothing to deserve them.'

Simon drew back. Good God, what was the matter with him? How could he, whose diplomatic talents had earned him the highest commendations, have so lost himself? What was there about this female with the aspect of a forest nymph and the tongue of a fishwife that caused him to fling reason to the winds every time he was close to her?

He swung away from her, gripping the edge of the desk and the last shreds of his equanimity. He sucked in another deep breath, and after a moment, he turned back.

'Please,' he said, taking both her hands in his, 'I do beg your pardon. That was a dreadful thing to say, and I did not mean it.' He grinned crookedly and Jane, to her intense irritation, felt her knees turn to blancmange. 'I cannot deny that you drive me to distraction, but perhaps that is because we so often seem to be working at cross purposes. I propose we call a truce. This afternoon, we shall join the others on their outing to the village, and we will enjoy ourselves.'

'It is certainly no wish of mine,' said Jane, feeling stiff and remarkably foolish, 'to brangle with you.'

'Then, I look forward to our outing. I must tell you that Roman remains are an interest of mine. In the meantime, I wish you would satisfy my curiosity.'

Jane's brows lifted warily.

'You have spoken of your family, and your plans for Winifred, but you have not spoken of yourself. What is it you wish, Jane?'

At this, Jane frankly gaped. No one had ever asked her what *she* wanted of life.

'I wish to travel,' she said hesitantly. 'I know it probably sounds foolish in a woman of my years, but I have always wanted to see the places described in the books I've read. I would dearly love to see – oh, the Roman forum, and I'd like to stroll down the Champs Elysées. And the Parthenon – by moonlight, perhaps!' She fell silent abruptly, feeling as though she had somehow just given away a piece of herself to this fascinating man.

'I don't think it sounds foolish at all,' Simon said softly. 'I have been to all those places and more, and I only wish they had brought me as much pleasure as you find in thinking about them.' As he spoke, he drew her down beside him on a settee that stood close to the long windows that overlooked a rose garden in full bloom. A tentative smile curved her lips as she lifted her eyes to his. The heavy scent of roses drifted in to envelop them and Simon found himself falling helplessly into the velvet abyss of her eyes. Without volition, his head bent to hers.

Seven

'Come, sit thee down upon this flow' ry bed,
While I thy amiable cheeks do coy....'
—A Midsummer Night's Dream, IV, i.

It must be the scent of the roses that was making her feel so very peculiar, thought Jane dazedly. A soft languor crept over her, and she felt mesmerized by Simon's brandy-colored gaze. The dancing flecks of gold in his eyes enveloped her in a mounting heat that had nothing to do with the summer morning. She seemed incapable of movement – or even coherent thought, and she held her breath as Simon's head bent closer.

'Simon! Are you in there, old man?' A booming masculine voice and a thunderous knocking on the door sounded through the room like a rifle volley. Jane jumped spasmodically, nearly slipping to the floor in her frantic effort to distance herself from Simon.

Simon, in turn, sprang to his feet, where he stood for a moment staring blankly at Jane. Abruptly, he turned toward the door. 'Yes, come in, Marcus.'

The viscount strode into the room. 'Ha! Thought I'd find you here. Tell you what, Simon, you've been working too hard, crouched in this wretched study like a troll in a cave.' He waved airily to Jane. 'Do you not agree, Miss Burch?'

Jane managed a shaky smile and a convulsive nod, but she was unable to speak.

'Come along, old man,' continued the viscount. 'We have just time for a game of billiards before luncheon.' With a beckoning gesture, he started for the door. Simon hesitated, darting a bemused glance at Jane, who returned it for a brief instant, flushing rosily.

'Do go along, my lord.' The words emerged in a strangled gasp.

'I have one or two matters to see to before I go downstairs.' She dropped her eyes and bolted from the room in a craven rush, hurtling up the stairs and down the corridor until she had reached the haven of her chambers.

She flung herself on the bed and stared up at the ceiling. For heaven's sake, she chastised herself, what was she in such a pelter about? Nothing had happened there in the sunlit intimacy of Simon's study. Nothing at all. Yet, she felt hot and itchy all over, and her heart was pounding as though she had been running a steeplechase. Her gaze fell to her arm, and it seemed as though she could still feel the imprint of his fingers where he had leaned close to touch her.

She flung her arms over her head, waiting for her breathing to return to normal. She was being perfectly ridiculous. Lord Simon Talent was but a tool in her machinations on behalf of her sisters. And, he had made it more than clear that he found her a thorn in his side. He had spoken of finding a comfortable wife. Well, if that's what he wanted, he certainly would not look in her direction. As for herself, she had no desire to marry at all. The thought of bending her independent spirit to the will of another had always been repugnant to her.

She sat up. Why, Simon Talent was a veritable tyrant, arranging the lives of those around him to his liking. Once he got an idea in his head, it was fixed there and no amount of calm reasoning could dislodge it. Married to a man like that, a woman's life would be a constant battle to maintain her identity. No, he was welcome to his biddable wife, and she wished him joy of her.

Fixing these laudable thoughts firmly in her mind, she rose from the bed and moved to the pitcher and basin on a commode near her bed.

Downstairs, Simon found he was having difficulty concentrating on his game. When he missed a cannon that he would ordinarily have made with ease, causing the ball to carom off the cushion and on to the floor, he gave up with a self-deprecating laugh and handed the stick to Gerard, who had kept up a steady stream of advice.

'Go to it, my boy,' he said, falling back into the position of observer. Marcus shot him a speculative glance as he made his own play, and the game continued with much good-natured banter.

After a few moments, Simon's mind slipped back to the scene that had just taken place in his study. He could not believe his reaction to the nearness of Jane Burch. He had behaved like the veriest moonling, almost losing control of himself over a pair of magical gray eyes. If Marc had not announced his presence at the door, he would have gathered that little witch into his arms and kissed her till her eyes crossed. If, that is, she had not slapped his face for his trouble.

Yet, she had not drawn back when he bent his head over hers. Would she have allowed an embrace? A kiss? He closed his eyes, and once again he felt the warmth of her body so close to his. Her nearness had filled his senses. The thought flicked through his mind that he would never again breathe in the scent of roses without thinking of 'my cousin Jane'. What would it have been like to press his mouth to hers? He had kissed many women. Surely her lips would taste no different from those of any other. A shock of excitement raced through him at the thought of her slenderness pressed against him, her soft mouth crushed beneath his.

He shook himself. This would not do. Dalliance with a wood sprite formed no part of his plans at Selworth. Not that Miss Burch was the type of female one could dally with. Beneath that ethereal exterior, she was a dedicated meddler and a thruster of spokes into wheels. In short, she was precisely the sort of woman he had always gone to great lengths to avoid, and he would do so again now.

He rubbed the back of his neck irritably. Why was he wasting effort plumbing the depths of Jane Burch's character? He had more important demands on his time and mental capability. With a renewed surge of desperation, he reviewed his plan for getting Winifred wed with all possible speed.

He listened with half an ear to the desultory conversation around him, coming to attention at the words '... to London to become an actress.' He jerked around to face Gerard, who was speaking with enthusiasm.

'I think it's a perfectly smashing idea. I wish *I* had her gumption. And I'll wager she'll make a go of it, too. I know squads of fellows who would put down their three shillings to watch Winifred spout Shakespeare.'

'Those squads of fellows are unlikely to get their chance,' said Simon sharply. 'For, Winifred is not going to go to London.'

'But ...' interposed Harry.

'Now see here, Simon,' interrupted Marcus. 'If the girl wants to be an actress, I do not see how you are going to stop her. This is something she really wishes to do, and I, for one, think she should be allowed her chance.'

'What chance?' said Simon with a snort. 'Just what do you think her reception would be in any theater manager's office. Why, she'd be shown the door – or the manager's bed – before she had time to untie her bonnet,' he concluded.

This undeniably accurate assessment was greeted with silence. Gerard exchanged a glance with Harry before speaking up. 'Well,' he said slowly, 'I don't suppose it would be a good idea for her to go there by herself.'

'The thing to do,' interposed Marc, 'would be to find her a sponsor. Someone who could—'

'No, Marc,' rasped Simon. 'The thing to do is to stop encouraging her in this lunacy. She is a gently bred female, and as such will find fulfillment in a good husband and a good home. I wish to hear no more on the subject.'

Three voices were raised in immediate dispute, only to be silenced by the sound of the luncheon gong. Simon moved away from the table and ushered the gentlemen out of the room, satisfied that he had nipped in the bud any incipient support for Winifred and her ruinous plans.

He did not notice that, as they moved along the corridor, Gerard and Harry whispered together at some length and in a most serious vein.

It was a merry group that set out for a far corner of the Selworth estate after luncheon. Since the route consisted of a barely worn path through overgrown fields, it was decided that everyone should be bundled into one of the farm wagons. Old clothes were donned and, with much laughter, the guests gathered in front of the house.

Simon sprang into action the moment the wagon trundled into sight.

'Here you go, Charlie,' he said, assisting the earl in clambering into the vehicle. Once Charles was in place, Simon turned to Winifred. 'You're next, m'dear.' Carefully, he handed her up into Charles's waiting arms and watched with a smile as Winifred nestled into the straw that lined the vehicle, and Charles settled beside her. Gerard and Harry were next, and they, in turn, assisted Jane into a place near them. Simon and Marcus brought up the rear. Simon's satisfaction increased as, with the bumping of the wagon over the rutted path, Charles found it necessary to place his arm about Winifred's shoulder to prevent her from tumbling about.

Jane's mood was far different as she watched Winifred turn her dazzling smile on the earl. Good lord, look at them, she thought in disgust. If he bends any lower over her bodice, he's going to fall right in. One would think that Winifred would behave with a little more decorum. She was always more than appreciative of masculine admiration, and now she was all but issuing an open invitation for the earl to plunder her charms at will.

Jane supposed she needn't worry. In a cart full of people, the earl would not be able to accomplish much in the way of amatory exploration.

Had she been privy to the conversation taking place between Winifred and Charles, she would not have been so sanguine.

'You do have a London town house, my lord?' asked Winifred, her violet eyes wide.

'Yes, indeed,' murmured the earl, allowing his arm to tighten ever so slightly. 'Perhaps you will come to visit me there someday.'

'Oh, I would like that above all things,' she cooed. 'Will you be going there when you leave here?'

'Why, as it happens, that is my intention,' returned Charles, who had intended no such thing. London was rather full of peril for him at the moment. It would not do for it to become known that he was in residence. But, now, come to think of it, London would be very thin of company at this time of year, and most people would be at their country residences. He allowed his fingers to trace the delectable curve of Winifred's shoulder. What a toothsome morsel, she was. Of course, if she did come to London, she would probably have a dragon in tow. Simon might overlook the lack of a proper chaperon here in the wilderness, but once in London, his little treasure was sure to be well-guarded.

He sighed and withdrew his arm slightly. He must have rats in his attic to consider dalliance with such a one. She might be unfurling all sorts of delightful petals in invitation, but she was an innocent for all that. She was gently bred, with all the hedges that the term brought with it. At his first attempt to lift her skirt, he would undoubtedly find himself either leg-shackled or on the business end of a horsewhip.

The earl lifted his eyes to encounter a glare from Jane Burch. Now, that one promised a little sport. Simon might spout propriety where she was concerned, but he had his hands full with the nubile Winifred. The Burch filly did not appear to have taken to him immediately, but he liked a challenge. He smiled into her disapproving gaze.

He behaved to Winifred with rigid decorum during the remainder of the journey, and when they reached the Roman villa, he attached himself at once to Jane.

'How fascinating, to be sure,' he murmured, placing an arm about her waist to assist her in stepping over what was left of a stone wall. 'To think of one's lands being overrun by Roman chaps hundreds of years ago.'

'That would be more like a thousand years – and more, my lord,' returned Jane, adroitly sidestepping his grasp. 'And in all likelihood, the people who lived here were Britons – Romanized, and subjects of the emperor, but English nonetheless.'

'You don't say,' said Charles, with an air of profound uninterest. 'At any rate, they didn't leave much, did they?'

Jane glanced around at the scattered stones that formed only the faintest outline of chambers, corridors, and outer walls. 'No, they left little but the proof of their existence, but I find that quite enough to set my imagination stirring.'

Charles's brows lifted slightly. 'Really?' he drawled. 'For me, I find present company quite enough to stir my blood.' His pale eyes glistened, making them look remarkably like peeled onions, as his gaze fell suggestively to the lacy curve of muslin covering her breast.

A withering set-down formed on Jane's lips, but after a moment's reflection, she swallowed it. The only purpose to be served in turning away his lordship's amorous advances would be to send him back to prey on Winifred. She smiled brightly. 'Whoever they were, they chose a beautiful setting for their home.' She waved her arm toward the distant downs, green and lush and garlanded with flourishing hedgerows.

'It is indeed lovely here,' said a voice at Jane's elbow. She turned to find it was Simon, who had approached so quietly that she jumped at the sound of his voice.

'Yes,' said Jane a little breathlessly. She glanced from Simon to Charles, marveling at the difference between the two men. It was odd, she thought, that while a gentleman's clothing covered all but a few inches of his person, they were remarkably revealing of character and personality. Lord Wye's fashionable garb merely made him look, in her eyes, slightly ridiculous, while Simon's conservative clothing, superb in its elegantly tailored simplicity, proclaimed his authority and his maleness with a careless grace. She found herself staring in unbecoming fascination at his muscled thighs, outlined in superbly tailored fawn breeches. Flushing, she jerked her gaze back to the ruins.

'I wander here often looking for artifacts, but I have found very little.' Jane was having difficulty talking past the pounding pulse in her throat.

Charles, whose interest in antiquities was obviously minimal at best, yawned and strolled over to where Gerard and Harry were engaged in a game of catch. Winifred, Jane was pleased to note, was deep in conversation with Lord Stedford. Simon appeared to take note of them in the same instant, for he straightened suddenly and strode over to them. Jane followed.

'Oh, Marc!' Winifred was saying, and Jane grimaced at her highly improper use of his nickname. 'What a wonderful idea!' She swung about as Simon and Jane approached. 'Come listen,' she cried, her cheeks pink with excitement. 'I was just commenting on the beauty of the scenery and likening it to the setting of *A Midsummer Night's Dream*, when Marc came up with the most marvelous suggestion. Do tell them, Marc.'

Marcus grinned amiably. 'I just thought it might enhance the mood of the piece if we did the play outdoors.'

'Outdoors?' echoed Jane dubiously.

'Wouldn't it be wonderful?' Winifred smiled beatifically. 'Just think – Shakespeare under the stars! We'd have all the greenery we'd ever want right at hand without having to haul trees in tubs and ferns in buckets.'

Gerard, who had also approached with Harry, stared about him uncertainly. 'It seems a long way to come for an after-dinner entertainment,' he began. 'I don't see—'

'Oh no, silly,' caroled Winifred. 'Not here. We would do it on the south lawn just off the terrace. We could set up chairs on the lawn and string lanterns in the shrubbery. Why, it would be quite magical!' Winifred's violet eyes sparkled with their own witchery, and Gerard sighed audibly.

Jane's sigh was one of irritation. 'Have you considered, Winifred, that one cannot depend on the weather? A late evening shower would ruin your whole production.'

Winifred pouted prettily. 'Oh, pooh. We get very little rain in July, and if it did come on to sprinkle, we could still hold it in the Crimson Saloon.' Having thus dismissed the possibility of interference in her plans by the Almighty, she turned again to Marcus.

'You promised me you'd show me some of your acrobatic turns this afternoon.' She placed the tips of her fingers on his sleeve. 'Won't you do some now? There – over by that large room, or courtyard or whatever it used to be – outlined by stones.'

'Oh,' said Marcus, obviously a little startled. 'I have kept up a little with my routines, but I've not done anything for some years now. I'm afraid I'm no longer very limber. Perhaps if I practice for a few days—'

'But, I want to see something now!' Winifred's lower lip showed itself again in an enticing pout. 'Just a somersault. For me?'

'For God's sake, Winifred,' interposed Simon with a glare, 'do you want to see the young idiot break his neck? And since when do you call a gentleman with whom you are barely acquainted by his first name?'

'But we are already good friends,' said his ward in pretty bewilderment. Her eyes were round as she gazed from Simon to Marcus, who flushed hotly.

'It's all perfectly innocent,' he said stiffly, and his eyes sparked at Simon before he turned to Winifred. 'Perhaps,' he added, removing his coat, 'the young idiot can do a little something without breaking his neck.'

So saying, he jumped lightly into the air and before the assembled group had time to gasp their surprise, flew end over end several times before coming to a halt fifty yards or so away from them. Waving carelessly, he then repeated the process in reverse, landing with a flourish on the spot from which he had started.

The spectators burst into involuntary applause, and even Simon uttered a shout of congratulation.

'Oh, Marc!' breathed Winifred. 'That is,' she amended after noting Simon's minatory stare, 'Lord Stedford – that was perfectly awe inspiring.' She clapped her hands together. 'I know! You must do that in Act Five, the reconciliation scene between Oberon and Titania.' She curtsied coquettishly and moved to him.

' "Hand in hand with fairy grace, Will we sing, and bless this place?" ' she whispered softly, her violet eyes alight with what Jane could have sworn was love regained.

Marcus responded by sweeping her into the curve of his arm. ' "To the best bride-bed will we, which by us shall blessed be ..." ' He sighed, and pressed a tender kiss on her alabaster brow.

'Marcus Crowne!' A high feminine voice pierced the silence that surrounded the pair. 'Whatever are you doing?'

Marcus paled and leaped back so suddenly that Winifred was nearly knocked off balance.

'Lissa!' he cried, expelling the sound as though he had just received a blow to his midsection.

Eight

'You thief of love! what! have you come by night
And stol'n my love's heart from him?'
—A Midsummer Night's Dream, III, ii.

The group whirled to face the speaker, who proved to be a young girl hurtling down on them from the gig that had just deposited her at the edge of the ruins.

'Lissa!' echoed Simon, and Jane looked at the newcomer with some interest. Lord Simon had mentioned a sister; could this enchanting creature be she?

For the girl was fairylike in her grace and beauty. She was small and dainty, seeming to float over the grass toward them. Raven curls danced about her delicate features, and her eyes were a deep, pure black. At the moment, they were jet striking on flint, shooting sparks that seemed plainly visible to the small group that stood paralyzed before her.

Behind the girl, an older woman clambered down from the gig, assisted by the groom who had driven them. She, too, was small, and comfortably plump. She wore a great many necklaces and brooches, which persisted in catching in her shawl, making her descent difficult.

'Lissa,' repeated Simon, hurrying to envelop his sister in a bear hug. 'What in the world are you doing here?' Without waiting for an answer, he set her aside and moved to the older woman. 'Aunt Amabelle! I am so glad you are here. Did you have a good journey?'

By now, Marcus had been galvanized into action and he, too, hastened to Lissa's side. When he attempted to embrace her, however, she stamped her foot and pushed him away. 'Don't you "Lissa" me!' she cried indignantly. 'I traveled all the way up here with Aunt Amabelle because I thought you would be lonely. I see, however' – her dark gaze became positively incandescent – 'that you are quite well supplied with company.'

'Oh,' said a harassed Marcus. 'Ah.' He turned in relief as the older woman approached. 'Good afternoon, Lady Teague,' he replied in answer to her enthusiastic greeting. 'Very nice to see you.' He turned again to the still simmering Lissa and undertook an incoherent monologue that did nothing to soothe that young lady's sensibilities.

'Yes,' said Lady Teague rather breathlessly to Simon. She was a pretty woman in her fifties, whose light brown hair showed but a few strands of gray. 'We had an excellent journey. It is only two days here from Kent, you know. We might have arrived last night – that was Lissa's wish – but I thought it would be better to put up in Bramling and arrive fresh and rested today.' As she spoke, she attempted, somewhat ineffectually, to disentangle her necklaces from the fringe of her shawl, the laces on her bodice, and the many bracelets that encircled her wrists. 'Indeed,' she continued after a moment, 'I cannot think what possessed Lissa to behave in such a manner. We were told on our arrival, of course, that you and the, er, others were some distance from the house, and the butler said he would dispatch a footman to notify you that we were here. We were shown into a quite lovely morning room to wait with tea and biscuits, but nothing would do but that we commandeer a vehicle and hare off after you.'

Simon grinned and said in a low voice, 'I suspect it might have something to do with the fact that I wrote Jared and Diana of my ward's great beauty.'

Lady Teague flashed her nephew a speaking look, then turned at his direction to face the group assembled about them.

'Aunt,' he began, 'Lissa, allow me to introduce to you my ward, Winifred Timburton.'

Winifred made a polished curtsy to the older woman and, smiling, extended her hand to Lissa. Lissa swelled visibly, but good manners forced her to put forth a mittened hand in greeting.

Winifred took it in her own, and her smile widened. 'But, you are quite lovely,' she said unaffectedly.

Not unnaturally, the militant sparkle in Lissa's eyes dimmed for a moment. 'I beg your pardon?' she said uncertainly.

'You are absolutely exquisite,' said Winifred, gazing at the girl in frank admiration. She whirled to Simon. 'My goodness, who would think you would have such an attractive sister?' she added disingenuously.

Simon, grinning, made no response, but introduced the rest of the party to Lissa and Lady Teague. By unspoken agreement, all turned to make their way back to the house, amid a flurry of greetings and mutual expressions of good will. Charles, raising his quizzing glass for an examination of the lovely newcomer, encountered a look of such undisguised hostility from Marcus that, with a muttered oath, he fell back to his original position near Jane. Gerard and Harry fell silent, uttering meaningful sighs during the course of the short journey home.

Once at the house, the two recently arrived guests were seen no more until dinner, by which time they had been settled in their chambers, and given the opportunity to freshen themselves, and become acquainted with the manor.

'What a perfectly beautiful home, Simon,' said Lady Teague as she sat with her nephew in the Gold Saloon, waiting for the others to gather for dinner. It was an elegantly appointed chamber, furnished in the style of Louis Quatorze, with white walls trimmed with gold scrollwork, and gold hangings at the windows.

'How can you bear to think of selling it? To my mind, it's much prettier than Ashwood.'

'You may be right, Aunt, but I've always known that Ashwood would be my home eventually, and I've grown fond of it. When this business is done with – Winifred and Selworth – I plan to settle down there to a life of rural solitude.'

Lady Teague made no reply, but shot her nephew a skeptical glance. 'Well, the young lady is certainly a diamond of the first water. And you say her inheritance from her father and her brother is more than respectable, so you should have no difficulty in firing her off.'

Simon, unwilling to discuss at the moment just how difficult his task was liable to be, contented himself with a noncommittal grunt. Once again, his aunt lifted her brows, but said only, 'Tell me more about the young woman whom I'm replacing as duenna. I had no chance to speak with her – Miss Burch, I think you called her – but she is quite charming, as well. In fact, I fail to see how she managed to convince the neighbors that she is in any way qualified to act as companion for a young woman surely no more than a few years her junior.'

Simon was aware of a spurt of warmth burgeoning in him at the sound of her name, and was surprised at the tenderness he could hear in his voice as he chuckled. 'You should have seen her as she was when I arrived, Aunt. She looked a perfect quiz. You would think—'

'Simon! There you are!' A small whirlwind erupted into the room, rushing to perch herself on an armchair of straw-colored satin near him. Gowned in pomona green sarcenet, her hair caught into an airy Clytie knot, Lissa looked as though she had just stepped from a shady, forest glade. Her demeanor, however, was anything but cool as, after greeting her aunt, she sent a fiery glance toward her brother.

'Simon, how could you allow Marc to fall into the clutches of that – that brazen female?'

'Brazen? Clutches? Don't you think you're coming it a bit too strong, Lissa? Marc and Winifred are merely friends.'

'Friends! I know what I saw, Simon. He had his arm around her, and he was k-kissing her!' Tears welled in her sparkling, black eyes and she dashed them away furiously.

'On the forehead, for God's sake – and they were surrounded by people. At any rate, they were only rehearsing a play.'

'A play!' She sent him a look of injured astonishment. 'What do you take me for, Simon?'

Simon grimaced. 'At the moment, anyone would take you for a flea-brained widgeon. Winifred is putting on a play here at Selworth to which she plans to invite everyone for miles, and she and Marc were rehearsing a scene from it. Now see here, Lissa, you've been playing fast and loose with Marc's affection for three years now, and the moment he contrives some innocent entertainment for himself, you come flying down like a banshee, all green-eyed and spitting fire.'

Lissa spluttered for some moments, apparently mulling over which of these entirely unreasonable statements to refute first. 'Innocent entertainment, is it?' she said at last in a voice pregnant with righteous indignation. 'More like something from a bawdy house, I'd say. How *could* you permit that – that lightskirt to—'

'Her name is Winifred, Lissa,' said Simon in a voice she'd never heard him use, 'and the play she's producing is *A Midsummer Night's Dream*.'

'Oh.'

'Marc is playing Oberon to Winifred's Titania. She chose him to play the part mainly because of his athletic ability, I believe.'

'Oh.'

'Really, my dear,' interposed Lady Teague. 'I think Simon is right. You know how Marcus feels about you, and it seems to me that Miss Timburton showed no real affection for him. On the other hand, she seemed quite pleased to meet you.'

'Well,' said Lissa unhappily, 'it just seems to me that Marc was putting a lot of unnecessary feeling into that scene. How *could* he?' Tears threatened again, and Lissa rose to gaze unseeingly out the long window that gave out on to the south lawn.

'I think you will have to take that up with Marcus,' said her aunt tactfully, after a quick glance at Simon. 'In the meantime, I hope you will not treat Marcus to a scene. Nothing so puts up a gentleman's back as being accused of something when he perceives himself to be innocent.'

Lissa made no reply, but remained standing with her back to the room, one shoulder hunched defensively. However, when Marcus entered the room a few minutes later with an apprehensive expression on his face, she turned to greet him pleasantly.

'Lissa!' His face wreathed in a smile of relief, he hurried to embrace her. 'I'm frightfully glad to see you. You know,' he began hesitantly, 'back there – by the ruins – I hope you must realize that—'

Lissa grew a trifle rigid, but she kissed him on the cheek and tapped his arm playfully. 'Simon has already explained what you were doing. I suppose I must forgive you, but I trust your Miss Timburton will be able to find another Oberon.' Her lips curved in a confident smile.

A shadow crossed Marc's face. 'She's not "my Miss Timburton", Lissa, and as for my playing Oberon – well, we'll talk about that later.'

Lissa's pink little mouth opened as though she would dispute this statement, but after a glance at Simon, she subsided. She was not given the opportunity to say more, for at that moment, Jane entered the room.

Jane had experienced an extremely trying day. She had spent most of it eluding Lord Wye's busy hands and endeavoring to put Winifred in Lord Stedford's path at every opportunity. Her success in both these efforts had been minimal. She had, further, been incensed by the frequent glowers sent her way by Simon, who apparently thought she was flirting with the man she had chosen for his ward. Then, to top things off, she had no sooner paired Marcus off with Winifred with great success, she felt, for that kiss could not have been mere acting, than his lordship's wandering fiancée put in an appearance. Beneath the consternation on Marc's face, it was obvious that young Lady Lissa was the light of his life. Well, hell and damnation, thought Jane. If Marc was truly in love with Lissa, she could not in all conscience continue to throw him at Winifred. But what of Lissa? Did she truly love Marc, or had she rushed to Selworth in the spirit of a dog in the manger?

What a coil it all was, she thought dully, as she entered the saloon. She managed a cordial nod to Lissa and Lady Teague. Lissa did not seem a bad sort, she mused, although endowed with a rather short fuse. Jane had spent a few minutes with Lady Teague, showing her her chambers and escorting her about the house, and she found an immediate rapport with the older woman. Amabelle, Lady Teague, might seem a bit hen-witted, but Jane suspected a shrewd brain lurked behind the clattering jewelry and the dithery gestures.

Charles arrived a few minutes later and at the last moment, before the meal was served, Gerard and Harry skidded into the room, breathlessly apologizing for their lateness.

'Had to post a letter,' said Harry.

'An important letter,' said Gerard, with a significant glance at his friend.

Jane's forehead wrinkled. She did not at all like the sound of this. It had been her experience that when Gerard and Harry got up to something 'important', dire events followed. With some foreboding, she followed the group into the dining room.

Some minutes later, Simon glanced about in some satisfaction. So far, so good, he thought optimistically. He had managed to seat Lissa next to Marc, and both were still on speaking terms. Charles sat next to Winifred, preening noticeably as she laughed at one of his sallies. Lissa regaled the group with the latest *on-dits* from London, though Marcus did not seem to be as entertained by them as were the rest of the group. Winifred, however, hung on Lissa's every word.

'But, do you not go to the theater?' she asked.

'Oh, yes,' answered Lissa carelessly. 'Almost every night, when there isn't a ball or a rout or some such.'

'Have you seen Kean?'

'Mmm, yes, I think so.'

'You *think* so?' Winifred was incredulous. 'Surely you would remember if you had seen him as Hamlet.'

'Oh. Well, we see so many – but, yes, I'm quite sure we did attend *Hamlet*, and I do remember the gentleman who played the title role was quite, er, energetic.'

Simon laughed at the expression on Winifred's face. 'As similar as you two are physically, you do not seem to have much in common.'

Winifred and Lissa looked at each other curiously. Lissa's mouth turned down.

'Oh, I don't think—' she began, but was cut off by Winifred's delighted crow.

'Why, we do look alike, don't we, Lissa? We have different-colored eyes, but we both have dark hair and lovely fair skin – and we are both beautiful.'

Lissa blinked. Winifred bounced a little in her seat. 'I have just had the most marvelous idea!'

Simon's heart sank.

Winifred leaned forward to speak further to Lissa. 'As you know, I am putting on a production of *A Midsummer Night's Dream*. I, of course, am playing Hermia, as well as the part of Titania. But I need someone for the role of Helena, and you will be perfect.' She turned to encompass the rest of the table in her glance. 'Do you not all agree?'

'But—' began Lissa.

Winifred pressed a hand to her bosom. 'Sometimes I am truly amazed at my own cleverness. The fact that Lissa looks so much like me will greatly heighten the impact of both parts.' Her gaze roamed over Lissa's petite form in clinical detachment. 'You are not so tall as I, but I shall wear very flat sandals and we shall build yours up a little. You are not nearly so well rounded either, but,' she continued, oblivious to Lissa's gasp of indignation, 'perhaps we can feed you up between now and the performance date.'

'I do not *wish* to be in your stu— in your play,' said Lissa in a high-pitched, breathless tone.

'There, there,' said Winifred, as though to a recalcitrant child. 'Of course, you do. It will be great fun and you will have a good time.'

Ignoring the small choking sounds emanating from Lissa, Winifred sat back in her chair, a beatific expression in her violet eyes. 'I cannot believe how well things are going. Except for the vicar and Mrs Mycombe, of course. They will be here tomorrow to rehearse their parts as Theseus and Hippolyta, but I fear they are quite unsuitable. Why, the vicar must be sixty if he's a day, and his wife is not much younger, and thin as a bed slat besides.'

'Winifred,' said Jane sharply. 'The vicar and his wife are doing this as a favor to you. The whole idea of appearing in a play goes very much against the grain for both of them. You knew before you set out on this project that there are few around here who can measure up to your criteria for acting talent.'

Winifred sighed, and a frown creased the ivory perfection of her forehead. 'That's true.' She turned to Simon and flung out her arms, knocking over a glass of lemonade as she did so. 'That is why I must shake the dust of this backwater from my feet, my lord. Oh, just imagine what it must be like to perform with the like of Edmund Kean, or Mrs Siddons.'

Simon felt his stomach tighten. Across from him, Charles leveled his quizzing glass at Winifred. 'My dear Miss Timburton. Are you saying that you have an inclination to perform upon the stage in London?'

Damn! thought Simon.

Winifred turned to Charles, her lovely face a study in innocent enthusiasm. 'Oh, yes, my lord, I wish it above all things. It is what I was born for!'

Charles dropped his quizzing glass in astonishment, but Winifred did not notice, having abruptly lowered her head and her attention to the blancmange before her.

'But,' said Charles, still in a state of stupefaction, 'ladies do not perform upon the stage.'

'This one intends to,' said Winifred calmly, her eyes still on the blancmange.

'Of course, she is not going to London to be an actress,' interposed Simon irritably. 'She has been spouting this nonsense for some time, but I assure you, nothing will come of it.'

Winifred did not reply, but, spooning the last of the custard into her mouth, shrugged her shoulders expressively.

Later, alone in his study with Charles, Simon expounded on this theme.

'I don't know where or when she took this maggot into her head, Charles, but I assure you, I have no intention of allowing my ward to make a spectacle of herself upon the stage in London or any other locality. The thing is ...' He shot a speculative glance at his friend.

'The thing is, she's been so damned isolated here in Hampshire. All she's ever known are a parcel of raw bumpkins. She's never become acquainted with a real man of the world – a man of fashion, such as yourself.'

Charles polished his quizzing glass vigorously with a corner of his handkerchief. 'Oh,' he said. 'Ah.'

Simon's sally had not met with the reception he had hoped, but he pursued the topic, undeterred. 'Yes, I'm quite sure that when she gets out in the world a bit and is introduced to more men of your caliber, her attitude will change radically.'

Again, Charles refused to rise to the bait, satisfying himself with a noncommittal, 'Harrumpf.'

What the devil was the matter with the fellow? Simon wondered in angry bafflement. He had as much as said outright in their infrequent correspondence that he was looking for a mate, yet when he was handed a perfectly splendid specimen on a silver salver, all he did was bark and waffle.

The next day saw a visit from Reverend Mycombe and his wife. Winifred gathered everyone into the Crimson Saloon for a rehearsal that soon turned out to be an unmitigated disaster. The vicar had forgotten his spectacles and had difficulty reading his lines. His wife, a kindly soul, but possessed of a horror of all things theatrical, read her part in a barely audible monotone, frequently lifting her eyes heavenward as though asking forgiveness.

Meanwhile, Lissa had apparently convinced herself that if she was to protect her vested interest in Marcus, it behooved her to maintain a vigilant surveillance on 'that wicked cat', as she persisted in categorizing Winifred. Thus, with a great show of condescension, she reported for duty as Helena.

Charles, noted Jane with mixed feelings, had abandoned his pursuit of her own unwilling person for the moment. He was, instead, pattering after Winifred, his nose fairly twitching in anticipation, like a scrawny rodent scrabbling for crumbs on the kitchen table. Winifred accepted his blandishments with the aplomb of a seasoned siren, portioning out inviting smiles at regular intervals and fluttering her lashes. She allowed him to run his fingers over her shoulder, and to squeeze her hand with disgusting frequency. Once he even slid his arm about her waist, and was rewarded with a demure giggle. Jane could have slapped the girl.

Simon at first seemed pleased with this turn of events, but even he began to look uncomfortable at Charles's improper behavior. As it happened, however, Simon was soon distracted as Winifred at one point turned her attention to his acting skills. After fifteen minutes of the most minute critique of his performance, he looked ready to do murder. Jane smiled, and the next moment was shaken by a sudden and unwelcome urge to smooth away the lines in his tanned forehead with her fingertips and to press her mouth to the rigid line of his jaw.

Good Lord, what was the matter with her? Her thoughts flew to the scene in his study the day before. Simon Talent was a perfectly ordinary man – well, almost perfectly ordinary if one discounted those gold-flecked brown eyes and the authority he wore as casually as a comfortable cloak. Still, there was no reason her knees should turn to jelly every time he smiled at her or why her pulse should race like a wind-blown leaf every time his hand brushed hers. Get hold of yourself, my girl, she told herself firmly. He is a good-looking man, but you've known good-looking men before. And this one will be out of your life in a few weeks' time. She stiffened her shoulders and forced her attention to the scene being played out on the stage.

'My lord,' Winifred was saying. 'You have only one line in this scene, but it is an important one. You must show the audience your love for Hermia.'

'Winifred,' said Simon through gritted teeth. 'I have repeated the line twenty-four times in the last five minutes, with a different inflection each time. There are only so many ways I can say, "You have her father's love, Demetrius." The damned line doesn't make a particle of sense, anyway.'

'Well, of course it does!' gasped Winifred, as though Simon had just spit in church. 'Shakespeare always makes perfect sense. Lysander is telling Demetrius to relinquish his claim to Hermia.'

'Then why can't he just tell the stupid sod to push off?'

'Because,' replied Winifred patiently, 'they did not speak so in Elizabethan times.'

'Simon,' interposed Jane, her shoulders shaking with suppressed laughter, 'you know very well what the line is intended to convey, and I'll warrant you could recite it beautifully if you could just contain your spleen for a few moments. You are behaving like a child at table who must eat his vegetables before he can go out to play. Just do it, and do it quickly, and it will all be over.'

If anything, this piece of totally unwanted advice caused Simon's expression to further darken.

'My spleen is no concern of yours, Miss Burch,' he snapped, but turning, he recited the line once more, this time to Winifred's satisfaction.

A few minutes later, when he was able to exit the stage, he strode to where Jane sat in a far corner of the room, sheltered by a large potted plant, her lips moving as she memorized her lines.

'I wish to speak to you,' he said baldly, 'about – about my aunt.'

'Your aunt? Lady Teague?'

'Yes, that aunt,' he said replied acidly. 'I believe she is the only one of my aunts in residence at the moment – although, at the rate the house is filling up, I shouldn't be surprised to see one or two more drift in at any moment.' He shook himself. 'I went to her chambers to speak to her this morning, and found her sewing. She said she was working on a gown for you. I must tell you, Miss Burch, that I am appalled. I did not ask Aunt Amabelle here to see her relegated to the role of ladies' maid.'

'Good Heavens!' said Jane, stricken. 'I can't imagine – oh!' she said, her face clearing. 'Lady Teague is sewing costumes for the play.'

'What?'

'Yes, she took one of my old muslins and she's converting it into appropriate fairy attire. She says she thinks she'll even be able to manage wings. And you should see what she's creating for Winifred.'

'What?' repeated Simon incredulously. 'I don't believe this. How could you coerce that poor old lady into what's nothing less than – than slavery.'

Jane was somewhat taken aback by his thunderous tone, but she told herself he was merely allowing himself an outlet for the ill temper that had been building in him ever since he'd agreed to be part of the cast of Winifred's play. Well, if Lord Simon thought she was going to cater to his foul moods, he was very badly mistaken.

'Don't be silly,' she said calmly.

Simon took a step toward her, but, though her heart beat a little faster, she did not retreat. Gazing coolly into his hot brown eyes, she continued, 'It was your aunt's idea to make costumes for the players. She was telling me how much she regretted that there was not a suitable part in the production for her, then she asked if she thought she might be of some use with her needle. I must say we're fortunate to have her, for she's prodigiously talented.'

'I thought you said you were against Winifred's scheme to go on the stage.'

'I am, but the play is giving her a temporary outlet for her desires, and aside from that, it's providing entertainment for the rather large group of persons we seem to be accumulating.

'That brings me to another point, Miss Burch. If—'

'I thought we were going to call each other Simon and Jane,' said Jane innocently.

'All right. Jane, why do you continue to plot against me?'

'I beg your pardon?' asked Jane, her gaze wide with astonishment.

Good God, thought Simon dazedly, it was happening again. He was falling into her damned storm-colored eyes. He took a deep breath. 'I beg your pardon. I did not mean to sound so – so melodramatic. It's just that you seem bent on thwarting my wishes at every turn.'

She turned on him a look of such puzzled sweetness that he was torn between wanting to throttle her and a desperate need to take her in his arms.

'I beg your pardon?' she repeated stiffly.

'I have told you that I do not wish Marcus and Winifred to become – become entangled, and you persist in trying to bring them together.'

'I have not!' Her voice rose in indignation. 'At least, not recently. Particularly since Lissa arrived. Although I must say I think your sister is behaving very foolishly.'

Since this statement coincided precisely with Simon's own analysis of Lissa's behavior, he was momentarily at a loss for words. This perhaps accounted for his decision to take some sort of action instead. He moved closer to Jane, whereupon he found that her scent was making him dizzy. This perhaps accounted for his reaching for her to steady himself.

The next moment, he caught her in his arms and pressed his mouth on hers with an urgency that astonished and appalled him.

Nine

'Love looks not with the eyes, but with the mind;
And therefore is wing'd Cupid painted blind.'
—A Midsummer Night's Dream, I, i.

When Simon grasped her shoulders and pulled her toward him, Jane's initial response was a startled gasp. At the first touch of his lips on hers, however, she was overwhelmed by the unfamiliar and totally delicious sensations that swept over her. When his arms tightened about her, she was intensely aware of the feel of his body against her own, and she fancied that it was his heartbeat that thundered in her ears. She was also dimly conscious that only a large plant prevented them from being seen by the group at the far end of the room.

The kiss was over as swiftly as it had begun, for just as Jane's lips opened involuntarily beneath his, Simon jerked away from her. For a moment, he simply stood, gazing at her, his hands still on her shoulders, and to Jane it seemed as though his gold-touched brown eyes were drawing her into his innermost self. She stared back at him.

'Why did you do that?' she blurted.

'I have no idea,' he growled, 'but I apologize.' He released her and stepped back. 'You're enough to drive a man insane, do you know that?'

Jane did not know what she had expected him to say, but the unexpected bitterness in his tone hurt and infuriated her. She stiffened. 'If a little plain speaking causes you to behave—' she began, but fell silent at the sound of Winifred's chiming laughter issuing from what seemed like a great distance away. Lord, she and Simon would be missed from the group at any moment. She pulled away from him. 'If you will excuse me, my lord.' Turning, she fled precipitously from the dangerous intimacy of the little alcove.

Simon followed a few moments later, more shaken by the brief contact than he would have believed. Good God, what had possessed him to behave in such a manner? And toward a woman he could barely tolerate.

Barely tolerate? His mind careened back to the moment when he had stepped so close to her that her fragrance had temporarily robbed him of reason. It came as a distinct shock to him to realize that he had been wanting to kiss Jane Burch for some time now, to feel the softness of her lips against his own and to hold her lithe suppleness in his arms. It had taken everything in him to break away from her after that brief embrace, for he had wanted so much more. He wanted to bury his face in her silky cap of curls. He wanted to press heated kisses from her eyebrows to the base of her throat. He wanted ...

He shook himself. Never mind what it was he wanted. He must concentrate on what he was going to do, which was to avoid any further encounters in secluded nooks with the delectable Miss Burch. She was not the sort of woman with whom a man could indulge in dalliance, even if he were given to that kind of thing. She was the sort of woman who could make a man's life a living hell if given half a chance, with her incessant meddling and her boundless assurance that she knew what was best for everyone with whom she came in contact. He was strongly of the opinion that Winifred and Charles would be well on the way to a serious courtship by now if it were not for her interference.

He moved slowly out from behind the plant and watched Jane from a distance as she conversed with Lissa. She was still rosy from their encounter and his throat tightened at the remembered feel of her. He sighed. The last thing he needed was to become involved with a willful termagant, no matter how enticing. Although, if he were honest with himself, he'd have to admit that he even enjoyed his confrontations with her. But no more of that. The house was full of people. Surely, he could manage to stay out of her way.

For the next few days, he was able to keep to his resolution. He became increasingly absorbed in the running of Selworth, and as far as he could tell, all was proceeding fairly smoothly in the house. He saw little of Jane, and he suspected she was avoiding him as well. This notion did not give him the satisfaction he might have expected. He noted that Winifred and Charles were spending more time in each other's company. Lissa was apparently maintaining her sweetness of temper with Marc, so he had hopes that all was well in that quarter.

These pleasant expectations received a severe setback one morning when he happened upon the two in the orangery, where they had apparently stolen for a few moments of privacy.

'But you promised, Marc!' Lissa's voice was high with indignation.

'I did no such thing, Lissa,' replied Marc, his obvious anger barely held in check. 'It was you who arbitrarily decided that I should relinquish the role of Oberon.'

'Well – I just assumed you would not have any objections,' she said with what she no doubt knew was a perfectly adorable pout. Simon sighed in exasperation as he approached them.

'Now what are you two brangling about?' he asked.

In unison, they swung toward him, each speaking at once.

'Lissa is being an unreasonable little twit,' said Marcus.

'Marc is being a perfect beast,' said Lissa.

Simon's first impulse was to turn and leave the hapless lovers to their own devices, but his conscience held him in place. Or rather, it was his lively fear that Diana and Jared would blame him for the rift in Lissa and Marc's lute which prompted him to set the pair back on the course of true love.

'Now, then,' he said, at his most paternal, 'just what seems to be the problem?'

'There is no problem.' Marc responded stiffly. 'It is merely that your sister believes me incapable of running my own life.'

Lissa gasped. 'That's not true! I merely asked him to do a small thing for me, and—'

'Small thing! You want me to give up a harmless activity that is bringing me a great deal of pleasure, all because you have jumped to an utterly false conclusion.'

'It is not I who am jumping to false conclusions. You spend every waking minute with that overblown siren. Why, this is the first time you've condescended to give me a moment since I arrived!'

'That's not true. It's just that every time you want to talk to me, it's about my shortcomings, and if you want to know the truth, I'm getting a little tired of it.'

Simon, raising his hand, said in a tone of great reasonableness, 'Now, Marc, just stop and think a moment. Lissa may have reason for her, er, unhappiness with your behavior. After receiving news that you left your home with very little explanation, she arrives here to find you in the company – the constant company – of a very beautiful woman. Naturally—'

He was interrupted as Lissa clutched at his sleeve. 'Are you implying that I am jealous of that mannerless hoyden?' she hissed.

'Of course not,' responded Simon hastily. 'Now, on the other hand, Marc has told you that he has no interest in Winifred beyond that of partner in a stage production. I believe him, and I think you should, too.'

At this, Lissa swelled visibly and her eyes turned to molten pitch. 'Men!' she said in accents heavy with loathing. 'You are all alike and you all hang together. Well, I wish you joy of each other's company.' She turned on her heel, but whirled again for a parting shot. 'And as for you, Mister King of the Fairies, I hope you fall off your mushroom and break your neck!'

With this she swept out of the orangery, and Simon would have been ready to swear she left a trail of blue smoke in her wake.

After a long silence, Marc turned to Simon. 'Well, you certainly handled that well. With your skill and understanding of human nature, it is no wonder you have made such a success in the world of diplomacy.' With which piece of withering sarcasm, he bowed and left the room, leaving Simon to curse his unwonted ineptitude.

For the next week, events continued on a fairly even keel, at least on the surface. Rehearsals for *A Midsummer Night's Dream* continued apace, and Simon took comfort in the fact that, in his role of Lysander, he had few lines to learn and was called on to spend little time on stage. Winifred continued to encourage the attentions of Charles and Harry and Gerard with equal good will. She could not be said to actually flirt with Marc, but her admiration for his acting and acrobatic abilities apparently knew no bounds. As for Marc and Lissa, they might have been two planets spinning in different orbits, each unknowing and uncaring of the existence of the other. Jane Burch, he noted with dissatisfaction, might have resided in a different galaxy altogether. To his dismay, he found himself looking forward to the rehearsals because they provided opportunities to see her.

Simon had been eminently correct in his assumption that Jane was avoiding him. She quickly learned his routine and made it her business to carry out her own duties wherever he wasn't. She was dismayed to discover that she missed him. How could one possibly miss a man whom one disliked intensely? she wondered in some irritation. The fact that she had experienced such a shattering response to his kiss merely infuriated her further. Her reaction certainly proved, she told herself, that anyone could fall victim to a handsome face and a lean, taut body. It was not long, however, before she was forced to admit that it was more than Simon's physical attributes that drew her toward him. Irritating as she might find his methods, she could appreciate his concern over those near and dear to him. In addition, their confrontations exhilarated her. A verbal bout with Lord Simon left her feeling as though she'd been drinking champagne – invigorated and slightly giddy.

A warning voice inside her head told her that enjoyment of his company might be far more dangerous than a simple physical attraction. Thus, she kept scrupulously to her plan of playing least-in-sight where Simon Talent was concerned.

She found herself spending more and more time with Lady Teague, whose combination of lighthearted nonsense and basic common sense greatly appealed to her. Often she would visit the older woman in her chambers, where she busily plied her needle. It was apparent that making the costumes for the play was greatly to her liking. 'For,' she said earnestly one morning after breakfast, 'I am used to being busy at Stonefield. When Jared, Simon's brother, married Diana – she's Marcus's sister, you know – Diana took over my chores as chatelaine of the place, but now that she has a babe, and another on the way, her time is mostly taken up with maternal duties. She is such a love, you know.'

Jane hesitated. 'I expect Lord Simon is much missed at Stonefield,' she said after a moment.

'Gracious, yes. It was hard to say good-bye to him again. It seems he was always leaving. The time he was at Waterloo was the worst, of course.'

'Waterloo,' murmured Jane, and felt a fluttering in the pit of her stomach at the dangers he had survived and the horrors he must have witnessed.

'Yes,' said Lady Teague quietly. 'We hoped he would stay when he returned at last from the war, but he became restless at Stonefield after he sold out, and at that time, he had no home of his own. When he was offered a position on Castlereagh's staff – it was a very junior position, but it promised better things – he snatched it up, and it was nearly three years before we saw him again.'

'But now he has returned for good,' said Jane.

'Well, as to that,' replied Lady Teague with a laugh, 'he says he longs for peace and quiet, but – well, he has retained his connections with Castlereagh's people, and has promised to take on tasks as needed. However, I believe he intends to reside at Ashwood. He seems to have great plans for the place.'

Jane's heart sank, a response for which she instantly chided herself. It mattered not to her when Simon left to take up his life – and his search for a biddable wife. She had known when they met that their acquaintance would be brief, and that was, after all, the way she preferred it. The sooner she could get on with her own plans for Winifred, the better. She rose and smiled at Lady Teague. 'I've enjoyed our coze, my lady, as always, but I must leave now. I promised Mrs Rudge I would go over the week's menus with her. Goodness, when the poor woman signed on with us as housekeeper, she had no idea she'd be catering to such a houseful.'

The older woman smiled apologetically. 'I fear we have set your household at sixes and sevens.'

'Nonsense,' said Jane stoutly, pausing to give the plump little woman a quick hug. 'Winifred and I were expiring of boredom before you all came. In addition, if Simon had not caused all of you to come here, I would never have had the opportunity to meet you, my lady, and that would be a shame.'

Dropping a light kiss on the older woman's hair, she ran lightly from the room.

She made her way thoughtfully along the corridor and descended the stairs to the hall. Turning toward the service wing, she was stayed in her path by the tumultuous entrance of Gerard and Harry from one of the nearby saloons. Harry's round, blue eyes were even rounder and bluer than usual and his yellow hair seemed endowed with a life of its own, its ungovernable spikes fairly quivering in excitement. Gerard's eyes, too, those windows to his emotions, blazed a message that filled Jane with foreboding.

'What is it?' she asked in trepidation, but she barely had the words out before a knock sounded at the front door. It was apparent the two scapegraces had been watching for whoever approached, for without waiting for Fellowes, Gerard tore to the door and flung it open, Harry close behind him.

'Uncle James!' he called to the gentleman who was just stepping down from a fashionable curricle. The word 'nondescript' might have been fashioned to describe this gentleman, thought Jane in some bemusement. Somewhere on the far side of forty, he was above medium height and rather stocky, dressed in a conservative ensemble of gray waistcoat and dark coat and breeches. His movements were unhurried and precise as he set his whip in its holster and made his way stolidly from his vehicle to the door. When he removed his shallow-crowned hat, his hair was revealed as thinning and of a brown so light as to be almost without color, matched by his brows and even his eyes, which were the most expressionless Jane had ever seen.

Gerard and Harry clustered about him, pelting him with unintelligible questions, but when they were inside the door, Gerard turned to his sister. 'Jane, may I present Sir James Beemish. He is from Gloucestershire and, being on his way to London, has stopped to visit with Harry.'

Sir James said nothing, but nodded and pressed his lips to Jane's hand in a vague salute.

Jane, quickly digesting the fact that stopping at Selworth on the way to London from Gloucestershire would have involved a considerable detour, also said nothing for a moment, merely returning Sir James's nod. The next instant, coming to herself, she extended her hand in welcome.

'What a nice surprise, Sir James.' She shot a significant glance at Gerard and was dismayed to find her suspicions confirmed as that young gentleman flushed guiltily. 'Do please come into the morning room and I'll ring for tea.' She noted with some wonderment that Sir James seemed to find her greeting odd, for at the word 'surprise', his brows lifted questioningly.

Once the little group entered the morning room, a forced laugh burst from Gerard's lips. 'Actually, Sir James's visit is not all that much of a surprise, is it Harry?' He turned to his friend in some desperation.

'No, no indeed,' chimed Harry. 'Been in correspondence with m'mother, doncherknow, and when she told me Uncle James would be trotting up to London – well, we've always been close, so I wrote him, asking him to stop for a visit. I hope that's all right,' he said, his blue eyes appearing ready to start from his head as he transferred his gaze to Jane.

Sir James smiled. Or at least Jane supposed it was a smile, for it consisted only of a slight thinning of his lips. 'I am dreadfully sorry, Miss—?'

'Burch,' answered Gerard promptly. 'My sister, Jane Burch. She's a visitor here, too, as are Harry and I. Well, no,' he amended awkwardly, 'not precisely a visitor. She's been acting as our cousin's companion, except that she's not anymore – only she is still ...' He trailed off despairingly.

Sir James's features creased in what might have been an expression of cordiality. 'It seems to me, Miss Burch, that these two young scamps have been taking advantage of your good nature. If my being here is an imposition, there is a perfectly adequate inn not two miles down the road.'

Despite his unassuming manner, Jane sensed a certain shrewdness behind the bland smile.

'Nonsense,' she replied with a cordial laugh. 'You will find us rather full of company at the moment, but we have plenty of room. I think we can put you up in tolerable comfort.' She rang for a footman, who soon bustled off to notify Mrs Rudge that yet another visitor had arrived. Mentally, Jane resolved that when she next spoke to the housekeeper, she would promise to recommend to Lord Simon that the household staff be enlarged to accommodate their sudden increase in resident population.

It was not very long before Mrs Rudge, a matronly female in starched bombazine, appeared to conduct Sir James to his chambers. Waving him on his way with further expressions of welcome, Jane waited until the door had closed behind their guest before rounding on Gerard and Harry.

'All right, you two, what is going on?'

Despite the guilt writ large on their faces, making them resemble schoolboys with their fingers caught in the jam pot, both young men insisted that Sir James's visit was the result of the most casual invitation issued by a loving nephew.

'No need to make such a pother about it, Janie,' said Gerard, rumpling her hair. 'You said yourself, the house is big enough to accommodate another twenty people without feeling the strain.'

'That's very true, you young whelp,' said Jane, jerking away from him to smooth her curls. 'But what I want to know is what is he doing here? You were obviously expecting him with bated breath, and I want to know what foul plan you two lackwits are hatching.'

'Janie!' said Gerard accusingly.

'Really, M-Miss Burch,' said Harry. 'It was all the merest happenstance.'

The pair steadfastly refused to deviate from their obviously carefully rehearsed story, and Jane was at last forced to give up.

'All right,' she said, as she moved toward the door. 'But, if he's in any way involved in one of your disasters while he's here, I'll know where to lay the blame.' With a minatory scowl, she swept from the chamber to inform Lord Simon that his responsibilities as host had just increased by one.

When family and guests gathered for luncheon in the Gold Saloon, Sir James was introduced all around. He greeted one and all with stolid courtesy, and to Jane's surprise, when he was presented to Winifred, his response, instead of the usual look of dazed wonder, consisted of a bow and a vague expression of pleasure at meeting her. It would be an overstatement to say that Winifred was taken aback, but the speculation in her glance was plain, as the gentleman, admittedly almost old enough to be her father, bent over her hand.

Simon welcomed the newcomer with cordiality, and Marcus acknowledged his presence with a smile and a nod.

'But where is Lissa?' asked Marcus, as footmen began bringing in trays.

'And Charles?' asked Simon.

Jane, glancing around, realized that she had seen neither of them all morning, and she was gripped by a sense of unease. Apparently, Marcus was seized by the same intimation, for he strode grimly toward the door.

He was forestalled as the door opened to admit Charles and Lissa, mud stained and disheveled and laughing uproariously.

'Lissa!' roared Marc.

'Lissa!' echoed her brother. 'Where the devil have you been?'

To Jane's dismay, and the obvious consternation of Lissa's

nearest and dearest, the young girl paused to press a light kiss on Charles's cheek before turning to face the group.

'It's been such a lark!' she cried blithely. 'Charles and I have spent the last three hours together in a deep, dark hole!'

Ten

'Wherefore was I to this keen mockery born?
When at your hands did I deserve this scorn?'
—A Midsummer Night's Dream III, i.

'"Lord, what fools these mortals be!" '

Jane, as Puck, spoke the words in her clear treble to Marcus, who was acting as Oberon. On cue, Marc delivered his lines with all the spirit of a man on the way to his own hanging.

Lord, what fools indeed, Simon thought morosely. The group was gathered on Selworth's south lawn, for Winifred had brought the rehearsals outside. Several potted trees and shrubs augmented Nature's efforts, so that the stage, an area raised on boards and covered with rugs, indeed resembled a forest bower.

A little way off, Lissa disported with Charles as they waited for their own entrances. Nearly a week had passed since the unnerving contretemps brought about by Lissa's disingenuous announcement. The whole episode, it turned out, had been completely innocent. In the company of a maid and a footman, Charles and Lissa had gone to inspect the Roman remains on their own. They had rambled over the ancient villa and had fallen into a pit lying within an unexcavated section of the structure.

Neither was harmed. The pit was, in reality, neither deep nor dark, but was sunk enough to make it necessary for the footman to return to the house for a shovel and another pair of hands, while the maid remained *in situ*, twittering anxiously at them from the rim of the pit. The two had apparently amused themselves by searching for artifacts and had, in fact, returned with a few coins and pottery shards.

It was obvious, however, that an alarming degree of intimacy had sprung up between them over the incident, though Lissa certainly did not appear to have lost her heart to the weedy peer, for she flirted outrageously with Gerard and Harry, as well as middle-aged Sir James, who took it all in good part.

Marcus retaliated by devoting every waking hour to Winifred. If he had appeared to be glued to the beauty's dainty fingertips before, he now seemed surgically stitched to every portion of her anatomy that he could touch without getting into trouble. Lissa, of course, conducted herself as though she were completely oblivious to the apparent defection of the man she had once declared the center of her universe.

Simon could cheerfully have strangled them both.

Almost immediately after Sir James's arrival, Winifred had appropriated him for the role of Egeus, Hermia's father. While denying in himself any talent whatsoever, Sir James, whom Jane had euphemized in her mind as 'the mysterious uncle', placidly agreed to take part in the play and, surprisingly, so impressed was Winifred by his performance, that she assigned to him the role of the clown Snout, as well.

Most of the actors had memorized their lines by now, and Simon was forced to admit that the production was coming together. Winifred, however, declared herself in despair. Marcus and Lissa spoke Shakespeare's rollicking dialogue in accents gloomy enough for a production of *King Lear*. Charles, though displaying an unsuspected flair for comedy, complained continually over the indignity of having to wear an ass's head, and Gerard and Harry experienced such difficulty in memorizing their lines that Winifred declared in some dudgeon that they would make pretty fools of themselves, blundering about the stage with their playbooks hanging about their necks.

The vicar and his wife, with the best will in the world, spoke their pieces in a colorless monotone, with an uncomfortable stiffness totally at odds with the personalities of the Duke of Athens and the Queen of the Amazons.

Winifred scarcely spoke two lines in sequence without stopping to give someone a direction, and it seemed to Simon that the only one caught up in the magic of the play was Jane, who breathed an airy lightness and fire and wit into the part of Puck.

'We shall just have to work harder,' said Winifred firmly after dinner a few evenings later. Everyone had gathered on the west terrace to enjoy a particularly magnificent sunset. 'Nothing was ever won without effort, after all.'

Her words were greeted with some surprise, since she had never been seen attempting anything more strenuous than lifting a sugared strawberry to her lips.

'That is very true,' said Aunt Amabelle with a wise nod of her head, her fingers busy with yet another costume for the play. 'And I'm sure if everyone puts his knuckles to the grindstone, we'll come through splendidly. If everyone' – she cast an austere glance at Marcus – 'simply concentrates on what he is supposed to be doing, the play will be a success. Or, no,' she said abruptly, 'that's "nose to the grindstone", isn't it?' She rubbed her own with some vigor.

Jane laughed aloud, and Simon watched her with a stab of tenderness. 'My cousin Jane', the frumpy spinster, had vanished completely. Her pointed nose seemed deliciously shaped now that it was not nearly so pink, and her eyebrows had grown out again, as had her lashes, which formed a dark fringe about the silver pools of her eyes.

Simon shook himself from his reverie, assisted by the unwelcome sight of Marc moving to seat himself close to Winifred. Very close to Winifred. 'I think,' said the young man in an intimate tone that hinted as assignations in secluded nooks, 'that I have a solution to your problem in scene two, act three.'

'Oh,' replied Winifred prosaically. Simon had noted that when the goddess was absorbed in her muse, she had no time for flirtation. 'Where Oberon is still on stage when Demetrius enters with Helena. Yes, that is a bit of a knot, isn't it? You can hardly be expected to stand in two places at once.'

'Well, perhaps I can,' said Marc with a lazy smile. From her perch on a nearby bench with Sir James, Lissa stiffened. 'What if, when Oberon tells Puck to stand aside, he retreats behind one of those large trees at the back of the stage? I could nip across behind the shrubbery while Puck is giving her little speech – she'd have to draw it out a little – throwing a toga or something over my costume. Then I could enter from behind yet another tree with Helena as her newfound swain.'

'Mmm,' said Winifred, 'that might work. We can try it out tomorrow. We'll do your scene with Helena first thing.'

'I don't think that will be possible,' Lissa said with a sniff. She edged closer to Sir James. 'I shan't be able to rehearse Helena's part tomorrow. I have other plans.'

Winifred's eyes widened. 'Plans? But this is the play! What could you have to do that is more important than that?'

Lissa rose from the bench, her skirts fairly vibrating, and Jane was put into mind of a small, furious cat, its tail a-twitch.

'A great number of things,' she said, with only the slightest tremor in her voice. 'Sir James is taking me up in his curricle tomorrow to go into the village.' She sent a provocative glance toward Harry's uncle, who ran a deprecating hand over his mouse-colored hair. 'Neither of us has seen any of the country hereabouts,' Lissa continued, 'and we have decided to go exploring.'

Winifred's eyes took on a feline cast of their own as they narrowed to steely purple slits. 'That,' she purred, 'will not be possible. We are going to be doing the first scene of act one just before luncheon, and I shall need Sir James. He is Egeus, you know, my – that is, Hermia's father, and he is critical to the scene.'

Lissa turned a haughty shoulder to Winifred and swayed toward Sir James, her lips curling into an appealing smile. 'What say you, sir?' she asked prettily. 'Shall we escape the tyrant's dictates for a little while to pursue our own pleasures?'

At this, Marcus stepped forward with fists clenched, but was forestalled by Sir James, who lifted a large hand. Turning an avuncular eye on Lissa, he murmured in a colorless voice. 'Now, now, my dear. The day is long, after all. We can just as well postpone our voyage of exploration until the afternoon. According to the schedule drawn up by Miss Timburton, neither of us will be required after luncheon for the rest of the day. We shall have hours to plunder the delights of the village and to wander leafy glades and verdant meadows.'

Lissa blinked, and Sir James blushed a little as though embarrassed by his sudden uncharacteristic flight of fancy. Marcus, his blatantly hostile stare undiminished, subsided into his seat beside Winifred.

'Well,' said Lissa ungraciously, 'I suppose that would be all right.' She cast a quick glance at Marcus who, having turned to watch with enraptured fascination a desultory game of catch being conducted by Gerard and Harry a few paces away, apparently did not notice. 'If you will excuse me,' she continued with great dignity, the tremor in her voice more pronounced, 'it's been a busy day, and I think I shall retire.' With a nod to the group, she swept from the terrace.

Immediately after her departure, Marcus rose to sit alone on a balustrade, his stony gaze transferring itself from Gerard and Harry to an undetermined location in the distance.

Watching, Jane fell prey to mixed emotions. While she could not in all conscience promote a match between Winifred and Marc if he and Lissa were truly in love, her conscience was not quite so nice when it came to two people who seemed bent on remaining at loggerheads with each other. She noticed the mental daggers cast by Simon at Marcus when that gentleman had appeared to be whispering honeyed temptation into Winifred's ear. Simon, she concluded, still believed that Marcus was Lissa's sole property, appearances to the contrary.

She cast a disdainful glance at Charles, who had sidled into the place next to Winifred vacated by Marcus. It was plain as a pikestaff, thought Jane. Winifred's scandalous scheme had borne its first fruits. She was already being thought of as a lightskirt.

And just look at Simon over there, grinning as though he were watching his horse round the bend ahead of the pack. He was apparently under the illusion that Charles's attentions to his ward indicated a burgeoning desire to make her his bride. True, Charles was not leering at Winifred through his quizzing glass as he had done at Jane, nor was he fondling her bare arm as though it were a spaniel, but Jane was as sure as though the man had hung out a sign that the light in his eye boded ill for Winifred's virtue.

She sighed. It appeared that another confrontation with Simon was in order. Not that Simon's problems were any of her business, but if Charles and Winifred were to be caught in a compromising situation, the fact that Charles was mistaken in his interpretation of Winifred's character would count for naught. Simon would have the two of them married before the cat could lick her ear, and Jane was determined that neither her friend nor her younger sisters would live under the same roof as the lecherous peer.

She came to herself with a start to realize that darkness was setting in and various insects of the night had come out to make nuisances of themselves. As the group moved inside to the Emerald Saloon to await the teatable, Simon hastened ahead to open the door for his aunt, and unobserved by all but Jane, Charles's hand slipped down to brush Winifred's shapely derriere. Winifred, to Jane's fury, merely smiled at Charles, her violet eyes quite blank.

Once inside, Winifred fell into conversation with Sir James.

'Oh, yes,' she said, dimpling, in answer to his question, 'I have every intention of becoming a professional actress.'

'I have heard that it is not an easy life,' murmured Sir James. 'Rehearsals begin early and go very late. Sometimes it is necessary to play in towns other than London, just to make ends meet.' He smiled at her, his rather hard eyes assessing. 'The acting life, it seems to me requires a great deal of dedication – and discipline.'

Winifred did not take umbrage, but considered his statement thoughtfully. 'It is true,' she said at last in an uncharacteristic moment of objective self-appraisal, 'that I have never had to earn my own way, and I suppose I am dreadfully spoiled, but I want this very badly. No one seems to understand that.' She smiled at him, for once without a trace of coquettishness. 'I am ready to do whatever is necessary to make a success on the stage.'

Across the room, Gerard and Harry exchanged significant glances, and when, a few moments later, Sir James rose to place his empty cup and saucer on the tea table, they joined him there for a few moments of intense, quiet conversation.

When, at last, everyone began to drift off to their beds, Jane lifted a hand to stay Simon, but dropped it again immediately. While Simon's attitude toward her had, on the increasingly rare occasions when they were together, been aloof to the point of rudeness, Jane recalled her vow to avoid being alone with him in intimate circumstances. The Emerald Saloon was spacious; but still, it was night, and the company would be taking most of the candles with them upstairs. She had no intention of spending so much as five minutes seated with Simon in the shadowed intimacy of a pool of candlelight. Alone. Tomorrow, in broad daylight, his study would do just as well. Or, no, not his study, she amended quickly, remembering the scent of roses from an open window. She must catch him in safe territory, someplace she could speak with relative privacy, without courting an undesirable closeness.

She had sufficient time to ponder this detail, for after blowing out her candle and climbing into bed, it was many hours before she fell asleep. Outlined against the bed hangings, she saw a face all too plainly delineated, with mahogany-colored hair falling over a compelling brow, and eyes the color of a forest pond, with flecks of gold dancing in their depths. A firm mouth seemed to smile at her in wicked invitation. That this last was wholly a product of her imagination did nothing to draw her toward sleep, for she next envisioned what it would be like to respond to that invitation. When at last she turned her face into her pillow, it was with a regretful sigh.

Despite her restless night, Jane was up early the next morning, and she proceeded immediately to her wardrobe for her shirt and breeches. She had ridden out in her boy's clothes almost every morning since the disastrous confrontation with the master of the house. From time to time she spied Simon in the distance, and he occasionally waved to her, but he never approached her, nor did he speak later of observing her. Ordinarily, this course of action suited her for, despite the fact that she felt no guilt over her morning forays, she did feel a residual awkwardness over the manner in which she had been found out. On this particular morning, however, she had other plans in mind. After a quick stop in the kitchen for coffee and a slice of bread, she headed for the stables, and soon thereafter was mounted on Talavera.

As luck would have it, she exited the stable yard just as Simon was returning from his own early morning gallop. He raised his hand in a perfunctory greeting and would have ridden on, but at Jane's gesture, he pulled up.

'Ride with you?' he asked warily in response to her demure invitation.

'Yes, just for a little way,' replied Jane, a little disgruntled at his reluctance. 'I shan't keep you from your breakfast for long.'

He grinned. 'It's not my stomach I'm worried about. I'm a man who believes in learning from experience, and it's been my experience that when you wish to talk to me, I am about to be treated to a constructive discourse I do not at all wish to hear.'

This was uncomfortably close to the mark, and Jane felt heat rise to her cheeks. She did not answer, but waited for him to turn his horse about. For some minutes they rode together in a silence that was oddly companionable. Jane was intensely aware of Simon's nearness and found herself musing in a most unmaidenly fashion on the muscular frame that showed to such advantage in well-cut riding clothes.

'How well,' said Jane at last, speaking with some difficulty, 'do you know the Earl of Wye?'

'Charles?' Simon asked in surprise. 'Well, we are not precisely bosom bows, but I've known him for some years now.' He scratched his chin thoughtfully. 'Actually, I do not know him all that well. The time we served together was fairly brief, and our correspondence since has been – well, intermittent. Why do you ask?' he concluded cautiously.

'Umm, what makes you think he is a proper husband for Winifred?'

He turned toward her, and in his eyes, Jane read his displeasure. 'What possible concern can my choice of a husband for Winifred be to you, Miss Burch?'

Oh, dear. 'Miss Burch.' Jane sighed. He was indeed displeased.

'Winifred is my friend,' she answered smoothly, biting her tongue as she almost added, 'and will be playing hostess to my two sisters.' Instead, she lowered her gaze demurely. 'I have reason to believe that the earl is not the sort of man you think him.'

'Ah. And what sort of man do I think him?'

'You believe him to be eminently eligible because of his title and his wealth. And, I suppose, you believe him to be a gentleman.'

'Well, of all the presumptuous ... Of course, he is a gentleman. He—' Simon stopped abruptly, recalling the lickerish expression on Charles's face that first evening at Selworth, when he'd inquired as to Jane's status in the household. 'Why?' he asked baldly.

Jane drew a long breath, and launched into a description of the earl's behavior toward her since his arrival. She had not yet come to the incident the night before when Charles had availed himself of Winifred's enticing proximity, when Simon interrupted her.

'He actually put his hands on your – on you?' he asked, his fists clenched so tightly on Storm's reins that the animal's head drew back indignantly. 'Why the devil didn't you tell me?'

Jane shifted in her saddle, feeling herself on shaky ground. 'I did not want to cause a row,' she said at last. 'Lord Wye is your friend – and your guest. I was afraid—'

Simon snorted. 'You must have done something to encourage him,' he said through tight lips.

'What!' gasped Jane in outraged astonishment.

'Not purposely, of course,' continued Simon hastily. His lean cheeks took on a dull flush. 'That is – you have not the slightest sense of decorum, and you must have inadvertently said or done something that led him to think – quite falsely, of course, that—'

Had Jane not been astride a horse, she would have slapped him. Instead, she wrenched on her reins, backing away from him.

'Never mind,' she said breathlessly, almost choking on the rage and hurt and humiliation that boiled within her. 'I deeply regret having brought this matter to your attention. I might have known that you would take Charles's part. You are both men, after all.' She spat the words with loathing. 'I realize what I am about to say is quite useless, but I did *not* encourage Charles – in word, gesture, or deed. The earl is, quite simply, a lecher. I can, of course, understand why this makes no difference to you. He is wealthy and a peer. Those facts quite outweigh any minor character flaws and make him eminently suitable as a *parti* for your ward, of whose moral standards you have so loudly proclaimed yourself the guardian.'

White-faced, Simon lifted a hand in protest, but Jane hurtled on, giving him no chance to respond. 'Winifred is an innocent, and gently bred, but I am sure in time she will become accustomed to her husband's distasteful gropings as well as his tendency to molest the housemaids, to say nothing of the drain on the household budget caused by the demands of his mistresses. She will also, no doubt, learn to deal with the malicious barbs that are sure to be flung at her by the oh-so-proper members of the *ton*.' She drew in a deep, shuddering breath. 'It is unfortunate that I shall be unable to leave Selworth until after Winifred's play, but please be assured that I will keep well out of your way for the remainder of my stay. In fact, it is my devout hope that I will not have to speak to you again while I am here.'

Unable to forestall any longer the tears that rose in a painful tide behind her eyes, she spurred Talavera, and in a few moments had sped away.

Simon watched her straight back disappear into the golden morning mist. He sagged in his saddle. Lord, he thought, bitterly, in her boy's shirt and breeches she was more seductive than any female he had ever beheld in revealing décolletage and winsome furbelows. He groaned. She had come to him, openly and in all sincerity to be of help to him, and he had returned her generosity by blurting out the most hurtful thing he could have said. He had not meant any of it, of course. He cursed silently. He was so damned obsessed with getting Winifred married off that he could not see beyond his fear of having to marry her himself.

He was forced to admit to himself that he had already observed that Charles was less than the perfect gentleman, but it was his feeling that he and Winifred deserved each other. Besides, if he were to admit that Charles was totally unsuitable husband material (and right now, his most urgent desire was to smash his fist into Charles's face, hard and repeatedly), it would be necessary drive the earl from his house with a fiery sword. This course of action would leave him with nothing but a curse and a prayer between him and a meeting with Winifred before the vicar and a church full of well-wishers.

To be sure, Winifred was not the fright he had feared she would be. She was a beautiful girl and, once she had been turned from her ludicrous plan to go on the stage, she would settle down, at which time she would no doubt be a credit to any man's home. He, personally, would rather be hung by his heels over a pit of alligators than marry her. Particularly, since he was already—

He stopped suddenly, his fists once more clutching the reins. For a long moment, he remained utterly still. At last, he said the words aloud. 'Particularly, since I am already in love with Jane Burch.'

He listened to himself in amazement. He had been stupifyingly buffle-headed. At some time during the past few weeks, his dream of a comfortable wife adorning his home, and presenting him with the required heir, had dissolved like snow crystals on a hearth, replaced by his need for a slender creature of fire and air with the soul of a sergeant major and a tongue like a whip thong.

And he, in his cataclysmic ineptitude, had just ensured she would, in all probability, never speak to him again.

Turning Storm about, he rode slowly toward the house and a future that seemed to promise only despair.

Eleven

'Here come the lovers, full of joy and mirth.'
—A Midsummer Night's Dream, V, i.

Jane rode aimlessly for a long time, letting Talavera have his head. Unheeded, tears fell to soak her shirtfront and, raising her head at last, she observed through blurred eyes that she had reached one of her favorite spots on the estate – a rounded knoll overlooking a lush, green valley.

She dismounted and flung herself on the grass, burying her face in its sun-laved warmth. On the far side of the knoll, a small grove of beech trees swayed gracefully, their glossy leaves rustling in the slight breeze that brought the scent of saintfoin and clover. She turned her face to the drifting clouds, seeking solace. How could everything look the same? The sun still wheeled in the sky, beaming impartially on the world beneath. Birds sang and bees buzzed mightily as they went about their tasks, just as though the earth had not opened up to let Jane Burch plunge into the depths of despair.

How could he have spoken to her so? She did not know which was worse, to be accused first of actually encouraging Charles's smarmy attentions, or next, to be told she was the kind of witless widgeon who would throw out lures without even being aware of it. It was a very good thing for Lord Simon that she was not in the habit of carrying a riding crop!

She was dimly aware that she was feeding her anger, willing it to spread into a conflagration that would blot out coherent thought. For, truth to tell, though Simon had spoken to her very little over the last week or so, it seemed to her that of late he was coming to view her with – well, not with cordiality, perhaps, but once or twice she had intercepted a glance from him that was almost ... No. She was imagining things. He had as much as told her he disliked her intensely, all because she dared thwart his grand plans. Oh, how she detested that man!

She came to her feet abruptly. Why the *devil* was she moping about here in the back of beyond? She had plans of her own to tend. If she were not careful, Simon would carry out his nefarious scheme to marry Winifred off to that lecherous snake, the Earl of Wye. Recalling the cordiality of Winifred's recent responses to Charles's overtures, it seemed a distinct possibility that she would accept the knave should he propose. She was determined not to let her friend fall into the evil clutches of the wicked peer.

Even to her own ears, Jane's words sounded as though they had come directly from a very bad melodrama, but at the moment she was in no mood for constructive self-appraisal.

As she remounted Talavera and headed for home, she vowed that she would put a spoke in Simon's plans. By God, she would remove Charles as a threat to Winifred's well-being and the virtue of her little sisters.

Somewhere, deep down in her core throbbed a hurt so painful she could not bear to bring it out for examination, and she tried to keep it at bay by mouthing more maledictions at Simon. By the time she reached the stables, she had quite exhausted her supply of pejoratives in her own language and had begun on her meager French.

Her instinct was to flee to the shelter of her chambers, and she looked carefully about as she entered the house. If she were to meet Simon at this moment, she felt that she would either explode or simply slide to the floor in a noisy flood of tears. Tiptoeing through the corridor to the back stairs, her attention was caught by the faint sounds of a commotion emanating from the main part of the house. Curious, she made her way to the entrance hall, where she was brought up short, her jaw dropping in amazement.

A young woman stood in the center of the hall. She was Junoesque in stature, and though her dark eyes were very fine, her features were sharp and unpleasant, giving her face the aspect of two polished pebbles surrounded by an outcropping of small rocks. She was dressed in the height of fashion in a traveling gown of gray twilled silk, over which she wore a matching spencer, embellished with rows of braid in a darker shade of gray. Next to her stood an older woman, also elegantly dressed, but small and pale and nervous. Behind these two stood yet another female, apparently a ladies' maid. Through the open door, a traveling coach could be discerned, disgorging, under the supervision of a distraught-looking Fellowes, a steady procession of luggage.

The young woman disdained to take notice of Jane, who was acutely conscious of the highly improper appearance she made in her shirt and breeches, but Fellowes, catching sight of her through the open door, hastened into the house.

'Oh, Miss Burch!' he exclaimed, his sensibilities apparently strained to snapping. 'We have visitors. I have sent for Lady Teague and Lord Simon. I offered to escort the, er, ladies into the morning room, but—'

'I,' said the young woman, apparently noticing Jane for the first time, 'am Lady Hermione Stickleford.' She spoke in a high nasal voice as her disapproving gaze swept over Jane, and she might have been announcing the arrival of the Princess Royale. Her nose twitched slightly as Jane merely responded with a blank stare. 'I can scarcely credit it, but it appears I am not expected.'

'Well,' said Jane, completely at a loss. 'I don't believe—'

'Hermione!'

The word was uttered in such a horrified squeak that Jane was obliged to turn to see who was speaking. Charles tottered in a doorway at the far side of the hall. His eyes were wide and staring, and his face was whiter than the pristine shirtfront that lay under his incandescent waistcoat.

'Wye!' uttered Lady Hermione in a faint scream.

Why what? thought Jane confusedly. Her face cleared almost immediately. She had almost forgotten that Charles was officially the Earl of Wye. Good Lord, this insufferable female was using the familiar form of his title! That must mean that he and she were ... good Lord!

'Hermione!' Charles cried again weakly, lurching across the floor to gather her in an awkward embrace. She allowed a chaste kiss on one cheek before drawing back to bestow a minatory stare on him.

'Wye, these people' – she glared austerely about her – 'apparently had no idea that I would be arriving this morning. Did you not—?'

She was interrupted by the arrival of Simon and Aunt Amabelle, who wore identical expressions of bafflement. Since Charles seemed incapable of speech, or even coherent thought, Jane moved forward.

'Aunt Amabelle, may I present Lady Hermione Stickleford? Lady Hermione, Lady Teague and Lord Simon Talent.' Jane, feeling she had acquitted herself with fortitude, stepped back after shooting a meaningful glance at Charles.

The earl's mouth contorted into a ghastly smile, and when he opened it, the only sound to emerge for some seconds was a rusty croak. 'Lady Teague,' he mumbled at last, 'Simon, Miss Burch, may I...?' His voice trailed off unhappily, but after a moment he began again. 'May I present my f- my f-.' Once again, his words slid into a strangled, incomprehensible knot of sound, until with all eyes on him, registering various degrees of expectancy he blurted, 'My fiancée.'

'What?' gasped Simon, an almost ludicrous combination of astonishment and fury written on his face.

'Oh, my,' said Aunt Amabelle, her jewelry vibrating discordantly.

Jane remained silent, as did Lady Hermione, who contented herself with a small sniff.

'Well,' continued Aunt Amabelle, bustling forward to fill the void, 'welcome to Selworth, Lady Hermione.' She sent a questioning glance to the older woman, who had remained silently in the background.

'My mother,' responded Lady Hermione with great condescension. 'Gertrude, Lady Wimpole, relict of the fifth Earl of Wimpole.' She paused expectantly, but when no response was forthcoming, she added stiffly, 'We reside with my brother, the sixth earl, in Oxfordshire, but for most of the year we can be found in Grosvenor Square.'

Lady Wimpole offered a wan smile and nodded her head, but said nothing.

'Well,' said Aunt Amabelle again, once more stepping into the breach. 'I'm afraid we were not expecting you, but we are happy to welcome another guest. The more, the merr— well,' she concluded after a slight pause and a glance at Lady Hermione's unpromising countenance, 'at any rate, we have plenty of room. If you will accompany me to the morning room, we can have a nice cup of tea while your rooms are being prepared.'

Lady Hermione turned to her betrothed. 'I would like an explanation, Wye,' she said, in a tone that boded no good for the hapless peer. 'However, I do not propose to discuss it at this moment.' She nodded to Aunt Amabelle before turning to her mother. 'Come, Mama. Fletcher' – this to the maid, who stiffened to attention – 'see to my things.' Lady Wimpole hurried after her daughter. The maid scurried out the front door to where trunks and portmanteaus were still being unloaded from the carriage, or rather, both carriages, since another vehicle had drawn up behind the first. Nearby, the two coachmen, several footmen, and a small covey of additional maids clustered in a vociferous group, raising their voices in question. Jane exchanged an involuntary glance with Simon. How long did her ladyship plan to stay, for Heavens' sake?

Answering an unspoken plea in Aunt Amabelle's eyes, Jane remained in the hall as the others proceeded in stately fashion to the morning room. She beckoned to Fellowes, who was still laboring outside.

'Do we have rooms that can be readied for these people?' she asked in an urgent whisper.

'Oh, yes, miss,' replied Fellowes kindly. 'As you are aware, the west wing is still empty and, although the chambers there are not usually kept in quite the state of readiness as the others, it will merely require the removal of the Holland covers from the furniture, fresh linens on the beds and, perhaps, the placing of a few vases of flowers.'

'Fellowes,' breathed Jane in humble gratitude, 'you are a prince among butlers. How about their staff? Goodness, those two women travel with a retinue fit for the Regent.'

'The abigails will have rooms adjacent to, er, Lady Hermione, is it? And…?' He paused diffidently.

'Lady Wimpole. She is Lady Hermione's mother.' Jane screwed up her features, glared down her short nose, and said in haughty accents, ' "The relict of the fifth Earl of Wimpole." '

A twinkle appeared deep in Fellowes' eyes. 'Yes, miss. The two abigails will be housed in rooms adjacent to those of the ladies. The footmen and the coachmen and the other females will be, er, suitably housed elsewhere.'

'Thank you, Fellowes,' said Jane. 'I had better change and join the others. Lord Simon seems somewhat disgruntled.' She grinned impishly at the butler and hurried toward the stairs.

A quick glance at Simon, when she entered the morning room some minutes later, revealed him to be no more gruntled than before. He sat silent and fuming over the teacups as his aunt produced from somewhere a flow of inconsequential chatter. She stopped midsentence as Jane seated herself, as though, with the promise of reinforcements, her mind simply stopped functioning. Her bracelets clanked disconsolately.

'Well!' said Jane brightly. 'I hope you had a pleasant journey. Did you come from London or Oxfordshire?'

'From Oxfordshire, naturally,' replied Lady Hermione with a sniff. 'London is quite insupportable at this time of year.'

To this, Jane could find no response. 'My brother is just down from Oxford, temporarily,' she said in some desperation.

'Our estate is near the northern border of the county,' said Lady Hermione. 'We never go to Oxford. It is filled with students, you know.'

'Yes, I suppose it is,' said Jane unsteadily. She turned to Lady Teague. 'Do you know where the boys are?' she asked. 'Or Winifred and Lissa – and Sir James?'

'Gracious,' said Lady Wimpole, speaking for the first time. 'Are all those people guests in the house?'

'Yes, all except for Winifred,' replied Simon through clenched teeth. He shot a searing glance at Charles, who quailed visibly. 'Miss Winifred Timburton, that is, my ward.'

'No, I don't, dear,' Lady Teague responded vaguely. 'Know where they are, that is. I saw Gerard and Harry set off earlier with fishing poles over their shoulders, and I believe Lissa is attending to some correspondence in her room. I have no idea where Winifred and Sir James might be.'

As if on cue, the door to the morning room opened to admit the pair in question. Winifred, gowned in rich ivory linen embroidered in an intricate design of pale green leaves, and her hair caught into an graceful knot atop her head, looked as though she had just stepped from a temple frieze. Lady Hermione's eyes fairly started from her head.

'Fellowes said we have guests,' said Winifred disarmingly. Her gaze swept about the group questioningly and if, as introductions were made all around, she sensed Lady Hermione's obvious hostility, she gave no sign. Lady Hermione nodded distantly to Sir James before turning away. Obviously, a mere baronet, particularly one so unassuming as the nondescript gentleman bending over her hand, was beneath her notice. Conversation became general then, and in a few moments Fellowes appeared to report that all was in readiness for the newcomers. With a crackle of her skirts, Lady Hermione rose from her seat, and moved regally toward the door, her mother trailing in her wake like an obedient shadow. Before proceeding through the door, the younger woman swung about.

'Wye,' she said evenly, in her well-modulated voice, 'I shall wish to speak to you directly we are settled in and rested.'

Charles started, but appeared resigned to his fate. 'Yes, my love,' he replied meekly.

As soon as the two women had left the room, the others moved to the door as well, Charles in the lead.

'One moment. if you will, Charles,' Simon called firmly, reaching to place a hand on the earl's shoulder. 'I'd like a word with you.'

As the two stepped into the corridor, Simon knew an almost overpowering urge to shake Charles until his ears fell off. He maintained his hold on the earl's shoulder until they reached the study, whereupon he thrust him into the room before him.

Plunging the hapless peer ungently into a chair, Simon sank into the one behind his desk.

'So, Charles,' he said in a voice of awful calm, 'you are betrothed.'

Charles shifted uncomfortably, his long legs angled in front of him. 'Simon, I swear I meant to tell you, but ...' He trailed off in a painful pause.

'But, what?' growled Simon.

'Well, the thing is, nothing's really settled yet.'

'Odd. Lady Hermione appears to feel the matter is settled.'

'Yes, well – I did propose.'

'And?' Simon experienced the eerie sensation that the furniture was advancing on him, closing him in, and that the air in the room was pressing down, making it hard to breathe He noted absently that Charles's shirtfront was no longer pristine, being quite damp with perspiration.

'And she did accept,' concluded Charles in a despairing whisper.

Simon leaned forward on his elbows, steepling his fingers before him. 'Ah. And you have her family's permission.'

'Lord, yes,' muttered Charles. 'Her brother practically embraced me when I went to ask for her hand. But,' he continued eagerly, 'nothing has been signed yet – no settlement papers, dowry – that sort of thing. I was hoping – that is ...'

'You sound less than anxious to enter the married state, Charles.' Simon marveled at the steadiness of his own voice.

Charles heaved a martyred sigh. 'To tell you the truth, old man, I've been hoping desperately for something to happen so that I won't have to go through with it.' Catching Simon's expression, he ducked his head shamefacedly. 'I know how that sounds. I mean, I did ask her, but only because m'sisters and m'mother have been after me like terriers. Don't give a fellow a moment's peace. "Eminently suitable", they say. "So well bred". But, good God. Simon, did you get a good look at her? She has a face that would curdle custard and a disposition to match. I know I should have told you she was coming, but I kept hoping something would stay her.' He glanced reproachfully at the ceiling as though calling a recalcitrant Deity to His duty.

'Poor lad,' said Simon. He rose and came around the desk. 'Stand up, Charles.'

Instead, Charles cowered in his chair. 'You ain't going to hit me, are you?'

'Hit you? For letting me think I was entertaining an eligible *parti* for my ward?' He reached down and wrenched Charles to his feet by the scruff of his neck. Though Charles topped Simon by at least four inches, it was Charles who drew back in fear. 'Or,' continued Simon in a voice of iron, 'for putting me in an absolutely untenable position, so that I now find my life in ruins? No, I'm not going to hit you for that.'

Whereupon he reached back and brought his fist forward, plunging it into the center of Charles's face, knocking the earl to the floor, where he sprawled in an awkward heap.

'Aaugh!' cried Charles, his hand pressed to his nose. He pulled it away and examined his fingers in fascinated horror. 'I'm bleeding!' He fished in his coat pocket and produced a handkerchief, with which he attempted to stem the flow. 'You said you wouldn't hit me!'

'You're lucky I'm not going to do it again, and a few more times after that. I promise you I'll do much worse if you ever so much as breathe heavily on Miss Burch again.'

'M-Miss Burch?' An expression of contrived innocence spread over Charles's features, and Simon's foot fairly twitched with an impulse to kick him.

'Yes, Miss Burch. She told me what occurred between you – and after I had taken pains to explain to you that she is under my protection. I should demand that you marry her, I suppose, but it seems unfair to serve her such a turn.'

Charles blanched. 'I'm terribly sorry, old man. Don't know what came over me. It won't happen again, I assure you.'

At the conclusion of this disingenuous speech, Simon was inclined to pull the earl to his feet for another lesson, but after a moment, he nudged him with his toe.

'Get up, Charles. And get out of my sight.'

Charles did not need to be told twice. With surprising agility in one who had been so utterly brutalized the moment before, he leaped to his feet. The next moment, handkerchief still pressed to his nose, he whisked himself out the door.

Simon retreated to his chair behind the desk, and for many long moments he sat there, his head in his hands.

Dear God, what was he to do now? Within two weeks, if his ward had not received a serious declaration of intent, it was he who would be down on bended knee before her. A vision of life with Winifred rose before him, and a groan of anguish welled up from the depths of his soul.

He found little solace in the fact that Winifred's requirements for a husband apparently included an exalted title and a great deal of money. Simon was a wealthy man, and though he was not a peer, he was closely related to one which, in Winifred's mind, probably amounted to the same thing. No, there was little doubt that she would accept his proposal. His expressed determination that she would never set foot on the stage would carry little weight with Winifred, given her unshakable confidence in her ability to sway men to her desires.

He uttered another groan before reaching for the pile of papers left earlier for his perusal by Minster, the estate agent.

Only a few yards away, Jane entered the library. It was, she thought, one of the pleasantest rooms in the house. Unlike the libraries in so many gentlemen's residences, it was light and airy, painted white and embellished with garlands of gilded carvings. The atmosphere of restful luminescence was further heightened by the bookcases of bleached lime which lined the walls.

She always welcomed an opportunity to slip away from the household for a few minutes among her favorite books, for Winifred's father, though his taste in women was dubious, had a magnificent collection of volumes of every genre. Jane favored the classic tales of adventure and love, and she was currently enthralled with *The Song of Roland*.

She had scarcely removed the book from the shelf, preparatory to curling up in one of the comfortable leather chairs that dotted the room, when the sound of the door opening caused her to turn. At the sight of the figure who stood there, she knew a moment of panic, and clutched the huge volume to her breast in a protective gesture.

The next moment, she dropped the book on a nearby table, and strode toward him.

'I was just leaving, my lord,' she said to Simon as he stood frozen on the threshold. 'If you will excuse me.'

She attempted to push past him, but he grasped her shoulders and pulled her inside the room, closing the door with his foot.

'Jane – please. I must speak to you.'

'You have already spoken to me, my lord, with what results I do not care to consider.'

'I know, but you must listen.' He tightened his grip as Jane began to wriggle in his grasp.

'Is this how you attained your success in diplomacy – my lord?' Jane said scornfully. 'By coercion?'

Simon immediately loosened his grip, but he did not release her. Instead, he moved with her farther into the room, pausing before an oak library table.

'I deserve all the contempt you can heap on my head, Jane.' He spoke with great effort, she noted, and he looked as a man might who had just been handed a heavy burden. 'Just give me five minutes. Then, if you wish to leave, I shan't try to stop you.'

Reluctantly, Jane ceased struggling, and Simon lowered his hands.

'Thank you,' he said. Jane looked into his eyes and immediately wished she hadn't. The golden flecks swirling against their velvety brown background disoriented her and caused strange, wonderful sensations to curl in the pit of her stomach. 'Actually,' he continued, 'I merely want to apologize.'

Though she was no longer in his grasp, Simon did not move away from her, and she could feel the warmth of his breath on her cheek. The all-gone feeling produced in her stomach by his touch, the soap and lotion scent of him, totally unnerved her, and she raised her hand, as though she would brush it away.

'What I said was absolutely unforgivable, and I did not mean a word of it.'

Jane found it hard to breathe, and she pulled away from Simon, seeking deep within herself for the anger that had sustained her earlier. 'Then why did you say it?' she asked levelly.

Simon was silent for a moment. 'I'm not sure if I can answer that.'

he said at last. 'As I told you before, I am – anxious to get Winifred married, and I thought I had found the perfect partner for her. So desperately did I cling to that belief, that when you told me something that threatened to shatter it, I – well, I scrabbled around for a – a theory that would allow me to deny what you said.'

Jane was still angry, but she was puzzled as well. 'I do not understand,' she said, 'this great determination to find a husband for Winifred right this minute. Winifred is not getting any younger, but surely – if you just wait until you can take her to London for the Season—'

Once again, Simon paused for a long moment before replying. 'I don't think I can explain that either,' he said with a sigh.

Jane knew a surge of disappointment. She schooled her features to immobility, however, as she said briskly, 'There seems to be a great deal you cannot explain, my lord.'

She would have moved to the door then, but was halted by the look of unhappiness that flooded Simon's eyes. A strange, sad feeling swept through her, and she put her hand out. Before she was aware of what was happening, Simon had pulled her against him.

His arms encircled her, and he pressed his cheek against her hair. Jane felt him shudder against her, and her resentment melted in a wave of longing that caused her to curl against him. When he drew back to cup her chin in his hand, she raised her lips to his.

Twelve

'Lovers and madmen have such seething brains ...'
—A Midsummer Night's Dream, V, i.

Simon reveled in the feel of her against him. He knew he had no right to enfold her in his arms. She had given him no encouragement, beyond the lightening of her storm-cloud eyes and her lifted hand, but so deep was his need of her at that moment, that with her gesture, he was lost to reason. In the turmoil of the desire she stirred in him, he became aware that she had brought her arms about him. She lifted her mouth, and with a choked sigh, he placed his lips against hers.

This time the kiss was not urgent, but deep and tender and seeking. Simon's hands moved on her back. God, she felt good! When she pressed against him, he pulled his mouth from hers to drop kisses on the vulnerable, petal-softness of her eyelids, then along her cheeks, and the infinitely tender line of her jaw. The scent of lavender enveloped him, and the small noises she made in the back of her throat drove him to the brink of insanity.

He drew his hand over the lovely, womanly fullness of her breast, and she gasped. It was at that moment that the realization of what he was doing forced its way into his mind. Apparently, Jane was brought to reason at the same moment, for she drew away abruptly, leaving him bereft.

For a moment, she simply stared at him with her great, misty eyes, her fingers pressed against her lips.

'You have to stop doing that,' she whispered brokenly.

'Yes, I know,' he said, his breath catching. 'I am in danger of making it a habit. I think it's that scent you wear.'

She laughed shakily. 'You are blaming me?'

I love you, Jane Burch. I love you and I want you and I need you as I need air to breathe. He clamped his teeth on the tide of words that seemed ready to burst from him. How could he speak them, knowing the antipathy she felt for him and knowing that by this time next week he might be betrothed to someone else?

'Of course, I blame you,' he said gruffly. 'I have already told you, I am not responsible for my actions where you are concerned. It was either kiss you or strangle you, and I understand they have laws about that sort of thing.'

Jane drew a shuddering breath. 'You make a joke of it, and I suppose, in a way it is, but I warn you, I will not allow this to happen again. Contrary to what you must believe, I am not in the habit of allowing men to kiss me – repeatedly – on a whim.'

At this, he stiffened at the reminder that he was still unforgiven for his earlier blunder.

'No one is more aware of that than I,' he said in a low voice. 'Please believe me.'

He turned to go, but swung about as he reached the door.

'By the by, I do not believe Charles will importune you again.'

'No.' Jane's lips curved upward. 'I am sure he will be kept well under guard from now on.'

Heartened, Simon permitted himself a small grin. 'That is not what I meant, but you are quite right, of course. I think we can regard Charles as more or less a spent force.' He gazed at her for a long moment then, turning, he left the room, closing the door softly behind him.

Jane discovered that her knees would no longer hold her up, and she sank into the nearest chair. Her first instinct was to fan the feeble spark of anger that still lay deep within her at the words he had spoken earlier in the day. The despicable cad had not only hurled false accusations at her, but had had the temerity to maul her like a common chambermaid. She should have given him a piece of her mind and then slapped him.

But she had done neither. In fact, at the time, she would have had difficulty in locating her mind at all, let alone giving pieces of it away. When he had pulled her to him with his need written plain in his eyes, rational thought had deserted her. She knew only an irresistible need of her own, to press into him, to feel the lean strength of his body against hers. When his mouth had covered hers with such urgency, her response had been immediate and overwhelming.

Her lips had parted eagerly beneath his, and at the touch of his hand on her breast, she had thought she would shatter with wanting.

He had said he did not mean the words he had flung at her, and she believed him. What she had a hard time believing, and therefore forgiving, was his motivation for saying them in the first place. He was keeping something from her, and while he had every right to do so, the thought that he felt he could not trust her completely was like a small knife whittling away part of her insides.

The notion occurred to her that she had not been altogether forthright with him about her scheme for Winifred, but that was really a very small omission. What possible interest could he have in her dreams for her sisters? No, the important thing was that there was something he was not telling about his grand scheme for Winifred's future, and she meant to have it out of him.

Having settled all this to her satisfaction, her thoughts returned, very much without her permission, to that shattering kiss. How, she wondered again, her mouth suddenly dry, could she have responded so wantonly to the fire of his embrace? How could she have permitted such intimacy when she was still so overset by his earlier behavior? The answer came swiftly and suddenly, as though it had lain in the back of her mind for some time, just waiting to be released.

Because you're in love with him, you twit.

She was, she noted almost detachedly, not as surprised by the idea as she should have been. Somewhere in the fringes of her mind, she had become aware of the attraction he was beginning to hold for her. She had admitted long ago, that despite the adversarial nature of their relationship, she enjoyed being with him.

He was, she mused, despite his regrettable tendency to order people's lives, an eminently lovable man. He was intelligent and witty and decent. She smiled wryly. Admirable features all, but the simple fact was that she had lived on a heightened plane of existence ever since the morning she had greeted him in her disguise. Since then, she seemed really alive only when she was with him, and strangely inanimate when she was not.

There was no getting around it, she concluded with a shiver of excitement. Somehow she would always be bound to him, no matter if she never saw him again after this fateful summer. She loved him.

She supposed she could try to draw Simon to her by initiating some of the feminine inducements of which she had heard. The truth was, however, she was not good at that sort of thing. During her London Season, in addition to the fact that she was small and colorless — 'a little dab of a thing' as she had heard herself described – she was an abysmal failure in the art of flirtation. She had not a single wile in her arsenal. How then did she expect to attract the likes of Lord Simon Talent? She could only hope that if he kissed her when he was infuriated with her, he might be induced to propose marriage if he became truly enraged.

Forced to laugh at her own nonsense, she left the library, leaving *The Song of Roland* lying on the table, forgotten.

Dinner that evening was hardly a memorable event. The increasing crowd at the board made for a noisy group though, oddly, Lady Hermione was not the cynosure of all eyes, as might have been expected. Gerard and Harry, seated near Winifred, devoted their attention, as usual, to their deity.

Winifred, also as usual, spared neither of them so much as a glance. This evening, her attention was absorbed by Sir James, who had casually mentioned his town house in London. Jane eyed him curiously, wondering not for the first time what had brought this rather odd, middle-aged gentleman to Selworth. She shot a glance at Gerard, who, with Harry, followed with fascination the conversation between Winifred and 'the mysterious uncle'. What, Jane wondered again, were they up to? Sir James, continuing his discourse, admitted with a rueful smile that the town house was not located in a fashionable area, nor was it very large, but it was situated in Soho, a mere stone's throw from several of the city's most prominent theaters. Winifred had pricked up her ears, and was now interrogating Sir James on the denizens of his neighborhood.

Lissa and Marc were seated next to one another, and in rigid silence, pushed food around their respective plates. Both were obviously miserable. Both were obviously determined to ignore the other.

Simon, with Lady Hermione seated at his right, regarded the proceedings as more of an endurance contest than a meal, since it took every ounce of *bonhomie* at his command not to give the insufferable female the set down of her life. Having learned that Simon was the brother of the Marquess of Chamford, she had unbent sufficiently to dole out slices of genteel conversation at judicious intervals. Her main topic of conversation was her family seat in

Oxfordshire, and she reported with relish its manifest superiority over every other country house in the realm.

'Papa and Mama visited Stonefield Court once when I was a child,' she declared with some relish. 'Mama was much struck by its beauty and its situation, but, of course, Papa pointed out that it has not the prospect of Wimpole Park, nor is the design so salubrious.'

'Oh,' said Simon.

'How fortunate that you have such a large dining room here at Selworth.' Lady Hermione glanced about the chamber, and Simon felt that the oak table and chairs, the mahogany sideboard and every other stick of furniture in sight were being appraised to the penny by her polished-stone eyes. She tittered amusedly. 'Of course, the state chamber at Wimpole Park could hold several times this assemblage.'

Simon gritted his teeth. 'Ah,' he replied.

Gerard and Harry, in the meantime, joined Winifred and Sir James in their discussion, which had drifted from the theaters of London to Winifred's current work-in-progress.

'Yes,' Harry was saying, 'but if Charles has to say that speech through his ass's head, he's going to have to put more volume behind it.'

Lady Hermione swiveled to face the young man. 'What did you say?' she asked blankly, uncharacteristically heedless of the social solecism she was committing by leaning forward and talking down the table.

'I said that Charles is going to have to talk louder,' responded Harry cheerfully.

'No, before that,' Lady Hermione snapped.

'Oh. I was talking about his ass's head.'

'I *beg* your pardon!'

Jane, suffused with laughter, intervened. 'Harry is referring to Charles's performance as Bottom in our home production of *A Midsummer Night's Dream*.'

'Wye?' asked Lady Hermione in patent disbelief.

'Why should he not?' interposed Harry, puzzled.

'I was expressing my surprise,' returned Lady Hermione frigidly, 'at his consenting to participate in such an activity.'

'I've done it before,' said Charles in some irritation.

Before her ladyship could respond to this, Winifred leaned past Sir James to say in a kind voice. 'All the main parts are filled, Lady H. but I can use you as one of Hippolyta's attendants.'

For a moment, Lady Hermione remained silent, every fibre of her speaking its affront. 'I think not,' she said at last in a voice of chilled granite. Winifred opened her mouth, but the next moment closed it with a blink of her eyes and, for once, she made no argument.

Lady Hermione turned to her betrothed. 'What I was trying to convey,' she continued in the same tone, 'is my difficulty in accepting the fact that you would so lower yourself as to take part in a common theatrical.'

Charles frowned pettishly. 'Perhaps you do not recall that I took the part of Tattle in *Love for Love*.'

Lady Hermione smiled with an air of patient resignation. 'But that was the Duchess of Capsham's production.' The implication was clear that the duchess might indulge in pastimes regarded as wholly unfit for persons of a lesser order. 'You will wish to withdraw immediately, Wye.'

'I am enjoying myself, Hermione.' Charles's jaw thrust forward mulishly, his reluctance to perform from inside an ass's head apparently forgotten. 'And I see nothing untoward in Winifred – er, that is, Miss Timburton's – plans to put on *A Mid-summer Night's Dream* in the privacy of her own home.'

Lady Hermione's smile grew a trifle strained. 'We will have a little talk about it later, dearest,' she said quickly.

When the cast assembled the next morning in the Crimson Saloon, since it had come on to mizzle directly after breakfast, it became obvious that Lady Hermione had accomplished her little talk with Charles. It was equally obvious that the results of this discussion were not what she had hoped, for not only was Charles vocal in his intention to perform, but he insisted on wearing the ass's head during rehearsal, which he had steadfastly refused to do before. In addition, he played his role with particular élan, fashioning new bits of business for the hapless Bottom and broadening the role in a way that quite convulsed the others. All but Lady Hermione, of course, who sat by the window with her embroidery, wearing a martyred air. Beside her sat Lady Wimpole, a silent, contrapuntal presence.

Jane eyed Simon surreptitiously. He seemed tired and drawn today, and left the room frequently for reasons that he did not elucidate. His manner toward her was courteous, but somewhat distant, and if their encounter yesterday had left a lasting impression with him, he gave no indication.

Later in the morning, the vicar and Mrs Mycombe reported for duty, and Jane watched regretfully as whatever spark that had been ignited by Charles's performance promptly fizzled and died. The vicar and his spouse recited their lines as though they were expecting a summons from the bailiff at any moment.

'No, no, Mrs Mycombe,' called Winifred from the back of the room. 'Hippolyta is flirting a little with Theseus here. You must try to be a little more playful. Come now, again – "Four days will quickly steep themselves in night ..." '

Mrs Mycombe turned stiffly to her husband, and placing her plump hand on his arm, rolled her eyes and fluttered her eyelashes as though a large insect had just flown into them. She uttered a strangled giggle and repeated the lines.

'Umm,' said Winifred. 'Perhaps we do not need quite so much business. If—'

The vicar and his wife exchanged glances and stepped down from the stage.

'Winifred, dear,' began Mrs Mycombe, 'we – that is the vicar and I feel – that is ...' She trailed off uncertainly and cast an anguished glance at her husband.

'Winifred, dear,' repeated the cleric, 'Mrs Mycombe and I have been discussing our appearance in your play, and we have come to the reluctant conclusion that it just won't do.'

'What?' gasped Winifred.

'We are neither of us actors.' He chuckled ruefully. 'Well, I guess we do not need to tell you that. Nor do we have the inclination to attempt such a thing. I'm afraid, my dear, that we must regretfully step down from the boards.'

'I fear,' Mrs Mycombe interposed gently, 'that you will have to find someone else to play Theseus and Hippolyta.'

Winifred had expounded at length only the evening before on the deficiencies of the Mycombes' performing skills, but no one needed to tell her that a Duke of Athens and a Queen of the Amazons in the hand, no matter how inadequate, were worth however many might be hidden inaccessibly in the bush.

'But, you can't!' wailed Winifred. 'You can't just – just resign. I have no one to replace you!'

'Now, now,' said the vicar in a kind but implacable voice. 'There must be other persons in the vicinity who – the Bintons, perhaps.'

'The Bintons?' echoed Winifred is an incredulous squeak. 'The greengrocer and his wife?' Her face puckered. 'I would be a laughingstock!'

'Now, now,' Mrs Mycombe said in some distress, but as determined as her husband to relinquish her budding stage career. 'I'm sure you will find someone.'

Having expressed their decision, the couple evidently felt it wise to make a judicious exit, and promising to attend the play, left Selworth in haste.

Winifred sank on to a brocade settee. '*Now* what am I going to do?' she asked in despair.

Lady Teague, who had entered the room some moments before with an armful of costumes to be fitted, moved to sit beside her. 'You must look on the bright side,' she said, disentangling one of her bracelets that had somehow attached itself to the laces embellishing Hippolyta's kirtle. 'The Mycombes are perfectly delightful people, of course, but you were quite correct in saying they were not right for their parts. Now, you are free to search out someone with more ability.'

'But there is no time!' Winifred fairly shrieked. 'We are putting the play on in two weeks, and I have already sent out the invitations. How am I going to find two people with a modicum of talent and with the ability to memorize lines quickly?'

'Perhaps the best plan,' said Simon from his place on the stage, 'would be to cancel the whole thing. We can still have the dinner party, but we'll offer, ah, impromptu recitals by the ladies for entertainment.' He glanced about him with a satisfied smile, as though expecting nods of agreement from the rest of the cast. What he received was a fiery glance from Winifred.

'The play,' she said mutinously, 'will go on as scheduled. In fact, since so many of us are playing two roles, I wonder if there is not some way you could play Theseus, and Jane – why, Jane, Puck does not appear with Theseus on stage at all, so if you ...'

'No!' Simon and Jane spoke in unison.

'That is,' continued Jane, I am much too short for the Queen of the Amazons, don't you think? And I'm sure I could never learn so many new lines.'

'And I cannot do Theseus,' said Simon. 'No.' He raised a hand to stem Winifred's incipient protest. 'Filling the part of Lysander is as far as I am willing to go in pandering to what I can only call your unhealthy obsession with the stage. Now, I promised that I would not forbid you to put on the play, but if you will take my advice, I would give it up now instead of harassing us all.'

'Well, really!' gasped Winifred, but she was talking to the empty air, for Simon turned on his heel and left the room.

Jane knew a surge of irritation at his peremptory manner. Winifred might be irritating in her single-minded dedication to her craft, but she could not really be blamed for that. When one wanted something very badly, it would take a person of far greater self-discipline than Winifred to rein in her needs. She wondered if Lord Simon Talent had ever wanted something very badly. She rather thought not.

Lady Teague also left the room, and Harry and Gerard moved to take her place, Gerard seating himself on the settee, and Harry sitting cross-legged on the floor before Winifred in a worshipful attitude.

'You know, Winifred,' began Gerard, his gray eyes sparkling, 'Harry and I do not appear with Theseus and Hippolyta – at least, we do not all speak together. What if I were to play the duke, and Harry could don that kirtle thing and play Hippolyta?'

Winifred, momentarily startled from her fit of gloom, gazed at Gerard as though he'd taken leave of his senses. When she glanced floorward, the vision of Harry in kirtle and peplum evidently caused her some anguish, for she placed her rosy fingertips against her mouth.

'Do but think, Winifred,' continued Gerard eagerly. 'All the women's parts in Shakespeare used to be taken by men. Harry has all that yaller hair, dontcher see, and he's pretty short, so—'

It was obvious to the meanest intelligence that Harry did not share Gerard's enthusiasm for the proposed project, but he nodded manfully, valiantly attempting to twist the spikes of his hair into ringlets.

'I played a chambermaid once in a skit some of the fellows got up at Oxford,' he said valiantly.

Winifred was forced to smile despite herself. 'That is very kind of you – both of you, but I fear it will not serve. No,' she sighed profoundly, 'I shall ask the Bintons if they will perform, though they will no doubt quite ruin the whole production.' She lifted her hand in a disconsolate gesture. 'I had hoped to have actually acted in a play before going to London. I thought my appearance in a Shakespearian production might help get me an audition. Now, I wonder if I will ever get into the theater.'

At this, Gerard and Harry shot a significant glance at Sir James, who sat some distance away, leafing through a copy of *The Gentleman's Magazine*. Though he appeared not to notice their fixed stares, he rose and made his way to the small group.

'Miss Timburton,' he said portentously, 'I am sure you are taking much too dim a view of things. If you will permit, may we take a stroll through the rose garden? Perhaps nature's beneficence will put you into a happier frame of mind.' With barely a glance at her stalwart supporters, Sir James extended a hand to Winifred, who accepted it somewhat listlessly.

Watching their goddess exit the room, Gerard and Harry conducted a furious, though whispered, discussion between themselves for several moments before getting to their feet. Nodding to those remaining, they, too, left the chamber, followed by Lissa and Marcus, who studiously avoided each other's gaze.

Jane, left alone in the center of the Crimson Saloon, sighed. She gazed around the empty room, her glance lingering on the stage where Bottom's ass's head lay discarded along with Titania's silver-tipped wand.

' "O weary day," ' she murmured, quoting Shakespeare's broken-hearted Helena. ' "Oh long and tedious day, abate thy hours!" ' Sighing once more, she shook her head and walked dispiritedly from the room.

Thirteen

'I have a device to make all well.'
—A Midsummer Night's Dream, III, i.

The remainder of the hours before luncheon passed quietly for the household, and it was a rather subdued group who returned to the house after their various activities to freshen themselves for the midday meal.

Jane, whose morning had consisted of nothing more exciting than inspecting linen with Mrs Rudge, repaired dispiritedly to her chambers to comb her hair and wash her face. She felt strangely suspended of late, as though she drifted in and out of a vaguely remembered dream. Irritated with her own missishness, she scrubbed her face furiously, and was pulling a comb through her tangled hair when her attention was caught by a sound that drew her to her window. There she caught sight of a carriage just rounding the last bend of the drive before it disappeared from her view on the way to the main entrance. Dear Lord, she thought dazedly, not more visitors! She sped downstairs to be met with the sight of Winifred standing in the center of the hall, greeting a tall gentleman and a lady, both dressed in the first stare of fashion.

As Jane ran lightly down the stairs, Winifred turned to face her. Her spirits seemed entirely restored, for her face glowed with pleasure.

'Ah, here you are!' cried Winifred before turning back to face the newcomers. 'Lord and Lady Chamford, may I present my cousin Jane? Jane, these are Lord Simon's brother and sister-in-law, the Marquess and Marchioness of Chamford – or should I say?' she added, her voice rising in glee, 'The Duke of Athens and his intended bride!'

Jane stared, openmouthed, and not unnaturally, my lord and his lady also looked somewhat taken aback. The marquess was a striking gentleman, very tall and rather harsh featured. Dark hair, cut shorter than the dictates of fashion, curved over a broad brow, and his eyes, even darker, were alive and penetrating. In contrast, the marchioness was very fair. She was a woman of extraordinary beauty – tall and slender and possessed of a striking mane of hair the shade of antique gold. Her eyes were a clear, light gray.

'Jared! Diana!' It was Simon hurrying across the hall to envelop them in a laughing embrace. 'What the devil are you two doing here? Have you come to see if I've run my new estate into the ground yet?'

'Oh, Simon,' gasped Lady Chamford, divesting herself of her bonnet, 'it is perfectly dreadful to descend on you without notice, but when we re – that is, Jared has conceived the notion that I require some diversion, and suggested – well, no, insisted on this impromptu visit.'

Lord Chamford, his chiseled features softening as he gazed on his wife, laughed. 'You must absolve me, Simon. Young Peter has been running his mother ragged, and now that she is to be confined again' – he cast a significant glance at his wife's almost imperceptibly swollen waistline – 'I felt a little respite was in order.'

'At any rate,' said Simon, planting a noisy kiss on Lady Chamford's cheek, 'you are both—'

He was interrupted by a tumultuous shout from Marcus. Lissa, entering at the same time from another doorway, drew back momentarily on catching sight of him.

'Danny!' cried Marc. 'Jared!' He swept his sister into a sweeping hug, and clasped his brother-in-law's hand.

Lissa moved forward then to fling herself into her brother's embrace with a soft, teary, 'Oh, Jared, I am so glad you have come!'

Lady Hermione descended the stairs at this moment, followed by a sulky Charles, and introductions and explanations were undertaken once again.

Jane moved forward to take Lady Chamford's bonnet and her linen spencer, forestalling the maid, who hovered respectfully in the background.

'My lady,' she began, only to be cut short by the marchioness's musical laughter.

'Please, do call me Diana, and I know Jared will wish to be

informal, as well. You must be Jane,' she said, gazing at her rather intently. 'We have heard so much about you from Aunt Amabelle and Lissa.'

Jane felt herself blushing. 'Thank you – Diana. Luncheon will be served soon, and I know you will wish to refresh yourself. It will take a little time to ready the state bedchamber, but if you would care to repair to my chambers—'

'The state bedchamber!' echoed Diana. 'Oh, please do not. I shall be quite eaten with remorse should we put you to so much trouble.' She glanced around the increasingly populated hall. 'It looks as though you have been through a great deal already.'

'Nonsense,' responded Jane stoutly. 'This is a big house, and we have bedrooms aplenty.' Her eye was caught at that moment by the sight of Fellowes, who had just hurried into the hall, coming to a lurching halt as he beheld yet another contingent of invaders. 'If,' she continued smoothly, 'you would prefer something a little more, er, intimate than the state chamber, we can have something ready for you very quickly.' She gestured airily to Fellowes, who with commendable aplomb, turned to Mrs Rudge standing by with two maids at her side. Jane breathed a silent prayer of gratitude that the housekeeper just that morning had hired two more girls from the village and another footman as well.

Pausing only a moment to avail herself of another embrace from her brother and to murmur a few words to her husband, Diana accompanied Jane up the broad staircase, where they encountered Lady Teague at the top.

'Diana!' cried Aunt Amabelle, her jewelry tinkling a joyous accompaniment. 'My dear child!'

Hearing her, Jared ran lightly up the staircase and there was another interval of kisses and embraces. Finally, Jared returned to the group below, and Lady Teague accompanied Jane and Diana to Jane's chambers. Once there, Diana once again apologized for their abrupt descent on the household.

'We are all happy to see you here, my l— Diana,' said Jane. 'I could tell that Simon was enormously pleased. He told me shortly after he arrived that he regretted he had such a short time to spend at Stonefield before journeying up here.'

'That's true,' replied Diana, laughing. 'He and Jared had time to re-fight only half the battles of the Peninsular War to their satisfaction, and there is still much they have to catch up on.'

'Would you care to lie down for a few moments?' she asked. 'We could put luncheon back for awhile.'

'Lie down?' asked Diana in some surprise. 'Oh, you mean because of ...' She glanced down, patting her stomach. 'Oh no, I am disgustingly healthy, and even more so when I am increasing. Jared is always trying to cosset me, and now and again I will feign delicacy just for him, for it pleases him to think I am a fragile flower.'

Diana's glowing cheeks and sparkling gray eyes lent truth to her declaration, and after she had washed her face and permitted her maid to repair the damage done to her hair by her travels, she and the other ladies returned to the ground floor, where they found the others ensconced in the Emerald Saloon, ready to begin their meal.

'Did you have a good journey?' asked Lady Teague as the footmen began serving salad and cold meat.

'Yes, it was very pleasant,' replied Jared. 'We made good time, and would have been here even sooner if my bride had not insisted on stopping every five minutes for sustenance.'

'Yes,' agreed Diana, laughing. 'I seem to be absolutely ravenous all the time. It was the same way when I was carrying Peter, you know. If—'

'Have you heard that I am putting on a play?' interrupted Winifred.

Diana, stopped in midsentence, turned a surprised look on the girl.

'Winifred!' barked Simon, and he was echoed by Jane, who continued sharply, 'Lord and Lady Chamford will think you the most complete hoyden.'

'Oh, I am sorry.' Winifred laughed unrepentantly. 'It is just that I am so pleased to see them here. They arrived just in the nick of time, did they not?'

Simon, feeling a familiar tide of irritation rise in him, said, 'What the devil are you talking about?'

'Why the play, of course. Lord and Lady Chamford will make a perfect Theseus and Hippolyta!'

'Oh, for God's sake.' Simon gestured impatiently, which, since he was holding a forkful of salad, was a rather unfortunate circumstance. Charles, sitting near him, found himself the recipient of several lettuce leaves on his collar.

'Sorry, old man,' said Simon, without the least hint of apology in his tone. He turned again to Winifred. 'I will not have you harassing the remainder of my family about your da – wretched play. Do you understand?'

Since no one in the room had ever seen the self-possessed Simon Talent in such a taking, an astonished silence fell over the room.

'What is the name of the play?' asked Diana at last, in an effort to fill the uncomfortable moment.

'We're doing *A Midsummer Night's Dream*, and *I* am playing both Titania and Hermia.' Winifred went on to describe the parts being performed by the rest of the family and guests at Selworth.

'Marcus is to play Oberon?' asked Diana, concealing a smile.

Winifred nodded. 'And Demetrius.'

'I might have known,' sighed Jared.

'Did you know,' continued Winifred breathlessly, 'that Marcus is an accomplished acrobat?'

Marcus was, by this time, looking extremely uncomfortable. Glancing at Lissa, Jane noted the tightening of her lips, as well as the tears that welled in her eyes. Farther down the table, Simon's expression revealed his disapproval of Winifred's fulsome admiration of Marcus and his unhappiness at the state of affairs between Marcus and Lissa. Jane felt her heart twist on his behalf.

'Oh, yes,' said Jared dryly in answer to Winifred's untimely comment. 'His, er, exploits in that area have become quite a legend in our family.'

'I remember the play well,' said Diana, sending a quelling glance to her husband. 'In fact, I produced an abbreviated version of *A Midsummer Night's Dream* at Madame Du Vrai's seminary.'

This statement, of course, necessitated a brief history of Diana's life in Paris as the adopted daughter of a French merchant, at the end of which she concluded, 'And I think it would be *trés amusant* to take part in your production, Winifred. What do you say, Jared?'

Jared bent a harassed glance on his brother before turning back to his wife.

'Diana, what in God's green world makes you think I can act, or would want to do so?'

'Oh, but, Lord Chamford,' interposed Winifred eagerly, 'The Duke of Athens has a fairly small part. I'm sure you would be able to memorize the lines. Lord Simon is in the play, too, you know.'

'Mmm – yes,' said Jared, his dark eyes gazing enigmatically on his brother. 'I am wondering how that came about, Simon.'

'I'll talk to you about it later,' said Simon hastily. 'At any rate, if Diana would find pleasure in—'

'Miss Timburton! Lord Simon!' It was Lady Hermione, who had spoken very little during the course of the meal. 'Lady Chamford is being most gracious, but you surely cannot expect her, or his lordship, to participate in what is really nothing more than a low romp.' Her nose pinched unbecomingly until it resembled a misformed pebble stuck just below her eyes.

After surveying her in silence for a long moment, Jared turned back to Diana. 'If it would give you pleasure, my love, to take part in this little romp, I shall be happy to oblige,' he said, and the intimacy of the smile he turned on his wife made Jane look away.

Lady Hermione flushed to the roots of her hair and sniffed in outraged affront.

At that, Winifred insisted that luncheon was over, even though most of the raspberry tarts prepared that morning by Cook lay on a plate uneaten. Winifred dragged the company almost bodily into the Crimson Saloon, where she shepherded Jared and Diana on to the makeshift stage, and handed them playbooks, ready to begin the task of showing them their positions.

By the end of the day, Jane decided that she liked Diana very much, and when the teatable was brought into the Gold Saloon that night, it seemed as though she had known the affable marchioness for years instead of a few, short hours.

'Oh, dear,' said Diana, yawning for the five or sixth time that evening behind her fingertips. 'Perhaps the journey tired me out more than I thought. I do believe I shall retire, my love. No, no,' she said hastily, as Jared rose to his feet. 'I know you will want a comfortable coze with Simon. I shall get Goodbody to tuck me away and I'll see you when you come up.'

The other ladies declared their intentions to seek their beds as well, and when Jane offered her arm to Diana, that lady accepted it with her usual gracious charm. Aunt Amabelle toiled behind them, chattering all the way, and when they reached Diana's bedchamber, Jane and the older woman entered with her.

'I trust everything is satisfactory, Diana,' said Jane, a question in her voice.

'Very much so. You have seen to our every need and then some. This is such a lovely house, Jane,' she continued, seating herself in a dainty wing chair and gesturing Jane and Lady Teague to seats nearby. 'I should imagine Simon will hate to leave here when he has Winifred's affairs straightened out.'

'He seems quite anxious to return to his home – Ashwood, is it?' asked Jane hesitantly.

'Yes, but I hope he will spend some time at Stonefield first. He was in such a tearing hurry when he came home, that we feel very much put upon.'

'I don't understand why he found it necessary to hurry to Selworth so soon after his arrival home.' Jane was guiltily aware of the gaucherie of her statement, but her curiosity had been unsatisfied for far too long, and she felt surprisingly comfortable with Diana Chamford.

The marchioness was staring at her in blank surprise. 'Why, so that he could get Winifred fired off, of course. He was almost quivering in fear the whole time he was home that he would be forced to marry the chit himself. Not,' Diana added quickly, 'that she is the horror we were led to expect. At least, not quite, but ... Oh, dear.' Diana's hands went to her generously curved mouth. 'I forgot, she is your relative, is she not? I am so sorry; I only meant that ...'

She trailed off helplessly, but Jane, still absorbing the first part of her statement, did not hear. 'Marry her himself?' she echoed, a cold feeling settling into the pit of her stomach.

'Oh, my dear,' chimed Aunt Amabelle. 'You did not know?'

'Know?' Jane wanted to scream the word. 'Know what?'

'Oh, my,' sighed Diana, exchanging a glance with Lady Teague. 'It appears Simon did not want anyone outside the family to be aware of his dilemma.'

There was a moment's silence before Lady Teague and Diana spoke to each other in unison.

'Oh, but don't you think...?' asked Lady Teague.

'On the other hand ...' said Diana.

By now, Jane was ready to explode. 'I do not wish to pry into a family matter, of course,' she said through gritted teeth. She rose and turned toward the door. 'If you will excuse me.'

'No!' The two voices again spoke as one, and Diana continued. 'It was foolish of Simon to be so closemouthed about the whole thing, and since you – that is ...' She exchanged another sidelong glance with Lady Teague. 'That is, since it is your cousin who is involved in this whole ridiculous mess ...' She drew a deep breath. 'The fact is that if Simon does not find a husband for Winifred within the next two weeks, he will have to marry her himself.'

At this, Jane felt as though she had already exploded. 'What?' she asked faintly.

'It was part of that wretched agreement between Simon and Wilfred Timburton,' said Aunt Amabelle, almost in tears. 'Why Simon let himself be so imposed upon, I cannot imagine, but once he considers a thing to be his duty, no amount of reason will sway him.' Lady Teague's jewelry provided a cacophonic background to her words.

Haltingly, Diana recounted the terms of the agreement signed by Simon after Wilfred's death.

Jane sat down suddenly. 'But that is just – just wicked,' she gasped. Then, as a thought struck her, she asked, 'Does Simon actually have to marry Winifred, or merely ask her?'

'I don't know,' replied Diana, 'but doesn't it amount to the same thing? I mean, what woman in her right mind would refuse a proposal from Simon?' She uttered a strained laugh. 'Admittedly, I am biased in my opinion of him, but he is eminently eligible, and a wonderful man, besides.'

On the brink of tears, Jane silently acknowledged the truth of this statement.

There was a long silence in the charming little sitting room, broken only by the crackle of the fire in the hearth and the sighs and recriminations voiced by the participants in the discussion.

'It is too bad that Charles is betrothed to Lady Hermione,' said Diana thoughtfully.

'Yes,' replied Jane glumly.

'Odd, I have not seen an announcement in any of the papers.' Lady Teague shot her niece a speculative glance.

'Well,' Jane mused aloud, 'I don't think it's been officially announced yet.'

'The earl does not seem altogether pleased at the idea of marrying Lady Hermione,' said Diana, tapping her fingers abstractedly on the arm of her chair.

'Well, who would be?' blurted Jane. 'That is – I should not speak ill of a guest in the house, but—'

Lady Teague uttered a sound remarkably like a snort. 'To dish it up unsalted, the woman is absolutely insufferable.' She swung about to face the marchioness.

'Diana, what have you got in mind? You are looking particularly angelic at the moment, and you have me quaking in my shoes.'

'Why, nothing, Aunt. It just occurs to me that there may be a way out of this situation ...' She exchanged a conspiratorial glance with her aunt and her hostess. 'If we put our heads together.'

Fourteen

'Every one look o'er his part.'
—A Midsummer Night's Dream, V, i.

Over the next week, rehearsals for *A Midsummer Night's Dream* finally came together to Winifred's satisfaction. She declared that if she had been given the opportunity to handpick a lady and gentleman from throughout the realm to play Theseus and Hippolyta, she could have done no better than Jared and Diana. Jared, she said, to a chorus of wholehearted agreement from the other players, eminently fulfilled the commanding presence of the Duke of Athens, and Diana's queenly bearing as the duke's intended bride brought sighs of admiration from the other ladies.

Lissa and Marcus, while their performances lacked anything resembling sparkle, managed their roles with competence. Marc's agility lent verisimilitude to his role as Oberon, and Lissa, while by no means a skilled actress, infused her part with an unaffected sweetness. Winifred, more secure in the growing capability of her cast, began to polish her own delivery, and Charles convulsed the group regularly with his antics as the bucolic Bottom. He even went so far as to declare he no longer minded the cumbersome ass's head, constructed by the local carpenter of balsa wood and covered with rabbit skin.

Winifred knew a moment's unease when Sir James announced that it was necessary to travel to London for a few days, but he earnestly assured her, shaking his head ponderously, that he would return in plenty of time to perform his role of Egeus and that of the clown, Snout.

Even Simon, despite the rapid approach of what he termed his rendezvous with doom, was beginning to enjoy himself. His role was not a demanding one, and he found it somewhat of a relief to submerge his concerns in Shakespeare's pleasant diversion. He found particular delight in the scene in which he crouched at Jane's feet in the shrubbery, shouting maledictions supposedly mouthed by Puck in Lysander's voice and directed at Demetrius. He rather relished Jane's obvious discomfiture as he pressed himself against her shapely leg.

Only one person refused to participate in the gentle hilarity that grew as the performance date approached. Lady Hermione, steadfast in her decision to maintain a watchful presence at every rehearsal, sat with her mother by the window in the Crimson Saloon, assiduously plying her needle and sending poisonous glances at the proceedings onstage. During Titania's scenes with Bottom, wherein the fairy queen caressed and kissed her hairy long-eared lover, Lady Hermione became quite rigid with fury and those observing marveled that Winifred did not bear marks at the end of the day as a result of her ladyship's venomous stares. Even on the morning when several of the village children gathered to rehearse their parts as attendant fairies, Lady Hermione did not relax either her vigil or her expression. While the others laughed and played games with the youthful performers, Lady Hermione pulled her skirts aside with frequent, acid requests that 'someone please remove this dirty child'.

Poor Charles could not so much as set out for the village tobacconist to replenish his snuff supply without his fiancée's company. On the rare occasions when he slipped his leash, he would find Lady Hermione awaiting him on his return, her chiseled nose twitching suspiciously.

There were those, of course, who felt that Lady Hermione's fears were far from groundless. Charles, in the rare moments when Lady Hermione relaxed her surveillance, continued his attentions to Winifred. The two could be seen scurrying off at odd moments together, to reappear some time later, flushed and laughing. Jane remonstrated with Winifred to no avail, for the flighty maiden would simply toss her head and say, 'Oh, don't be so missish, Jane. You know I love to flirt, but it's all perfectly harmless. I do the same with Gerard and Harry and Sir James, after all.' Which was perfectly true, but did nothing to reassure her dwindling number of well-wishers.

Lissa, for example, made her rising fury apparent as she watched the pats bestowed by the beauty on Marcus's cheek and the delicious laughter that rippled from her at his every sally.

Fortunately a diversion occurred before battle lines could be firmly drawn. Aunt Amabelle completed the costumes and, while they were not yet worn at rehearsals, the cast tried them on at every opportunity, preening and pluming themselves in their make-believe finery. The gentlemen – Simon, Jared, and Marcus – demurred strongly against the Grecian tunics provided for them. Nothing, declared Simon, echoed by the other two, would prevail upon him to appear in front of the world dressed in short skirts. This contretemps was fortunately smoothed over when Aunt Amabelle lengthened the tunics and found sturdy, knee-high buskins for them, thus insuring against an unseemly display of bare shins or knees or even worse. All the principal male players except Charles were provided with floor-length cloaks of a light wool in various attractive shades. These, it was declared, lent a richness to the rather plain muslin tunics worn by those gentlemen cast in the more aristocratic roles.

The others declared themselves highly pleased with their costumes. Winifred, in particular, fancied herself in Titania's splendor. From one of her old gowns of celestial blue silk, Lady Teague had fashioned a piece of glittering magic, sprinkled with spangles and trimmed with silver stars. A pair of spider-gauze wings fluttered from her shoulders, and on her brow rested a sparkling tiara, embellished with a crescent moon. Winifred whirled and pirouetted before the others, reveling in their expressions of admiration. Gerard, in a burst of inspiration, compared her to a cloudless evening sky bedecked with heaven's own glory. As for Charles, compliments fell from his lips like water dripping from a spout.

Jane's ensemble consisted of a brief tunic of pure white muslin, belted with a silver cord about her slim hips and cut in a jagged Vandyked hemline that revealed enticing views of her shapely legs. Her wings were of gossamer, tiny and fragile, and she was sprinkled with brilliants from head to foot. Candlelight made haloes on her silvery curls, and she was, thought Simon, so ethereally beautiful that it hurt to look at her.

The forthcoming play was the talk of the neighborhood. Since the arrival of Lady Teague, visitors had been welcomed at Selworth, and in return, particularly since the ménage now included such exalted company as a genuine marquess and his wife, its inhabitants had been feted at small dinner parties. Jane, who had faced the first of these outings with some trepidation, was relieved to discover that her story of a new modiste and an illness that caused her to lose weight seemed generally accepted, widened eyes and puzzled glances notwithstanding.

The vicar and Mrs Mycombe, though no longer part of the production, kept close tabs on its progress, and frequently traveled from the vicarage to watch the rehearsals.

'If only,' said Simon to his big brother one drizzly afternoon, 'I didn't have this life sentence hanging over me, life might be bearable.'

He sat at his desk in the study, where he and Jared were sharing a decanter of Madeira. He stared gloomily at the streaks of rain on the window, so precisely reflecting his mood.

'No possibilities on the horizon?' asked Jared.

'None. I sent out a few feelers shortly after I arrived here, but they came to nothing. I was not overly concerned at the time, because with Charles on the scene, I thought I was home free.' He slammed his hand on to the desk. 'If only I had more time! I could get her to London – get her fired off into society – she'd be snapped up in no time. But now, come Thursday next I shall be thrust into the ranks of the affianced.' His head sank despairingly into his hands.

'It seems to me there's a good possibility she will refuse your offer,' suggested Jared. 'She doesn't appear to be precisely enamored of you.'

'And thank God, fasting, for that, but it's nothing to the point. She's as selfish as she can hold together and badly spoiled to boot. She's not going to take well to the idea of a life of penury. She'll view me as her lifeline.'

'But what about this fixation of hers? Going on the stage? Surely she knows that if she married you, she'd have about as much a chance of accomplishing that as she would of opening a brothel.'

'No, I do not believe she does realize that. She is so confident of her ability to twist any man around her pink little finger, that I'm sure she thinks it only a matter of time before I'd be sitting up and barking at her command.'

Jared laughed shortly. 'She doesn't know you well, does she?'

Simon grunted, but made no response.

Jared glanced at him speculatively. 'Well, at least your heart is not engaged elsewhere. Is it?'

Simon looked up swiftly. 'What do you mean by that?'

'Only that I've noticed you casting sheep's eyes at the charming Miss Burch, brother.'

Simon sat up suddenly, ready to refute this remark, but after a moment, slumped in his chair. 'Has it been that noticeable?'

'Only to your nearest and dearest,' said Jared with a laugh. 'I take it you have made no, er, overtures?'

'Of course not!' exclaimed Simon. 'Well – perhaps – of a sort. Not that they met with much success.' A memory of Jane's warmth pressed against him in the cool intimacy of the library swept over him. 'That is – she didn't slap my face – but ... Oh, dammit, Jared, she thinks of me as an overbearing boor! In addition to which, how can I press my suit when I'm on the verge of becoming betrothed to someone else?'

For a moment he reflected on the fact that Jane, though she had hardly spoken to him since that devastating moment in the library, had bestowed one or two glances on him that actually approached cordiality, and it was all he could do to keep from seeking her out in some secluded niche and catching her in his arms and kissing her breathless. What would be her response, he wondered, if he were to ask her out for a stroll some evening, and then, when they were hidden from view, if he were to throw honor to the winds and reveal to her what was in his heart?

He grunted. She would probably inform him briskly that no, she could not marry him because she disliked him excessively.

'And she has every reason to view me with distaste,' he said to Jared. 'I've thrown the most heinous of insults at her and beyond that have done nothing but growl at her without provocation. Well, perhaps not quite without provocation. She seems to have ceased her efforts to throw Winifred and Marcus together – oh, yes, did I not tell you about that? She, too, is anxious for Winifred to marry – though I don't think she has been entirely honest with me on that subject – and when Marc arrived with me, he became her prime target, despite my telling her that he was already spoken for. As I say, she has apparently given up her plans in that quarter, deciding that Marc and Lissa truly love each other, but I have an uneasy suspicion that if those two idiots do not settle their differences soon, she will be back at the old stand, that busy little brain of hers hatching more misguided plots and schemes.' His voice rose, and he leaped to his feet to stride around the desk. 'She is the most exasperating female I've ever met.'

'And you're head over tail in love with her.'

'Of course, I am!' replied Simon angrily. He sat down again behind the desk.

Jared chuckled. 'This conversation is beginning to bear a marked similarity to the one you and I held together shortly after Diana arrived at Stonefield.'

'Mmph,' replied Simon. 'I remember. You were so busy trying to convince yourself that she was nothing but an adventuress, you couldn't see that *you* were head over tail in love. I have no such misconceptions about Jane, but I can see no future for us.'

'Perhaps,' said Jared enigmatically. He unfolded his muscled length from his chair. 'I truly sympathize with your dilemma, old man, but I must be on my way. I'm promised to Diana for a game of piquet.' He moved to the door, turning to add, 'Don't give up hope, Simon. You're not leg-shackled yet, and in a week, anything can happen. Diana, for example, seems to feel sure of a last minute reprieve for you.'

Simon grinned mirthlessly. 'You mean I might be struck by a bolt of lightning, or swept away by a flood?' But he spoke to the empty air, for Jared had closed the door softly behind him.

Indeed, it began to seem to Simon that some sort of natural cataclysm was all that could save him from his rapidly approaching entanglement in the bonds of matrimony. At dinner that evening, Diana, speaking to Charles, waxed enthusiastic about that particular state, and Winifred was the first to agree with her.

'Oh, yes,' Winifred said, her cheeks flushed becomingly. 'I have become convinced that the married state is dreadfully important for a woman.' Her musical laugh chimed forth. 'I have decided that when I go to London I shall find a husband with pots of money. And I think a title would be helpful, too.'

An appalled silence greeted this ingenuous remark until Sir James, returned from London late that afternoon, cleared his throat. All eyes turned expectantly to the large gentleman as he lifted his hand in an awkward gesture. 'I wonder if I might trouble someone for another slice of that sole,' he said absently. Jane watched in some exasperation as Harry absorbed his uncle's request as though it had sprung from the Delphic oracle, and then turned to whisper urgently to Gerard.

Later, after everyone had gathered in the Gold Saloon, Jane sat in a damask wing chair, watching Diana at the piano. When Jared had asked his wife to treat them to a selection, there had been a round of enthusiastic applause from the members of her family, joined by not one quite so vigorous from those who were not. As soon as her slender fingers touched the keys, however, it became profoundly evident that the marchioness was a gifted pianist.

When she had concluded a short program, consisting of a Mozart rondo, a set of variations by Handel, and the first movement of Beethoven's 'Sonata in C-Sharp Minor,' she phased into an old folk song, and Lissa, Jared, Simon, and Marc gathered about the piano to sing.

Jane pondered the relationship between Jared and Diana. The marquess was the archetypical dominant male, yet he bowed to Diana's wishes, and their love for each other was obvious to the meanest intelligence. Her gaze drifted to Simon and she wondered, just for a moment, what it would be like to be married to him – to be held in Simon's arms every night – what it would be like to share a bed with him. What, she mused, would he look like stripped of that elegant coat, waistcoat, and fine lawn shirt? She gasped at her wayward thoughts, jerking her attention back to the singing.

The five regaled the audience for some minutes, before Diana's fingers drew the rest of the group into the rollicking strains of John Peel.

Even Lady Hermione was induced to join in the singing, and a rare moment of harmony hung like a benediction over the household.

The temporary peace was shattered the next day at dress rehearsal. Everything that could possibly go wrong did so with a vengeance. Gerard and Harry forgot their lines and the half dozen maids and footmen, whom Winifred had dragooned into acting as attendants for the Duke of Athens, forgot their stage cues. While they were nowhere to be seen when they were needed, they trundled on to the stage en masse some minutes later during a tender scene between the duke and his affianced bride. Charles inadvertently sat on his ass's head, crushing the fragile frame to bits, whereupon Lady Hermione delivered herself of a spiteful 'I-told-you-so' speech that set everyone's teeth on edge. To crown a perfectly wretched morning, Harry put his foot through Winifred's costume, resulting in a spectacular shower of stars and a fifteen-minute tirade from the queen of the fairies.

Winifred failed to appear at luncheon, and was discovered sitting alone in the center of the Crimson Saloon stage, bemoaning the ruination of her dreams. When Sir James lowered his bulky person into a seat next to her, saying prosaically, 'It is common knowledge in the theater that a wretched dress rehearsal ensures a successful opening night performance, or so I've heard,' she merely sniffed at him, refusing to join the others.

Simon went to bed that night in unrelieved gloom. Tomorrow was the deadline set by Wilfred's will, and it had become apparent that he could no longer hope for a miracle to save him. It was almost without surprise, therefore, that the household rose the next morning, the day of the long-awaited dinner party and theater performance, to gaze from the windows on a scene of leaden skies and wind-tossed trees. Breakfast was a silent meal, with family and guests picking morosely at their eggs and York ham and kippers. Not surprisingly, Winifred was particularly on edge and moved about the house, buttonholding cast members with endless bits of last-minute advice and suggestions until everyone declared they were being driven quite mad. Thus, when Sir James suggested rather ponderously that she drive with him to the village, she was unanimously urged to take advantage of his kind offer.

Simon moved about the house with an air of quiet desperation, for his moment of doom was upon him. By the end of the day, he would be betrothed to Winifred Timburton. He would mouth the time-honored words of proposal and, while she might cavil somewhat at the outset, she would eventually smile prettily and accept him, after which he would swallow his despair and accept the congratulations of his family and friends including, he supposed, Jane Burch.

The hope that Winifred would refuse him bobbed with insistent frequency to the surface of his gloom, but was pushed down with resolution. The girl was not overly intelligent, but when it came to her own well-being, she was a realist, and once the unpalatable facts had been impressed on her, she would accept her fate, if not with equanimity, with a reasonable degree of fortitude.

He would wait, he decided, until after the play. There was no sense putting an additional burden on Winifred's already overloaded sensibilities. Immediately after the final curtain, he would summon her to his study and accomplish the fateful deed.

What would Jane's reaction be to his proposal to Winifred? he wondered. Surely she would understand that his proposal was not made of his own free will. He snorted. What the devil's difference would that make? Whether she believed him to be acting under duress or that he was wildly smitten with Winifred, she was still as much beyond his reach as though she'd taken up residence on the moon.

Dear God, he was eight and twenty. He had gone through all those years heart-whole, and now, having found his 'bright, particular star', he was about to lose her. She would disappear from his firmament as though she had never existed. How was he to get through the rest of his life without her?

Fifteen

'The actors are at hand.'
—A Midsummer Night's Dream, V, i.

To everyone's vast relief, the skies cleared shortly after luncheon and the sun warmed the spirits of the players as well as the greensward where the play would be performed later in the evening.

The guests were to begin arriving late in the afternoon, and by lunch time, the cast was in a high state of anticipation. Simon, striving to resign himself to his fate, steadfastly thrust his own problems to the back of his mind in order to assist a near-prostrate Winifred in accomplishing the few last-minute details that remained before the performance. In this, he was tenaciously assisted by Charles, to Lady Hermione's obvious displeasure.

Jane, on the other hand, found herself unable to concentrate on anything beyond the fact that by the end of the day, the man she loved would be betrothed to another, and she was powerless to do anything about it.

She was perfectly aware that Simon did not love Winifred, despite the girl's beauty, but that knowledge only made matters worse. Aside from her own misery, she could not bear seeing him shackled to a woman he could barely tolerate. She tried to save a corner of her sympathy for Winifred, whom she knew did not love Simon, but failed rather miserably at that endeavor. Would Simon, she wondered, disregard his pledge to Wilfred if he were in love with another – herself, for example? At least, he would no doubt have made more of an effort to disentangle himself, provided he could maintain his wretched honor.

Luncheon was a somewhat chaotic meal. The members of the household had fallen victim to stage nerves, and those of the staff who were involved in the production had come down with the same affliction, so that slices of cold meat were dropped in laps and fruit fell from trembling fingers to the floor. Afterward, the ladies repaired to their chambers to rest, and the gentlemen resorted to billiards to calm their nerves.

Immediately after luncheon, Jane made her way to the formal dining parlor, where, for one last time, she went over the dinner menu and accommodations for the guests with Mrs Rudge.

'The chickens were delivered this morning, Miss Jane,' said the housekeeper with satisfaction. 'And fine, fat hens they are. Cook has the vegetables ready, and she is working on the sauces and the pastries now. As for the guests, all the bedchambers are in readiness.' A smile creased the plump contours of her cheeks. 'We shall be quite full at bedtime this evening.'

'Oh, that is excellent, Mrs Rudge,' said Jane with a smile. 'And the table looks lovely. I'll just set these.' She gestured with a handful of place cards. 'And everything will be complete.'

'Ah,' sighed Mrs Rudge, 'it's nice to be having a party again. This house was made for happy times, and it's been so silent of late.'

Jane felt her smile go a little rigid, but rising, she nodded her agreement. 'Let us hope it will be the first of many happy gatherings.'

Mrs Rudge came to her feet as well, and bobbing her head, left the room in a crisp swirl of bombazine skirts.

Jane moved along the table, trying to immerse herself in her task. They would seat twenty-eight for dinner, including the neighboring Earl of Granbrook and his wife and daughters, and she wished the evening to be a reflection of the beginning of Simon's status in the neighborhood. She thought of the years and years ahead, after she would be gone back to Suffolk. Would Simon follow through with his plans to sell Selworth after his marriage? Her fingers clenched as she formed the words in her mind. Or would he remain here with his bride? And what of Patience and Jessica? Winifred's marriage to Simon would create just the atmosphere she had hoped for them – a respectable household, headed by a well-connected man of wealth and prestige. But, dear Lord ... Live in the same house in London with Simon and his bride? She couldn't do it. She simply could not do it.

She collapsed into a dining chair, the place cards twisted in her hand, and wondered how she was going to get through the dinner party – and the play – and the rest of her life for that matter.

She was about to sink into a tearful swamp of self-pity, when she heard the door open behind her. Instinctively realizing who stood there, she jerked upright and began an intense and quite spurious inspection of the cards in her hand.

'Ah, here you are, Jane. I've been – Jane, are you all right?' asked Simon.

Jane turned and brought forth yet another of her seemingly bottomless supply of bright smiles. 'Why, yes, of course. I was rather deep in concentration, I'm afraid. Placing the guests is always a rather tricky endeavor. One must remember who is feuding with whom and who would like to be better friends with someone else. And, of course, there are those who cannot be relied upon to hold a decent conversation with anyone....' She knew her tongue was running on wheels, but she feared the silence that would fall between them if she were to stop speaking. 'Have you seen Diana? She promised she would assist with the flowers, and that is to be my next task.'

'Actually, I was speaking with her just a few minutes ago. Or rather, with her and Charles. The two were involved in a somewhat intense discussion in the morning room. Have you noticed, those two have become rather thick of late?'

'Yes, as a matter of fact I have, and so has Jared. He was twitting her yesterday afternoon on her new-found passion for scrawny, overdressed tulips. She looked a little self-conscious, but only smiled rather mysteriously.'

Simon laughed. 'I'm sure Jared realizes he has nothing to fear from that quarter, but I wonder what Diana is up to?'

'I think it must have something to do with Aunt Amabelle, for the two have had their heads together quite frequently of late. Perhaps they are planning a surprise for the guests after the play performance.'

Simon perched on the edge of the dining table, and for a long moment, he simply looked at her.

'I'm pleased to see you have become such friends with Diana – and Aunt Amabelle,' he said at last. 'I hope – that is, you must visit Stonefield Court sometime. I plan to bring Winifred there sometime soon, after – that is, before winter sets in.'

Jane felt her throat constrict, and she knew an urge to run from the room. The subject must be addressed, however. She drew a deep breath.

'I shall be leaving Selworth within the next few days, Simon. I was only waiting to be done with Winifred's play.'

'Oh.' Simon had gone quite pale, and he lifted a hand as though to protest her words.

'I would have departed before this, except that Winifred would have ...'

'Yes, she would have been vastly disappointed.' He rose to his feet, and his hand moved toward her. 'As would I.' He stopped, and seemed to search within himself for a moment. 'I understand your decision,' he said, so softly that she could barely hear the words, 'but I wish – oh, God, how I wish ...'

He stepped closer to her and his gaze enfolded her in that now-familiar boundless warmth. His mouth curved in the crooked smile that always turned her to custard. 'Despite our frequent, er, confrontations, I am pleased to have made the acquaintance of "my cousin Jane".'

He grasped her shoulders gently and, placing his hand where her curls hugged the nape of her neck, he kissed her with great precision on her cheek, just where it met the hollow of her temple. His lips were warm on her skin, and he withdrew them an instant later. In that moment, Jane felt suspended in an aching void. Was this how it would end? she wondered in anguish. With this butterfly touch on her face, leaving her in a despairing maelstrom of wanting? He would never be hers, but by God, she wanted something more to remember than this. Before her sense of propriety could stop her – almost before she knew what she was about, she reached up and cupped his face in her hands. Pulling him to her, she pressed her lips against his.

His response was instantaneous. His arms tightened around her and his mouth moved on hers, seeking, demanding a response that Jane gave freely. She felt herself opening to him like a flower, and she pressed herself against the length of his body as though she would memorize his every contour.

Jane was not sure which of them pulled away first. They stared at each other for a moment in appalled silence before Jane whirled and ran from the room.

The afternoon seemed to drag interminably to most in the house, but Simon found himself suspended in a storm of confusion, where time seemed to have lost its meaning. Good God, Jane had kissed him!

She had walked into his arms and offered her lips to him for the taking. His knowledge of the workings of the feminine psyche was limited, but surely, she would not have done such a thing if she disliked him. Would she? Was it possible that she...? He sat down rather suddenly in his chair behind the desk in his study.

He was possessed by a sudden exhilaration. If there was the slightest hope that she returned his feelings ... He must go to her! He fairly sprang from his seat, but paused with his hand on the door handle, as the cloud of depression that had followed him around for weeks settled on him once more.

A vision of her luminous eyes gazing at him from the pillow next to his rose up before him, followed by one of intimate conversations before the fire while winter storms raged outside, and long, slow kisses in shaded arbors. His gloom deepened and the cloud became blacker. In his blind joy at the possibility that Jane Burch was actually in love with him, he had forgotten that he was already slotted for a proposal this evening. It was unlikely that, after pledging his undying love on bended knee to Jane, she would take well to his rushing off to Winifred to accomplish a similar purpose.

For some moments, he stood in the center of the room, his shoulders slumped. Suddenly, he stiffened and his fingers curled into fists. By God, he was not going to let the chance of a life of fulfillment with Jane slip away. He was *not*, by God, going to marry Winifred! There *had* to be a way out of this.

After several minutes of furious pacing, an idea came to him. It was, he admitted, a trifle less than completely honorable, but ... Drawing on the coat he had removed on entering the study, he strode from the room.

In other corners and crannies of Selworth, some rather odd conversations were taking place.

In the billiards room, Gerard and Harry huddled together, whispering so as not to be overheard by Charles and Sir James who were just finishing their game.

'I am sure of it!' said Gerard, shooting a surreptitious glance at Charles. 'They're planning an elopement! My God, when I heard him telling her they are to meet in the stables after the play, I tell you, I came within an inch of calling him out, but damned if she didn't just giggle and say she'd be there with bells on! Harry, he's promised her five thousand pounds!'

'D'you think we should tell Jane – or Lord Simon?' muttered Harry nervously, his hair standing on end like that of Shakespeare's fretful porpentine.

'No! We can't do that. They'd shove Winifred in her room and not let her out till she's thirty. No, we have to put a stop to it ourselves.'

At this, Harry's hair nearly leaped from its roots. 'Stop them? How?'

'I don't know. I'll have to think about it. We'll talk later. Ssh!' said Gerard in sibilant accents, an eye on Charles who was looking at them curiously.

In the morning room, Diana and Lady Teague sat together on a settee, ostensibly poring over the latest fashions displayed in *La Belle Assemblée*.

'Do you think we've done the right thing?' whispered Lady Teague, looking over her shoulder, though there was no one else in the room.

'If you're talking about morality, probably not, but, yes, I'm sure we're doing the right thing. The idea of Simon's marrying Winifred Timburton doesn't bear thinking of. Not only would she ruin Simon's life, but just think of her in the family. Can you picture her at Stonefield at Christmastime and all the other family celebrations?' Both women shuddered. 'As for Charles and Hermione, those two certainly deserve each other, but I don't believe Hermione's affections are seriously engaged. It's my opinion she regards Charles as she would a pet pug who will get up to mischief if he isn't watched constantly.'

'Well, she's certainly right there,' muttered Aunt Amabelle, her bracelets clinking gently.

'As for Charles, I had barely begun my little campaign, you know, merely suggesting that it was a shame he was to be leg-shackled to Hermione when a beauty like Winifred was his for the asking. He clung to my every word as though I were handing him tablets from Mount Sinai. By our second conversation, he was already agreeing with me, and by the fourth, he was all eagerness to shed Hermione like a suit of old clothes. Oh. Aunt Amabelle, I believe this is going to work! Charles told me of the arrangements he has made for tonight.'

'Oh, my dear,' said Aunt Amabelle breathlessly, 'by this time tomorrow, Simon will be free! Do you think...?'

'Well, I certainly hope so. If Simon is not betrothed to Jane Burch by this time tomorrow, I shall think him the greatest slow top in nature. Those two were made for each other, and it's obvious that they're head over ears in love.'

Aunt Amabelle sighed blissfully. 'You're right, Diana. It cannot be considered wrong to give true love a push in the right direction. Now, tell me, dear, what do you think of this gown? I rather like the bodice, but do you not agree that the gathered skirt is the height of absurdity?'

In the small, curtained area on the terrace that overlooked the south lawn, where the play costumes hung in readiness for this evening's performance, Charles and Winifred stood entwined in a passionate embrace.

'Oh, my love,' muttered Charles, surfacing momentarily for air, then bending to press his mouth against Winifred's cheeks and her throat, continuing in a southerly direction. 'My goddess! Tonight you will be mine. We shall have all eternity to spend together, for all is arranged!'

His twitching fingers edged toward the bosom so enticingly thrust against him, but at that moment Winifred drew back.

'Not now, dearest,' she breathed. 'It would not be proper.'

'But, see what I have brought you!' exclaimed Charles in trembling accents. From a coat pocket he produced a fat packet, which he placed with great ceremony into her hands. 'Five thousand pounds, just as I promised. Enough to clothe you properly as soon as we reach London. After we ... It is all there,' he said somewhat testily, as Winifred opened the packet. 'You needn't count it.'

'Of course not,' cooed Winifred. 'I am just so overwhelmed at your generosity.' Still clutching the packet, she allowed Charles to draw her into his embrace once more. This time he was successful in slipping a hand inside her bodice. Her only response was a soft giggle as, opening one eye, she lifted the packet to eye level behind Charles's head and with her thumb, riffled through the notes.

It was only at the sound of approaching voices that, with a guttural groan, Charles ceased plundering Winifred's delights. Removing his hand from her décolletage, he lurched backward a step, allowing his goddess to rearrange her clothing. When Jane and one of the footmen entered a few moments later, Charles, though still breathing heavily and Winifred, blushing rosily, were able to greet them with a modicum of poise.

*

It was nearing five o'clock in the afternoon when the first guests arrived, although by now, the vicar and Mrs Mycombe hardly counted as guests, so frequent had been their appearances at Selworth of late.

Simon arrived out of sorts to greet the visitors and out of patience. He had been seeking Winifred for some time, and his quarry had proved singularly elusive. Either he entered a room to be told by a servant that she had just left, or catching a glimpse of her scurrying around a corner, he raced to the spot only to find that she had disappeared when he arrived there. Even when he dispatched a servant to find her, the young man came back unsuccessful.

Winifred was on hand, however, to greet the vicar and his wife, but afterward disappeared with the Mycombes and the stolid Sir James, much to Simon's frustration. The Earl of Granbrook and his wife, daughter, and young son arrived almost on the heels of the Mycombes, and after that, a steady procession of vehicles deposited guests at the great front door, making it impossible for Simon to carry out his planned discourse with his ward.

During his brief tenure at Selworth, Simon had met many but not all of the persons soon gathered in drawing rooms and saloons, thus for the rest of the afternoon he was kept occupied with his duties as host. Most of the guests eventually drifted upstairs to their assigned chambers to rest and refresh themselves before it was time to dress for dinner. When the gong sounded, Simon was still making polite conversation with the earl and Squire Beresford and young Mister Kent, who owned a sizeable property some fifteen miles distant.

'You can relax now,' said Diana to Jane as the two ascended the staircase to ready themselves for dinner. 'Your preparations are complete, and all you need do now is enjoy the day.'

Jane smiled. 'As you no doubt do when Stonefield Court is full of company.'

Diana's eyes twinkled. 'Of course not. I am always tense as a drumhead when we have guests, making sure all is well until the last one has disappeared over the horizon. I was merely passing on the excellent advice that Aunt Amabelle and our housekeeper, Mrs Ingersoll, always press on me during such occasions. What are you wearing this evening?' she asked nonchalantly.

'Oh, my midnight blue satin – the one with the acorns embroidered in silver. I wore it a few nights after your arrival, when we went to the Selwyns' dinner party.'

'Oh, yes, I remember it. Excellent! That is, it's terribly becoming to you – the silver seems to be reflected in your hair and it makes your eyes all deep and mysterious.'

'Why, thank you,' said Jane, somewhat startled.

'Umm,' added Diana. 'The thing is, I know how hard it is to find a color that goes well with gray eyes. I've always felt that mine are perfectly colorless, but Jared seems to like them – fortunately.' She stopped rather self-consciously. 'That is, of course – why there's Winifred!' she cried in apparent relief. 'Where on earth has the girl been all this time?'

Jane glanced swiftly in the direction indicated by Diana to observe Winifred entering the hall from the corridor that led to the courtyard and the back of the house.

'I don't know,' she replied grimly, 'but I am about to find out.'

She turned away from Diana and hurried down the stairs to where Winifred stood, her violet eyes sparkling with mischief, in easy conversation with Mr and Mrs Mycombe.

'Winifred,' she called in a deliberately casual tone, 'may I have a word with you?'

Smiling, Winifred excused herself from the vicar and from Sir James who came in at that moment from the front of the house, an odd smile curving his thin mouth.

Grasping the girl's arm, Jane gave her a surreptitious pinch as she led her up the stairs. 'Where have you been?' she exclaimed in an exasperated whisper. 'You're the daughter of the house, for pity's sake. You're supposed to be on hand to greet people when they arrive, particularly on a day we've been planning for so long. What on earth kept you?'

Winifred's glance, though still containing shreds of impish laughter, was mildly surprised. 'But you and Lady Teague and Simon were here. I still have some things to do in preparation for this evening, you know. The costumes were in disorder, and …'

'Oh, never mind,' snapped Jane. 'You're here now. For heaven's sake stay put and be charming. I've placed you next to Squire Pemberton at the dinner.'

'That old stick? Jane, how could you? He's the most boring man in this county and several adjoining ones besides.'

Jane's eyes glittered dangerously. 'Since,' she said through clenched teeth, 'you declined to participate in plans for the seating arrangements, I placed you where I thought you would do the most good. You will find Mister Kent on your other side, and you will probably get no conversation from him either, as he is always so dazzled in your presence that he becomes completely tongue-tied.'

They had by now reached the top of the stairs, and without giving Winifred time to respond, she gave the girl a little push toward her bedchamber, then hurried off to her own.

To Jane's vast relief, dinner went off without a hitch, and the smile on her lips remained fixed as Winifred graciously accepted the many compliments on its excellence. If some of the household members seemed inordinately preoccupied, the guests were too polite to take note, and after the meal, Winifred stood to announce that the play would begin in an hour and a half.

She made as though to leave the room, but Simon was before her.

'I must see you, Winifred,' he stated baldly.

'All right,' she replied composedly. 'We can talk in the morning.'

'No,' he said, his tone uncompromising. 'We will talk now. It will only take a few minutes.'

Winifred opened her mouth to protest this high-handed behavior on the part of one whom she had come to think of as one of her conquered, but closed it immediately on observing the expression in his eyes. Meekly, she followed her guardian from the room.

Sixteen

'The actors are at hand; and, by their show,
You shall know all that you are like to know.'
—A Midsummer Night's Dream, V, i.

Simon carefully closed the door of his study, and, moving to his chair behind the desk, he gestured Winifred to the one opposite. He could not help contrasting her at that moment with Jane, who had sat in that same place so many times, brangling with him over the management of those persons she held dear. There was no question that Winifred was by far the more beautiful but, he mused, almost smiling, what man in his right mind would chose a goddess over an enchanting wood sprite?

The deity sat watching him in silent expectancy, her amethyst eyes wide and impenetrable. He drew a deep breath. 'Winifred, you have been put in possession of the facts of Wilfred's bequest to me.'

An odd expression crossed Winifred's face, of startlement blended with relief. 'Yes,' she said, the word more a question than a statement.

'However, there was one pertinent piece of information that was kept from you, at my request.'

This time Winifred merely lifted her brows warily, but as Simon began his explanation of Wilfred's last plea, and the arrangement into which he had coerced Simon, her expression grew incredulous.

'Marry you!' she said some minutes later as he finished his tale. 'But – but, that's impossible!'

'I'm afraid not,' Simon said heavily. 'Not according to the provisions of your brother's will. I went over it – more than once – with Mr Soapes, Wilfred's agent, and he said the thing is absolutely airtight.'

Simon paused and shot Winifred a shrewd look. 'Now, while I hope you will not take offense, I have no wish to marry you, my feelings for you being no more than what is proper between a guardian and his ward. I believe it is also true that you have no desire to marry me.'

'Oh, no,' she said quickly. 'As a matter of—'

'Unfortunately,' continued Simon, 'the fact remains that since you have received no other proposal of marriage, I am obliged to offer for you myself.' He was now perspiring rather profusely and pulled a handkerchief from his waistcoat to draw over his forehead.

'But, that's impossible—' began Winifred again, only to be silenced once more.

'I know this has come as a shock to you, my dear, and l suppose I should have told you earlier what was to come, but I kept hoping – that is, I thought … Well, never mind what I thought. The thing is, I may have a way out of our difficulty.'

This time Winifred said nothing, merely staring at him in disbelief.

'What I propose is this. I am, as of this moment, requesting your hand in marriage, but …' He took a deep breath as Winifred's mouth opened. 'But, if you choose to refuse my offer, I shall give you the option of remaining at Selworth as long as you like, with the complete income of the estate to supplement your own inheritance, or I shall sell the place at the earliest opportunity and give you the profits.'

When, after a long moment, Winifred still said nothing, continuing to gape at him blankly, Simon went on in some desperation. 'I know you would be better off with a husband, but there is nothing to say you cannot have one later on.' He paused, realizing he sounded like a doting parent promising his offspring a toy. 'What I mean to say is, I shall still be your guardian until you do marry, or turn six and twenty, whichever comes first. But I would endeavor to interfere in your life as little as possible beyond hiring a companion for you – perhaps two. Do you think—?' He stopped as Winifred lifted a hand.

'What you're saying,' she began slowly, 'is that you are offering to marry me, but if I refuse, you will pay me a great deal of money – one way or the other.'

'Well – yes, that's pretty much it. If you need some time to think it over …'

'No,' The word was uttered with calm certainty. 'I will accept your offer. No, no,' she added quickly, as Simon turned pale, 'I mean the one about you giving me money.'

'Oh.' Simon almost sagged with relief. He straightened almost immediately and rose from behind the desk, and was at once overcome by a feeling of compunction. 'Are you sure?' he asked, listening with dread to his own words. 'You are very young, and I do not wish to take advantage of you.'

'Oh, no,' she said coolly, 'I shouldn't think you could do that. In any event, you are my guardian, and I shall, of course, be guided by your counsel. When must I decide whether I wish to live off the income from Selworth or whether I wish you to sell the estate?'

Her self-possession startled him. 'We have plenty of time for that. We should sit down with Mr Soapes and ask his advice. In fact, I shall have to go over all this with Soapes, anyway,' he said thoughtfully, 'but I cannot see where he would have any objection. He will remain as your man of affairs and will always see to your interests. In the meantime, may I say, Miss Timburton, and I hope you will not take offense, but you have made me a very happy man.'

Winifred rose and faced him, a mysterious smile on her lips reminiscent of certain very ancient Greek statues he had seen at the British Museum. She said nothing, but after a moment, laughed her silvery laugh, and ran lightly from the room.

Simon slumped against the desk, a dazed smile on his face. The next moment, he moved to the center of the room where, laughing aloud, he danced an impromptu jig. His exultation grew. He was free! Free to seek out his love and make her his own. If all continued to go well, that is.

He hurried from the room, but was again unsuccessful in his quest. Jane, it appeared was nowhere in the house. At last, as he made his way through the hall, a footman pointed through the open front door.

'Don't know where she was headed, my lord. The ornamental water, perhaps. It's pretty this time of evening.'

Thanking the young man, Simon stepped out into the gathering dusk. The night smelled of paradise, he thought. The scent of roses was heavy on the air, mingled with softer fragrances from the gardens and fields beyond. A swollen moon was rising, turning lawns and hedges to silver, and in the sky one, solitary star glittered like a jewel above the trees.

Simon turned his footsteps toward the water, and stood still when he saw her, seated on a rock, gazing into the pool. She had changed into her costume and, bathed in the luminescence of the moonlight, looked wholly a creature of the night. He had almost reached her when she turned to face him. He heard the startled intake of her breath as she rose to move toward him. The folds of her muslin tunic stirred in the light evening breeze and pressed provocatively against her body as she walked up the incline from the lake.

She said nothing as she approached him, but Simon was intensely aware of the almost tangible electricity that swirled between them. Her eyes did not reflect the moonlight, but were dark and mysterious and impenetrable.

'Jane,' he whispered, and almost before the word had dropped from his lips, she was in his arms, fragrant and supple and infinitely desirable. Their mouths met and clung in a kiss that was hungry and seeking, yet almost unbearably sweet. Her enticing curves and hollows seemed to be perfectly designed to fit against him, and the feel of her under his hands created swirls of pleasure in him that were eminently satisfying, even as they created a fierce wanting.

'Jane,' he said, almost groaning. 'Oh, my God, Jane.'

She drew back a little to look at him, a faint, sad smile on her lips.

'I have something to tell you, Jane.' He sensed the tension that suddenly filled her slight frame and continued hastily. 'This afternoon—'

'Janie! Jane, are you out there?'

It was Gerard, and Simon knew an urge to turn and strangle the young man.

'It's time to assemble with the others,' the young man said breathlessly as he approached them. 'Curtain in less than half an hour. Have you seen my tunic? It's supposed to be with Bottom's and the other clowns, but—'

Jane shot a glance at Simon, but spoke soothingly to her brother. 'It's all right, Gerard. Aunt Amabelle noticed a tear in it this afternoon and took it to her chambers to mend it. She is probably looking for you with it right now.'

'All right,' said Gerard, still apparently in need of mollifying, for he grasped her arm and began pulling her toward the house. 'But, you know, I'm supposed to stand in readiness to hand Marc his Oberon outfit as soon as he comes offstage from being Lysander, and I can't find the dam— dashed crown.'

'Oh dear,' said Jane. 'Well, perhaps Winifred moved it. I saw her rearranging things earlier.'

Her hand still lay in Simon's grasp, but when his fingers tightened on hers, she glanced up at him, her expression unreadable. Gently, she disengaged herself and allowed Gerard to hurry her toward the south lawn, where the players were gathering for the performance.

Simon swore softly under his breath. What the devil—? Jane must have sensed he was about to make a declaration. She had returned his kiss fervently. Surely that meant she felt something for him. What the devil! he thought again, unhappily.

Mindlessly, Jane trailed in Gerard's wake. She felt adrift in a sea of frustrated emotion. Dear God, she should not have allowed Simon to kiss her just then. And she most certainly should not have kissed him back. He had started to say something about this afternoon. Was he already betrothed to Winifred? No, surely he would not have come in search of her after a proposal to another woman. Still, no announcement had been made. Despite herself, her heart rose. Perhaps Simon had decided against offering for Winifred. As she turned this idea around blissfully in her mind, her heart reversed course. No, Simon was a man of honor. She must not chase rainbows.

Shaking herself, she glanced about her as she and Gerard reached the stage area. Most of the players were already in costume, others milled about, chatting nervously. Jane watched Charles, who displayed a suppressed excitement that seemed excessive even for normal opening-night jitters. He was fairly twitching as he thrust his ass's head over his ears, pulling it off again immediately, and repeating the same procedure again. When Winifred appeared, wearing the simple gown of rose pink in which she would appear as Hermia, Charles hastened to her side, speaking insistently in her ear as she passed among her cast. Where she had been almost wild with growing anticipation over the last week, Winifred now displayed a calm self-possession that surprised Jane. She patted Charles on his ass's head as she would a high-strung spaniel, and moved among the members of her cast, dispensing encouragement and assistance where needed.

Diana and Jared, in costume, stood to one side conversing with Aunt Amabelle, who had come armed with needle and thread, in case she should be required for any last-minute repairs. Diana's glance strayed frequently to Charles, and she frowned slightly at the earl's growing agitation.

Sir James, at Winifred's direction, and with Gerard and Harry in tow, checked the position of the candles in their tin holders, arranged in a semicircle at the front of the stage. From there, he moved to the prop table, inspecting the fairy wands, the flowers that supposedly held Puck's magic juices, and all the other items to be handled by the cast during the course of the play. He paused to reprimand several of the village children who, in their fairy costumes darted about, getting in the way and making mischief, just like the sprites they represented. Sir James, thought Jane, accomplished his tasks with quiet efficiency, looking surprisingly at home in surroundings that must be quite alien to him.

Marcus and Lissa stood near each other. Jane's lips tightened. The two were feigning indifference, each obviously very aware of the other's presence. At one point Marcus started forward as though he would speak to her, but Lissa, apparently engrossed in adjusting her costume, did not see, and turned away before he could complete his intention. Lissa did notice, however, when Winifred approached to consult with Marcus on a minor point of the performance, running her fingers over a muscled shoulder bared by his Grecian tunic. Lissa started forward, but immediately withdrew, turning a rigid shoulder to the scene.

Jane shook her head in exasperation. How could Lissa behave so stupidly? Was she simply going to let the man she loved walk out of her life without protest? If she would only talk to Marcus ... Suddenly, Jane stood stock-still, the buzz of excitement fading around her. Good Lord, wasn't that what she herself was doing? She loved Simon Talent and she was allowing him to sign his life over to Winifred without a peep from herself.

Her brain churned furiously. There was probably nothing she could do about Simon's damned sense of honor, but there must be something she could do about Winifred. She had always been able to talk sense into the girl – well, usually, at any rate. No announcement had been made. Jane repeated the phrase like a prayer. Simon must not have proposed to Winifred yet. Perhaps he was waiting until the last minute – after the play. She *must* intercept Winifred before Simon said something they'd all be sorry for.

Setting off to find her cousin, Jane paused to peer through the crack in the curtain that had been constructed in a frame and placed between the audience and the stage. Some two hundred chairs had been set up, and to her surprise, the original group of guests had been swelled by villagers and servants from neighboring houses until it had become necessary to bring out additional benches for the overflow.

Glancing about the backstage area, Jane saw Winifred standing in the midst of a questioning group of footmen who had been pressed into service as curtain pullers, candle lighters, and general factotums. Jane moved forward, only to be intercepted by Charles, who importuned her for assistance with his newly crafted ass's head.

At last, she was able to reach her quarry. 'Winifred,' she said urgently, 'I must speak to you.'

Winifred bent a gaze of dazzling radiance on her.

'Oh, Jane, I *am* so excited!'

'Yes, I'm sure you are, but I must—'

'Later, Jane. We are all ready to begin. I want to speak to you, too, for I have wonderful news!' She glanced around and lowered her voice to a whisper. 'I am not supposed to speak yet, but I cannot keep silent anymore, especially with you, oh, favorite of my cousins. After the play, I shall have the most interesting announcement! Lord Simon has made me an astonishing offer! It was truly all I needed to complete my happiness! But, I cannot say more now.' She hugged Jane briefly, and with a wink, hurried off to speak with Sir James, who had just beckoned to her.

Jane stood rooted to the makeshift floor. He had done it. He had actually proposed to Winifred, and she had accepted. Somehow, without realizing it, she had been hoping against hope that he would balk at the last minute. That he would be unable to enter into a loveless marriage. That he would realize that his true love waited right within his reach.

So great was her despair that she thought she would be sick right there in front of everyone. She shivered, and forced herself to breathe deeply. How could she have been so foolish as to think he might have come to cherish her unbiddable self above his duty?

Slowly, she moved offstage. At least, she thought wearily, she did not make her entrance until the beginning of Act Two, leaving her a little time to recover her equilibrium. Through a blur of tears she watched Simon take his place with Marcus and Lissa – and Winifred. At Winifred's signal, the curtain was drawn back, and the hired piper began his limpid prelude. In another few moments, Jared and Diana, looking truly regal in their tiaras and sceptered dignity, moved onstage.

'Now, fair Hippolyta, our nuptial hour
Draws on apace.'

The play had begun!

Some two hours later, Jane's clear laughter floated over the footlights.

'So, good night unto you all.
Give me your hands, if we be friends,
And Robin shall restore amends.'

Thus the play ended to a standing ovation from the audience. The players exchanged smiles of exhilarated gratification as they were called back for round after round of curtain calls. We did it! the smiles said, and indeed they had performed beyond their own wildest expectations. Oberon and Titania had been beauty and sorcery personified. The young lovers were all bewitched bewilderment. Bottom had coaxed guffaws from the audience with his antics, as had the rest of the clowns, and the Duke of Athens and his chosen bride, Hippolyta, Queen of the Amazons, had captivated the audience as well as their subjects. The players, grinning through their greasepaint, reveled in the applause, and Winifred, quite stupifyingly beautiful in Titania's magic glitter, accepted the shouted accolades with blushing pride.

'She's really good, isn't she?' murmured Lissa colorlessly to Simon, who, with the other players stood in a line to accept yet another curtain call.

'Yes, she is,' replied Simon wonderingly. 'She's proved herself an excellent director as well. I would not have thought that a group like ours – with no experience, and not much talent – could have been brought together with such results.' He bowed once more and beamed a smile across the footlights.

Lissa smiled frigidly. 'I can certainly see the attraction she holds for Marcus.'

The applause drew to a close, and the actors began to descend from the stage to mingle with the admiring throng.

'Look here, Lissa.' Simon reached up to assist her to the ground. 'Winifred may have been flirting with Marc – as she seems to do with everything in breeches – but have you seen him respond?'

'Well ...' said Lissa, her eyes glittering with tears.

'No, you haven't, and that being the case, I don't see why you don't make it up with him.'

'Oh, Simon, I want to so badly, but – well, you've seen how cold he is to me, all because I asked—'

'You didn't ask, you demanded, and you were pretty unreasonable, don't you think? In Marc's view, you tried to spoil his fun for no good reason.'

'Yes,' replied Lissa slowly, 'I suppose I did. Marc's love of play-acting is no worse than the way most men love hunting – or gambling, I suppose. Oh, Simon, I do love him so.'

'I don't think Marcus has been any happier than you have these past weeks, Lissa. I think if you were to tell him what you just told me—'

Lissa lifted her eyes. 'Oh, Simon, do you think so?' She smiled radiantly. 'I'll do it! I'll go and find him right now, and if I'm successful, you'll be the first to wish us happy – again.'

'Good,' said Simon. 'And,' he added with a broad grin, 'I may have some interesting news along that line myself very soon.'

He ignored her excited questions, and blowing a kiss, looked for Jane. He spotted her almost immediately. She was still on-stage, accepting extravagant compliments from a modish buck whose family's estate, recalled Simon, marched with Selworth.

With studied aplomb, he dispatched the young man, and took Jane's hand in his. He was a little startled when she withdrew it abruptly, but pressed on, undeterred.

'I've been trying to talk to you all evening,' he said significantly.

'Have you, indeed?' she responded frostily. 'I have been right here.'

'I meant alone,' said Simon, his puzzlement and unease growing. He attempted to draw her back into the area offstage which led to the dark invitation of the shrubbery beyond, but she refused to be budged.

'I do not think it would be proper for us to be alone, under the circumstances,' she sniffed.

'What circumstances?' asked Simon blankly.

She made no reply, but twitched herself away from his grasp. 'If you will excuse me,' she said stiffly, 'I must see to refreshments for the guests.'

The next moment she was gone, melting into the crowd, leaving Simon staring after her in angry bafflement.

Lissa, having watched with a smile as her brother hastened toward Jane, glanced around for Marc. Wondering that he was nowhere to be seen, she moved among the crowd that was beginning to drift toward the house. Some of the other cast members had disappeared as well, she observed, notably Winifred. Charles, too, was nowhere to be seen.

There! Wasn't that Marc, some yards up ahead? Catching only a glimpse of his fair hair glinting in the moonlight, and the dark green cloak he had worn as Demetrius, she hurried after him. She soon lost sight of him in the press of people, and was obliged to stop several times to accept the laughing congratulations of family and friends on her performance.

Still, in her haste, she reached the front door ahead of all but a few of the guests. Searching, she moved through the near-empty hall and then into the saloons which bordered its perimeter. Feeling oddly disturbed, she stood irresolute for a moment before proceeding toward the back of the hall and the little courtyard that lay beyond. She stepped quietly into the courtyard, and immediately a flash of something caught her eye. Turning, her hand flew to her throat and a small moan escaped her.

There, on the far side of the courtyard, silhouetted against the candlelight from within stood Winifred, her fairy crown tumbled to the grass. She was enveloped in the passionate embrace of a man. Lissa's first thought was that she had interrupted an assignation between Winifred and Charles but, though very tall, the man who was fairly raining kisses on Winifred's upturned face was not nearly as tall as Charles. His size as he bent over the beauty, was difficult to determine, hidden as he was under the folds of a voluminous cloak which was all too familiar.

'Marcus!' gasped Lissa in a broken whisper.

Seventeen

'Why, then you left me (Oh, the gods forbid!)'
—A Midsummer Night's Dream, III, ii.

For a long moment, Lissa simply stood transfixed, watching her world shatter. Then, with a sob, she turned and fled back into the house. She stumbled toward the staircase and took refuge in a small cupboard built in beneath it and remained there, shuddering and fighting back the waves of despair and nausea which threatened to engulf her. Never in Lissa's short and pampered life had she been hurt by anyone close to her. She, who was open and giving herself, had only to put out a hand to find herself cherished in return. Marcus Crowne was her first and only true love – and now he had betrayed her!

For almost an hour, Lissa stood in the shelter of the little cupboard, sunk in despairing reflection. At last, her eyes dry and her back straight, she emerged to seek out her aunt, whom she discovered in the Crimson Saloon. Drawing her away from the well-upholstered matron with whom she was conversing, she said in a voice that trembled only slightly, 'Aunt, I want to go home!'

Lady Teague observed her niece in some surprise. 'But you are home. Oh – you mean Stonefield? Now? My dear, whatever is the matter?' she asked, peering into the girl's face. 'Oh dear, is it Marcus?'

'I really don't want to talk about it, please. Could we just go home?' Despite her best efforts, the tremor in her voice increased alarmingly.

'But, we cannot, Lissa.' Lady Teague, in honor of the occasion had placed several more pins, pendants, necklaces, and bracelets on her plump person than usual, with the result that she sounded a little like an orchestra tuning up. 'We cannot just leave. Why do you not go up to your room, dear, and I shall come when I can?'

'I do not,' said Lissa, her body rigid, 'wish to go to my room. I want – to – go – home.'

She knew she was acting with the blind panic of a child, but she simply could not look at Marcus again, and she was sure that if she did not leave this room and Selworth within a very few minutes, she would fly apart in all directions at once.

The loquacious matron with whom Lady Teague had been speaking, grasped her arm and restarted the conversation that Lissa had interrupted.

'I cannot talk now, Lissa. Why – why don't you find Jared? Perhaps you can work something out with him.'

But Jared, when she ran him to earth on the front steps of the house, proved no more amenable to granting Lissa her most pressing wish.

'Don't be absurd, my girl. We can't just go haring off in the middle of the night. And we can't leave in the morning, either. It would look extremely odd, don't you think? Devil take it, Lissa, you can't expect everyone to drop what they're doing and minister to you every time you have a spat with Marc.'

His black eyes snapped at her and hers, darker yet, stared at him for a long moment before she turned on her heel and walked away.

'Lissa!' called Jared, but she did not stop. Hunching a shoulder in exasperation, he went to search out Diana, who could always be depended on to bring his tiresome little sister out of her sulks. Surely, that's all it was, he thought uncomfortably, remembering her white face and the anguish in her eyes.

Lissa ran out again into the hall, and this time, still in fear of meeting Marcus, hurtled up the stairs to the refuge of her bedchamber. She was halted in her flight by Gerard and Harry, who were coming down the stairs, nearly knocking her over in their haste.

'Lissa!' gasped Gerard, clutching at her. 'Have you seen Winifred?'

She shook her head stiffly and attempted to release her hand.

'Then, how about Charles?' His voice squeaked in agitation.

'I have not seen either of them,' replied Lissa coldly. 'Now may I please go on my way?'

'Oh. Sorry.' Gerard exchanged an anguished glance with Harry and the two bolted down the stairs, leaving Lissa to continue on her path.

Having gained the top of the stairs, Lissa hurried along the gallery that overlooked the hall and then into the corridor that led from it. Unseeing, she brushed past Charles, who was just coming out of his chambers in the company of a footman. So intent was he on the instructions he was imparting to the servant, that he did not even look up as Lissa hurtled past him. As for Lissa, absorbed in her own private hell, she heard only the words, '… and have the chaise at the stable yard gate at one o'clock.'

Her attention caught, she slowed and listened as Charles continued. 'I want the strongest cattle in the stable – your master won't mind, for I'll make it up to him later. They must take me to London with no stopping. No, I shan't require a coachman. I'll drive the team myself.'

London! Charles was going to London. Tonight! In her extreme agitation, she did not consider why a guest of the house would be taking such precipitate leave in the middle of the night, or why he required a carriage rather than his phaeton. Only the words, 'London', and 'no stopping', registered with her. She had plenty of pin money, and once in London, she could hire a carriage to take her to Stonefield. She knew the journey could be made in only a few hours. She turned to retrace her steps toward Charles, but caught herself immediately. He would, of course, not only refuse a request from her that she be taken up in his carriage, but would no doubt inform Aunt Amabelle and/or Jared besides.

She ran all the rest of the way to her room and flung herself on her bed, giving herself up to furious thought. How fortunate that Charles would be driving the carriage himself. It would be unlikely that he would discover an unscheduled passenger curled up in a very small ball under a rug inside. One o'clock, Charles had said. It was already a little after midnight. She would have to make her plans quickly. Good. The more she thought about a plan, the less time she'd have to think about Marcus.

A fresh burst of pain shuddered through her as she whispered his name. Would he miss her tomorrow morning? Would he even notice she was gone?

Downstairs, Charles circulated among the revelers, who were contained for the most part in the hall and the saloons surrounding it. Still garbed in his homespun tunic, he accepted with an affecting modesty congratulations for his performance as Bottom, but his smile grew ever broader as he passed through the assemblage until it threatened to split his face.

'Thank you so much, Lady Granbrook. By the by, have you seen Wini— Miss Timburton?' 'That's awfully kind of you, Lord Mumblethorpe. Has Miss Timburton been in here within the last few minutes?'

Perhaps, thought the earl, the little darling was upstairs preparing for their clandestine meeting at the stable gate in – by gad! – half an hour! Yes, that was probably it. In fact, he should be going up himself to change and to collect the portmanteau his valet was packing for him at that very moment. A tingle of anticipation shot through him as he moved toward the door of the Crimson Saloon.

'Wye! There you are.' At the sound of the nasal voice behind him, the smile dropped from his lips to be replaced by a grimace of alarm, which in turn was almost instantly replaced by one of crafty satisfaction. He turned.

'There you are, my dear. I've been looking all over for you.'

'Have you indeed?' said Lady Hermione, looking more than ever like a disassembled rock pile in a gown of granite gray embellished with knobby little tufts of embroidery. She placed her finger tips on the arm he held out for her and proceeded with him about the room, nodding graciously at the compliments directed at Charles as though she were personally responsible for any talent he might have displayed that evening.

'Now that you have dispensed with your duties here, Wye,' began Lady Hermione, 'I assume you are planning to return to London shortly.'

Charles jerked spasmodically and his head swiveled to meet her gaze. 'London? London?' were the only words he was able to produce at the moment, but he relaxed almost immediately. There was no way she could know about his plans, after all. The smirk returned to its place. 'Why, yes, I shall be leaving Selworth shortly. As, I assume, will you?'

'Most certainly.' Her ladyship shuddered. 'I can hardly wait to see the last of this place. I have been sorry ever since I arrived that I was obliged to come here.'

'Obliged?'

Lady Hermione uttered an unbecoming titter. 'Why, because of my feelings for you, dear Wye. I was so lonely at Wimpole Park. That is our seat in—'

'Yes, I know,' said Charles hastily. He peeled her fingers from his sleeve. 'I wonder if you will excuse me for a few moments, my dear. There is someone I must see.'

Lady Hermione giggled playfully. Lord, thought Charles, she'd been at the punch bowl too long. 'Yes, but only for a moment dearest,' she said with a coy smile.

Charles hurried away, leaving her wagging her fingers at him from the center of the room. He waded through the guests to the doorway, bumping into Diana and Jared as he did so.

Idly, Jared watched the earl's rather erratic progress into the hall. He turned to Diana with a laugh. 'He even moves like a hedge-bird. When, by the by,' he continued as he tucked his wife's hand in his arm, 'are you going to tell me what plot you and Aunt Amabelle have been hatching over his unfortunate head?'

Diana merely smiled mysteriously. 'All in good time, my dear.' She gazed about abstractedly. 'I wonder where Simon is. I wish to speak to him about something a little later on.'

'I don't know,' replied Jared with a pained expression. 'He's probably proposing to Miss-Godawful Timburton, I should imagine. I have not seen her of late, either. Lord, I hope she refuses him.'

Diana smiled demurely. 'I think he may have found a way out of his difficulties.'

Her husband bent a discerning glance on her. 'Yes?' he said encouragingly.

Diana flushed. 'Nothing.' Her gray eyes gazed up into dark ones that held a great deal of tender amusement. 'Oh, very well. I will tell you everything, if you promise not to put a spoke in our plans.'

'I may regret this, but very well.'

With some relish, Diana proceeded to detail the solution she and Lady Teague had concocted for Simon's difficulties.

'Oh, my God. Diana, an elopement? But Charles is betrothed!

'Simon told me that there have been no settlement papers signed. And truly, Jared, can marriage to Winifred be much worse than spending his life with Hermione? To say nothing of the fact that her ladyship will be much better off without Charles. She has no real regard for him, I'm sure, and it's obvious that she is clinging to him only because no one else has come up to scratch. I mean, Jared, the woman is at her last prayers!'

'My God, I never realized what a cat I married! Or what a devious hatcher of wicked schemes. Between the two of you, you and Aunt Amabelle could give lessons to the Borgias.'

Diana laughed. 'Why thank you, my dear.' She lifted her eyes to his once more and at the expression in her eyes, Jared's next words emerged a little raggedly. 'I wonder if it is too early to retire for the evening? I would Like—'

'Danny! Jared. Have you seen Lissa?' The pair turned to regard Marcus, who had come up behind them. He, too, was still in costume, though he had removed most of his greasepaint. His fair hair was in a good deal of disarray and fell over his brow in undisciplined curls.

'Damn, I forgot,' said Jared in some irritation. 'She came running up to me some minutes ago in high dudgeon. Said she wanted to go home – to Stonefield.'

'Stonefield?' echoed Marcus blankly.

'Mmm. She seemed more than usually upset with you.' He turned to Diana. 'I meant to ask you to go to her, but in the press of all this merrymaking, I quite forgot.'

A puzzled frown appeared on Marcus's face. 'I looked for her after the last curtain call.' He flushed a little. 'I thought, now that the whole thing is over, perhaps she and I ... At any rate, there were so many people milling about, I couldn't find her.' His gaze moved restlessly over the crowded room.

'Perhaps she has gone to change,' said Diana. 'I'll go upstairs. If she's in her chambers, I shall send word to you.' She bent a mischievous smile on her husband. 'I'll see you later – about that matter we were discussing.' With a soft rustle of the silk tunic she had worn as Hippolyta, she turned and hurried away.

Outside, at the back of the house, Lissa was also hurrying, to the stables. As she neared the yard gate, she stopped and huddled behind a convenient bush. Yes! There was the chaise, as ordered. Looking around carefully, she scurried across the lawn. Opening the door of the chaise, she discovered that Charles's portmanteau had already been placed there. She climbed into the carriage and, curling herself into a ball on the floor, she drew the rug that had been folded on one of the seats over her.

A few moments later, masculine voices and the crunch of footsteps on gravel warned her that people approached, and she cowered inside her hiding place. A sharp knock sounded on the door of the chaise and startled Lissa so that, despite herself, she uttered a small squeak.

Charles's laughter sounded loud in her ears through the door of the carriage and she shrank even farther into her corner on the floor.

'Ah! Winifred!' exclaimed Charles. 'You're in there already, my sweet bonbon. Come along then, Biggs.'

Lissa felt a lurch as the tiger mounted his post, and a second upheaval occurred as Charles climbed on to the driver's seat. Lissa shivered, terrified at her own audacity, and curled herself up as tightly as she could and clenched her teeth together as Charles cracked his whip and the chaise sprang forward.

In the house, Gerard leaned against a bookcase in the library, one of the few downstairs rooms not overrun with guests at the moment. His rough tunic was drenched with perspiration, for the night was warm and he had been in constant motion for the past hour and more. He straightened suddenly as the door opened, and exhaled a breath of relief when Harry skidded into the room.

'Well?' asked Gerard in a strained voice.

Harry merely shook his head, his yellow hair hanging in limp tendrils over his heavily bedewed forehead. 'She's nowhere to be found,' he gasped before sinking into a leather chair. 'Ain't seen hide nor hair of the earl, either.'

'My God,' breathed Gerard hoarsely, 'do you think they've flown the roost?' He ran thin, trembling fingers through his hair and his eyes were round as silver buttons.

'I dunno. Can't think of anyplace else to look.'

Gerard straightened suddenly, snapping his fingers. 'What a pair of loobies we are! We have only to check the stables. If Winifred and the earl are gone—'

'So will be the earl's phaeton,' finished Harry after staring blankly at his friend for a moment.

Five minutes later, the two stood outside the stables, immersed in unrelieved gloom.

'I cannot believe the earl – or Winifred, for that matter – would behave in such a cotton-brained fashion,' said Gerard. 'My God – to make off with Lord Simon's chaise and his best set of carriage horses. What if someone sees them haring off to God-knows-where? Her reputation will be in shreds. Not that she seems to care,' he added bitterly. 'And Wye must know that Lord Simon will discover their absence in short order, and then there'll be the devil to pay.'

'What if they're eloping to France?' asked Harry. He had only meant to be helpful, but his efforts were rewarded with a snarl.

'I tell you what, Harry, we have to go after them.'

Harry's only response was a faint whimper.

'No, really,' continued Gerard eagerly. 'The stable boy said they left only minutes ago. We should be able to catch up to them in ... What'd you say?'

'Nothing,' mumbled Harry, who had whimpered again.

'We'll take your curricle,' continued Gerard, his tone one of eminent practicality, 'and go after them.'

'And then what?'

'And then what what?'

'And then what are we going to do? Tell Lord Wye to hand Winifred over to us? You said she didn't sound unwilling. What if she tells us to sod off? Are we going to drag her back by her hair?'

'Oh.' said Gerard, daunted. He brightened almost immediately. 'We'll just have to talk her round. Don't forget your Uncle James.'

Harry snorted, his round, blue eyes crinkled in contempt. 'My Uncle James, indeed. Fat lot of good he's done us so far. I knew it wouldn't do any good to get him to come here. He's never done anything for anybody but himself in his whole life. But no – "he knows people in the theater", you said. "He'll be so smitten with Winifred, he'll help her do anything she wants", you said. Tchah!'

'Well, yes, but he told us at the start he would have to get to know her a bit – you know, feel her out – er, no, bad choice of words. See if she would meet his needs – well, no, that's no good either. You know what I mean,' Gerard finished impatiently.

'Yes, I suppose I do,' sighed Harry.

'Well, then, so all we have to do is – sst!' Gerard pulled Harry behind the stable yard wall. 'Someone's coming.'

They waited as one of the downstairs maids, giggling wildly and hotly pursued by the second groom, came peltering by them.

'Good God!' said Harry in tones of strong disapproval when they emerged from their hiding place. 'The thing is turning into a dashed orgy.'

'Never mind that,' snapped Gerard. 'Come on, we're wasting time.'

'Wait a minute!' cried Harry in some anguish as Gerard whirled away. Stumbling after his friend, he caught up to him at the stable door. 'What about Winifred – and her reputation? We mightn't catch up to them for miles, and it ain't going to look any better for her to be seen with us careening about the countryside in the middle of the night than it would be the earl.'

'Oh, my God,' said Gerard, halting.

'P'raps we'd do better to just go tell Lord Simon,' said Harry, with the air of one who had already said this several times during the course of the evening.

'No! That's the whole idea, here, isn't it? To rescue Winifred before she gets in terrible trouble with Lord Simon – and Jane, and all the rest?'

Harry felt that there was a flaw somewhere in this reasoning but, as usual in Gerard's schemes, it eluded him, and would probably continue to do so, he thought gloomily, until it was too late. He plodded after his friend, but was brought up short as Gerard stopped suddenly. He turned to face Harry, his gray eyes blazing with excitement.

'I have it, Harry! I know just what to do!'

Eighteen

'Hence, away!'
—A Midsummer Night's Dream, II, ii.

Jane entered her chambers, and closing the door behind her, leaned against it with a weary sigh. In a mirror on the far side of the room, she caught sight of herself and laughed mirthlessly. Still in her wings and fairy dust, she looked the part of bright, mischievous Puck, but inside, she felt more like Ophelia – some minutes after that luckless female's death by drowning.

Untying the silver cord at her hips, she moved toward the wardrobe. Dear Lord, she wished she didn't have to return to the party. She had never felt less like playing hostess than tonight. All she wanted to do right now was to climb into bed, pull the covers over her head, and stay there for the rest of her life. She turned as a scratch sounded at the door, accompanied by Hannah's muffled voice. Jane bade the maid enter.

'I have your midnight blue satin ready, Miss Jane,' she said, bustling into the bedchamber. 'It's on the bed.'

Jane remained for a moment at the wardrobe. Removing her silver sandals, she searched for the pair of comfortable slippers she always kept at the front of the cupboard. It was only after some rummaging, however, that she was able to locate them. Through a fog of preoccupation, her mind registered the fact that the contents of the wardrobe were in some disarray.

As Hannah slipped the blue satin gown over her head, she noticed that the maid seemed in considerable agitation.

'Hannah, what is it? Is something the matter?'

Hannah shifted uncomfortably. 'Well, I've been debating whether to mention this, but it seems there's been some strange goings-on in the stable tonight.'

'In the stable?' Jane tossed the question over her shoulder as she bent to pull on her stockings.

'Yes, one of the stable boys came into the kitchen while I was there, and he said Lord Wye had just taken off for London.'

'What?' Hannah now had Jane's full attention. 'In the middle of the night? In the middle of a party, for that matter?'

'And that's not all. The boy said that before he left, he was talking to his carriage.'

'I beg your pardon?'

'Well, to somebody inside the carriage, o'course. And the boy swears he heard his lordship call out the name Winifred.'

'*What*!'

Hannah nodded, expectations confirmed writ large on her face. 'I knew she would come to no good.'

'But, why didn't you come to me immediately? Or Lord Simon, or—'

Hannah shifted uncomfortably. 'Well, I didn't think anybody would miss his lordship, and as for Miss Winifred – well, the boy wasn't sure of what he'd heard, so ... All right,' the maid finished defiantly, 'that girl has been nothing but trouble to you and if she's gone off on the road to perdition, it seems like it serves her right, and no skin off your nose.'

'Hannah, how could you? Quickly, help me out of this.' Her hands fluttered in a futile attempt to undo the fastenings at the back of her gown.

'You're not going after her!' exclaimed Hannah.

'Winifred is my cousin, for heaven's sake – and my friend. I cannot stand idly by and watch her ruin herself.'

Nor could she stand by and see Simon publicly humiliated by the defection of his affianced bride, she thought, a knot forming in the pit of her stomach.

Hannah's lips tightened, but she said nothing as she assisted her mistress out of the satin gown.

'Good,' said Jane. 'Now go downstairs and find Gerard. Tell him to meet me at the stables immediately.'

As soon as the maid had left, in an almost visible cloud of disapproval, Jane hurried once more to the wardrobe. Pulling from it a gown of serviceable muslin, she was again struck by the disarrangement of her belongings. Shrugging the matter aside as unimportant, she searched for the oversized cap she had worn in her frumpy spinster days. She would, she thought, prefer to keep her face hidden during her proposed pursuit. After some moments of fruitless delving, she was forced to the conclusion that the cap was missing. And so, she discovered with some surprise, was her 'rig and tackle', as well as one of the generously proportioned gowns she had worn when in disguise.

Since she considered this singular circumstance by far the least of her problems, she shrugged once more and wriggled into the muslin. Donning shoes and cloak, she hurried from the room.

Downstairs, she turned toward the rear of the house, but was intercepted by Lady Hermione, her sharp nose quivering in agitation.

'A word with you, Miss Burch.'

Jane contained her impatience with difficulty. 'I am sorry, Lady Hermione, but I am in somewhat of a hurry and have no time for a chat. If you will excuse me.'

She would have brushed past her ladyship, but the woman grasped her arm. For the first time she seemed to take notice of Jane's apparel.

'Where are you going?' she asked suspiciously.

'Out,' said Jane shortly, attempting to pry Lady Hermione's fingers from her arm.

'Has this anything to do with Wye's disappearance?' asked Lady Hermione, her voice sharp.

The bottom of Jane's stomach seemed to give way, and she felt that her brain was plummeting downward to escape through the void thus created. 'Wh— what?' she croaked. 'Why...?'

'That's what I just said,' snapped Lady Hermione. 'I have been looking for Wye, and just a few minutes ago I heard two of the footmen whispering that he was seen leaving. What I want to know is – was that hussy, Winifred Timburton with him? I could swear I heard her name mentioned as well.'

Jane swallowed. 'Yes, I think Charles has left the house, and yes, I think Winifred may be with him.' She paused for a moment, debating as to how much of the situation she should impart to the woman who stood seething visibly before her. Coming to a decision, she spoke hastily. 'Lord Simon and Winifred became betrothed this afternoon.' She continued in a firm voice as Lady Hermione's eyes widened. 'I'm sure you will agree, my lady, that it is of the utmost importance that this matter be kept quiet, for Lord Simon's sake as well as yours. I am going to go after them, and if I hurry, I should be able to overtake them before they get very far. I intend to bring both of them back here with no one the wiser.'

'Excellent,' said Lady Hermione, 'I shall go with you.'

Jane opened her mouth to protest this high-handed declaration, but closed it immediately. With Lady Hermione on hand, Charles would be much more likely to abandon his flight, which in turn would make it much easier to corral Winifred back to Selworth. She nodded, and Lady Hermione, without another word followed her from the house.

At the stables, they were met not by Gerard, but by Hannah.

'He's gone as well, Miss Jane,' gasped the maid breathlessly, her chins aquiver. 'Him and that friend of his. I sent three footmen to scour the house for him and they're nowhere to be found.'

Jane threw her hands in the air, but murmured only, 'That wretched boy!' before hurrying into the stable. After speaking with the stable boy and receiving the same story as the one recited by Hannah, with the additional intelligence that Charles's destination was London, she ordered horses to be hitched to Harry's curricle.

'That's gone, too?' she exclaimed in response to the stable boy's information. Refusing to allow herself to be sidetracked by extraneous issues, she commandeered the first vehicle she beheld in the stable, a commodious gig. In a few minutes, Lady Hermione seated beside her in rigid disapprobation, Jane clattered out of the stable yard on to the path that led away from Selworth and thence to London.

Inside, Diana had returned to where Jared and Marcus stood in the Crimson Saloon.

'She's not there,' she said, frowning. 'I asked a few discreet questions among the guests, and no one's seen her since the conclusion of the performance.'

'She's probably sulking in a corner somewhere, waiting for someone to come and make a fuss over her,' said Jared.

Marcus turned on him, but was prevented from refuting this calumny against his beloved by the arrival of Lady Teague, who bustled up breathless and disheveled, her jewelry in full cry.

'Have any of you seen Lissa?' she asked distractedly. 'I spoke to her earlier and she seemed terribly overset. Now, I cannot find her, and I've searched everywhere. She is not in her room.'

'We've been looking for her, too,' said Diana.

'Oh, dear.' Aunt Amabelle inhaled sharply. 'Then perhaps I was not mistaken when – that is, when I was in her room, I happened to glance out her window, and I thought I saw her scurrying across the lawn – toward the stables. I thought I must be seeing things. Oh!' She started as Simon, who had silently approached the group, put a hand on her shoulder.

'Seeing what things, Aunt?' he asked casually. He flinched as everyone answered at once.

'Missing?' he asked blankly. 'Lissa?'

'Yes,' said Jared, 'and Aunt Amabelle thinks she saw her running toward the stables.'

At that, the entire group turned as one toward the door. Simon held up his hand. Lord, he thought, it needed but this to complete his evening. The woman he adored was not speaking to him, his ward seemed to have disappeared from the face of the earth – or, at least that of Selworth, and now his tiresome little sister was busily flinging spanners into his life.

'Wait,' he said to Jared. 'It will look dashed odd if we all leave while there are still guests milling about. Jared, you and Diana will have to stay here and man the fort. Diana, will you find Jane and apprise her of what's toward? Lissa mentioned something about wanting to go home to Stonefield, but I cannot imagine that she would have ordered a carriage put to and simply set off by herself.'

'Oh, no,' put in Aunt Amabelle tremulously. 'She's headstrong to a fault, but she has never gone beyond what is proper – that is—' She glanced up at Lissa's brothers, who were staring at her in disbelief. 'Well. Yes. Perhaps you'd best be on your way.'

'I'll check the stables,' said Simon, 'and if I find anything untoward, I'll take care of it.'

'I'm coming with you,' said Marcus mutinously.

Simon opened his mouth to protest, but after a glance at the young man's countenance, closed it again. 'Very well,' was all he said as, with a gesture to Jared, he turned and hastened from the room. Pausing only to change from their scanty Grecian tunics into more customary attire, they came together a few minutes later at the stables. It was only a few minutes after that that they were apprised of the departure from Selworth in rapid succession of Lord Wye and an unidentified female passenger who might or might not be Miss Timburton, of young Mr Burch and his friend, Mr Bridgeworth, and last, but by no means least, Miss Burch and Lady Hermione Stickleford.

'Jane!' exclaimed Simon. He leaned unsteadily against the stable door. My God, what could have caused this mass exodus? Much as he disliked the idea of further delay, he felt it necessary to put Jared in possession of these remarkable facts. His dudgeon rose like a hot air balloon at Jared's response.

'What do you mean you knew about Charles?' Simon growled. 'Where has he gone, and why the devil did Winifred go with him?'

Diana, who had remained at her husband's side, attempted to explain once more her cunning plan for Simon's release. For some moments, the rescuee remained speechless.

'You mean,' he said in a voice of awful calm, 'that you deliberately persuaded Charles to run off with my ward?'

'Well – yes, I did – but it was all for your own good, Simon. With Charles married to Winifred—'

Simon uttered an explosive snort. 'Is that what he told you – that he was going to marry her?'

'Mmm, yes,' interposed Jared. 'I wondered about that myself. He would have needed a special license for that, which he'd have to procure at Doctor's Common in London, and to my knowledge, he has not left Selworth since we arrived.'

Diana turned toward her husband, her gray eyes dark with concern. 'Do you think he lied to me, dearest. Oh, dear Heaven, what have I done?'

Clenching his teeth, Simon swung on Jared. 'You mean you knew of this – this lunatic scheme, too? And you did not tell me?'

A spark lit Jared's dark eyes. 'Calm yourself, little brother. I knew of it only moments ago. I cannot see, however, why you are in such a taking. Whether Winifred marries the benighted earl or chooses to live with him in moral turpitude, you're still off the hook.'

'Off the hook!' Simon thought he must be going mad. 'Jared, the girl is my ward. She is my responsibility. Do you think I can just stand idly by and let her become a Covent Garden nun?'

Jared sighed. 'It was a responsibility that was forced on you. In addition, aside from posting a twenty-four-hour guard on the little widgeon, I see no way you're going to be able to protect her from the consequences of her own folly.'

'If that's what it takes, that's what I'll do,' snarled Simon.

Jared sighed again, but said nothing more.

As Simon raced once more to the stable, he was forced to admit there was reason in what Jared had said. In fact, if he had Winifred here right now, he would strangle her with the greatest of goodwill. Not only had she plunged headlong to her own ruin, but she had involved Jane in her heedless flight. Where was Jane now, he wondered? Please God, she was safe. He did not know what he had done to earn the look of contempt she had thrown at him just as the play was about to start, but he prayed for the opportunity to make things right with her. The memory of the kiss she had bestowed on him warmed him, and he kept it hugged close to his heart like a talisman. The kiss must have meant something. It must have!

It could be said that there were two schools of thought on the subject of Jane's safety at the moment. There was certainly no denying that the coach was barreling along the London Road at a shocking pace. Lady Hermione had, from the outset of the journey, set up a continuous screeching, predicting their imminent departure from the road into the ditch, and their subsequent demise. Jane, paying no heed, grasped the reins firmly and gazed stonily at the road, as though she were on her way to church.

She was grateful that the moon, now high in the sky, was almost full, lending its light to the landscape below. Silvered fields and forests flashed past the curricle as Jane's gaze strained through the pale darkness for a glimmer of light that might signal the presence of another vehicle. She scarcely heard Lady Hermione's piercing remonstrations.

They had traveled for almost two hours before a sound, muffled by distance, caused Jane to utter a low cry. Lady Hermione shrieked.

'Was that a shot?' she said, gabbling in fright. 'It sounded as though it came from just ahead of us.'

'Yes,' said Jane, her voice strained, 'I think so.'

'No!' cried Lady Hermione as Jane urged the horses to even greater speed. 'Are you mad? Stop this instant! Who knows what might be up there? Perhaps there are highwaymen ... Did you hear me?' she screamed when Jane merely tightened her grip on the reins and slapped them again.

Her ladyship continued in this vein for the next mile or so, falling silent only when what appeared to be a vehicle was discerned on the road ahead. It had stopped, its passengers taking up positions at the side of the road. As Jane and Lady Hermione approached, it could be seen that there were not one, but two carriages standing motionless, one of which had left the road and was leaning drunkenly into the ditch. The vehicles were a curricle and a chaise, if Jane were not mistaken, and if she were not further mistaken ... She uttered an exclamation of concern as she neared the vehicles, observing that the passengers were familiar to her and they were clustered about a human figure lying on ground.

'Gerard!' called Jane as she drew the gig to a halt and leaped to the ground. Lady Hermione followed, abandoning her usually sedate demeanor.

At the sound of Jane's voice, those standing at the edge of the road whirled about.

'Jane!' said Gerard, a catch in his voice that was almost a sob. 'Thank God you've come.'

He ran to his sister, and flinging an arm about her shoulder, drew her toward the little group. 'It's Charles, Jane,' he gasped. 'I shot him – I think I've killed him!'

Nineteen

'Speak, speak! Quite dumb?
Dead, dead!'
—A Midsummer Night's Dream, V, i.

With a wordless cry, Jane sank to her knees beside Lady Hermione. Charles lay on the ground, sprawled at an awkward angle. There was a hole in his coat, high on his shoulder, from which blood flowed at an alarming tide.

'Who is responsible for this outrage?' asked Lady Hermione in a high-pitched voice, her fingers busy at Charles's coat buttons.

Jane, glancing about at the figures surrounding them, observed a plump female who was unknown to her, but who looked oddly familiar. Peering closer, she gasped. 'Harry! Is that you? What the devil…?'

For Harry – and indeed it was he – was garbed in a voluminous muslin gown and cloak, an oversized cap topping his ensemble. Good Lord, it was Harry who had appropriated her rig and tackle! Lacking the proper configuration of a plump, middle-aged female of generous proportions, he had apparently chosen to augment nature in certain critical areas with cushions. Unfortunately, the cushions were not of uniform size, and Harry's attempt to cover the discrepancy with a shawl was less than successful. At some time during the stirring events of the evening, the cap had become torn, so that part of the ruffle drooped disconsolately over one shoulder. Harry had insisted on wearing his own boots during his forced masquerade, and since his feet were sizeable, he looked as though he were trying to conceal a pair of andirons under his skirts. On the whole, he resembled something out of a third-rate farce.

Harry grinned weakly and muttered something unintelligible.

'You can explain later,' snapped Jane. 'Tell us what happened to Charles.'

'It was an accident,' whimpered Harry. 'We were—'

'Never mind that now,' Lady Hermione said abruptly. 'Someone help me here.'

Jane stared in astonishment as, with surprising efficiency, Lady Hermione, with some assistance from a trembling Gerard and Harry, eased Charles's shoulders out of his coat. Folding it, she made a pad to slip under his head. Coolly requesting Jane to retrieve her reticule, which had fallen to the ground nearby, she produced a pair of scissors with which she snipped away that part of Charles's shirt covering his wound.

In the lantern light his face was a deathly white, and Jane could see no sign of a pulse in his throat.

'Is – is he...?' she whispered.

'No,' said Lady Hermione, her voice displaying the merest tremor, 'but we must get him to a bed.' She looked around for a moment, then bent her gaze downward. Immediately, she grasped the scissors again, and, lifting the hem of her gown, began cutting her undergown into strips. Having fashioned a bandage, she pressed it to Charles's wound, oblivious of the blood that oozed from between her fingers and on to her skirt. The wound itself, once the blood had been stopped a little, proved to be a graze along the top of his shoulder. The ball had evidently passed through the tissue, for it was not embedded in his flesh.

Lady Hermione turned to Gerard. 'All right, tell me what happened.'

'It was an accident,' repeated Gerard, his own face ashen. 'We were pursuing Charles, and when we caught sight of his chaise, I hallooed at him to stop. Harry joined in with me. The next thing I knew somebody was shooting at us!'

'At *you*!' gasped Jane. 'But, how—'

'They must have thought we were knights of the road hauling up to rob them. Anyway, Harry's tiger, the stupid fool, grabbed up the pistol Harry keeps in a holster in the curricle, and when I tried to wrest it from him, it went off.'

'Good God!' exclaimed Jane, while Lady Hermione merely tightened her lips.

'Then,' continued Gerard, 'Charles lost control of the chaise and went into the ditch. When we came up to him, he lay as you see him there. I was never so glad to see anyone, Janie,' he concluded, 'for we none of us had the slightest inkling of what to do.'

'Obviously,' said Lady Hermione tartly. 'His wound certainly does not appear to be serious, but it disturbs me that he has not yet regained consciousness. Yes,' she said after further examination, 'it is as I thought. There is a bruise on his head. He must have hit it on something when he fell. We must move him,' she finished briskly.

'Yes, but – oh!' cried Jane, noting for the first time the figure that stood a little to one side in the shadowed lantern light. Dark curls tumbled in dishevelment over her forehead, and her fingertips were pressed to her trembling lips. Jane hurried to her and grasped her shoulder. 'There you are! Winifred, how could you...?' She jerked back suddenly, and peered into the girl's face. 'Lissa!' she gasped. 'What are you doing here?'

At this, the girl cast herself upon Jane's bosom. 'Oh, Jane,' she sobbed, 'I'm so glad you have come – and Lady Hermione.' She cast a dubious glance at her ladyship, who, after an initial start when Jane called Winifred's name, turned back to Charles and seemed to lose interest in her completely. 'I tried to help Lord Wye, but there was so much blood!'

Jane shook the girl slightly. 'But, what are you doing here?'

Lissa immediately broke into loud sobs. 'I have been so foolish, Jane!' Her voice rose in a hysterical pitch.

'Yes, yes,' said Jane soothingly, 'but you must tell me how you—'

Lady Hermione broke into the conversation. 'Could we continue this discussion at another time?' she said sharply. 'We must get Charles out of the night air.'

'Of course,' said Jane hastily. 'I think the gig would be more comfortable for him than the curricle, and—'

Lady Hermione interrupted again. 'I see some lights in the distance. Is it a village?'

She glanced around for corroboration and the tiger who had fired at Charles said anxiously. 'Yes, my lady, that there is Fitchling. It's just a wide place in the road, but they have a nice inn there – it bein' on the London Highway an' all – the Dog and Whistle, it's called.'

'Very well,' she said, bending once more to her patient. 'You there.' She gestured to Gerard and Harry and the second tiger, who were standing about looking rather forlorn. 'Help me.'

As they began to lift Charles, he uttered a groan and opened his eyes. Raising his head, he found himself nose to nose with Lady Hermione, and, giving vent to a startled yelp, he sank back into Harry's arms. He closed his eyes once more and, though he moaned pitiably, they remained firmly shut as he was carefully deposited into the gig. Lady Hermione climbed in beside him, accompanied by Charles's tiger. Gerard turned to clamber into the phaeton, but Jane laid a hand on his arm.

'Not so fast, my lad. Harry can take the curricle. You will ride in the gig with Lissa and me. It will be a squeeze, but you have a deal of explaining to do.'

Before mounting the carriage herself, Jane gave herself up to a moment's hasty reflection. The fact that it was Lissa who had set out with Charles instead of Winifred put an entirely different face on her own pursuit through the night. She had wished to spare Simon humiliation. Winifred was, in all probability, safe somewhere at Selworth, despite the fact that no one had been able to find her. On the other hand, the girl was obviously much taken with Marcus, her handsome fairy king. An unpleasant sensation churned in the pit of Jane's stomach. Lord, could Winifred and Marcus have eloped?

Jane sagged against the side of the gig, feeling desperately weary. What an incredible muddle it all was. In any event, matters had reached such a pass that Simon must be notified about Charles – and Lissa – and all that had taken place on the London Road this evening. She supposed he would have to be informed of Winifred's disappearance as well. Beckoning one of the tigers to her, she began a carefully worded monologue of instruction.

When she was finished, the diminutive young man mounted one of the horses that had by now been released from their positions, and galloped off into the night in the direction of Selworth. The gig, followed by the curricle, set off at a careful pace toward the little village. On the journey, Lady Hermione ministered to Charles. apparently oblivious to everything else. After an initial show of reluctance, Lissa told Jane of the circumstances that led to her concealment in Charles's chaise.

'I know it was a stupid thing to do,' she concluded tearfully, 'but I was so miserable – and I didn't want to face Marcus, and—'

'Yes,' said Jane, lifting her hand in a gesture of comfort. 'It was, perhaps, not the wisest course you could have pursued, but love makes us do strange things.' She smiled. 'At any rate, you are safe now, and as soon as we deposit Charles at the inn and get a doctor for him, we shall get you home.'

'O-ooh—' she moaned. 'Jared will kill me – if Simon doesn't do so first.'

Jane sighed. 'I do not think your situation is quite that desperate. I'm sure your family will understand.' She turned to her brother.

'Now, Gerard, it's your turn. I would like to hear an explanation of why you and Harry – in *my* personal rig – were haring around the countryside in the middle of the night.'

Gerard's tale, halting though it was, did not take long, and at its conclusion, Jane gave an unladylike grunt of exasperation. 'You wanted to protect Winifred from Simon's wrath? And mine? Of all the mutton-headed stunts you've pulled, Gerard, this one pretty much takes the prize. And you really thought that dressing Harry as a female would lend countenance to your mad scheme? Really, Gerard, if you—'

'Yes, but Jane,' interposed Gerard, possibly with the intent of diverting her attention from himself and his iniquities, 'it's a good thing Harry and I are here, don't you think? That is, how would a parcel of females manage on their own with a wounded man?'

Jane, her finger still raised in admonition, forebore to remind him that if it were not for him – and Harry – the females would not find it necessary to be managing a wounded man.

'Well, never mind.' She sighed wearily. 'The important thing is that we must get back home as soon as possible.' She glanced at Charles, lying back on the seat with eyes determinedly closed, and at Lady Hermione, who held him in her arms, murmuring to him unintelligibly and attempting to minister to him with a bottle of brandy, discovered in the chaise.

The village was not far away, and in a very few moments the curricle drew up to the Dog and Whistle. Gerard knocked peremptorily on the door, but it was some moments before it opened to reveal the proprietor and his wife in nightcap and gown, yawning and gaping as first Harry and then Gerard and Jane explained their needs.

Introducing herself as Mrs Biddle, the landlord's wife ushered the group inside the inn and then toward the stairs.

'You're in luck, Miss,' she said to Jane, her gaze still on Charles's inert form and the blood that seeped from his wound. Our best room is right at the top of the stairs, and it's empty. My Will can help get his lordship settled, and our boy, Samuel can go for the doctor. He lives just down the lane. My heaven,' she continued, 'what a thing to have happen. Highwaymen, of all things! And so close to the village.'

Gerard and Harry exchanged glances of congratulation on their perspicacity in blaming Charles's wound on land pirates.

Lady Hermione was taken upstairs, where she maintained a vigil at Charles's bedside until the doctor was announced some twenty minutes after their arrival. This worthy concurred in her evaluation of the wound, saying that the ball had not lodged in the flesh, but apparently had passed through the tissue in a glancing path. He sprinkled a quantity of basilicum powder on the wound and pronounced that, while it was his recommendation that his lordship remain in the inn overnight, if there was no further bleeding, and a fever did not develop, the earl could return home on the morrow. Measuring out a draught to help the patient sleep, he left the inn with instructions to be called if his services were required further.

Charles bore the examination with fortitude, though he drew in a sharp breath as the doctor began his probing, and when Lady Hermione extended her hand, he grasped it with gratitude. Immediately after the good doctor's departure, however, his eyes closed once more, and once more he began to moan.

'There, there,' said Lady Hermione, applying a cold compress to his head. 'I am here.'

Charles moaned all the louder.

'Charles,' said his betrothed with some asperity, but gently, withal, 'I know how you happened to be racing through the night in the company of that young girl, and I do not intend to scold you.'

One eye opened cautiously. 'You do not?'

'No, for I believe you to have been sadly taken in by that Timburton hussy. I saw her brazen overtures to you, and I will not blame you – at least for just this once – for being taken in by them. Now, do take your medicine, and a little of this broth, my love. It looks most fortifying.'

Obediently, Charles opened his mouth and Lady Hermione spooned first the doctor's draught and then a portion of the steaming broth into his mouth. When he lay back against his pillows with a sigh, she smoothed back a lock of hair that had fallen across his forehead, and plumped his pillows to a more comfortable position.

In a few moments, Charles's eyelids began to droop as the effects of the doctor's draught began to take effect.

'I'm afraid I was behaving very foolishly,' he murmured.

'Yes, I think so, too.' Hermione's words were softened by the gentle, almost maternal smile she bestowed upon him. 'We shan't speak of it any more. Just rest now, my love.'

Charles smiled blearily. 'You're a prince 'mong women, Hermione,' he whispered. 'Or, no – tha's not ri' is it?' He attempted to lift a hand in negation, but it dropped on to the bed almost immediately as his eyes closed yet again, this time in genuine repose.

Lady Hermione's lips curved in a small smile of satisfaction.

Downstairs, the rest of the group was reviving itself in the inn's coffee room with ale for the gentlemen, wine for the ladies, and sandwiches, put together with admirable efficiency by Mrs Biddle. The doctor's report on Charles set their minds at ease, and they now turned their attention to the pressing problem of the propriety of leaving Charles in the care of his tiger and the landlord and his wife until morning.

'If we were to leave now, we might arrive at Selworth before dawn,' said Jane, in a fever of anxiety about Winifred. 'But, I fear Lady Hermione will not wish to go with us, and I cannot leave her here unattended by another female.'

'I would volunteer to stay,' said Lissa, 'but—'

'That won't do, either. We must get you home as quickly as possible.'

'What a to-do over nothing,' said Gerard, with a snort. 'What do you think her ladyship and Charles are going to get up to, with Charles out like a light and a hole in his shoulder besides? Or perhaps you're afraid she might set up a flirt with the knives and boots boy?'

'Don't be absurd, Gerard. It's not what I think, but—'

She was interrupted by the sound of an approaching vehicle in the yard outside. Curious, Gerard went to the window to peer out.

'By Godfrey!' He swung about to report to the rest. 'It's Lord Simon! And Mar— Lord Stedford is with him!'

Lissa uttered a faint moan and turned beseechingly to Jane.

Gerard had no sooner drawn away from the window when the inn door opened to admit the two gentlemen in advanced states of anxiety and umbrage.

Twenty

'Cupid is a knavish lad,
Thus to make poor females mad.'
—A Midsummer Night's Dream, III, ii.

'Lissa!' roared Simon and Marcus in unison on beholding her.

'Jane!' Simon roared equally loudly as his glance scoured the room.

Pandemonium reigned in the inn for several moments as everyone tried to speak at once. Simon held up his hand.

'All right. First things first. Is everyone safe?'

By mutual consent, Jane took up the position of spokesman for the little group.

'Yes,' she replied, 'we are all well, except for Charles. But how did you get here so quickly? Surely the messenger I sent could not have—'

'We had already started out,' replied Simon impatiently. 'We met the tiger on the road. He wasn't making much sense – mentioned something about Charles being shot. We saw the carriage in the ditch – and blood.'

He turned to Jane questioningly, whereupon she launched into an explanation of the momentous circumstances that had taken place earlier in the evening, omitting to reveal fully her own motives in setting out after the adventurers. Her listeners hung on her every word, and when she had finished, Simon returned to the occurrence that interested him most.

'You mean?' he asked incredulously. 'Charles abducted Lissa by mistake?'

'Well, yes – more or less,' Jane replied a trifle unsteadily. 'I suppose one female in one's carriage is pretty much like any other – in the dark.'

Simon turned to Lissa, who still sat at the table, frozen. 'Which brings me to my next point. What the devil were you doing in Charles's chaise in the first place?'

'I would like to know the answer to that, myself,' said Marcus tightly.

At this, Lissa was galvanized into action. She started up from the table like a flushed pheasant to stand before Marcus. 'And, I would like to know, my Lord Stedford, what you have done with Winifred.'

'Winifred?' he asked blankly.

'Yes, Winifred – as in Miss Timburton – beauteous Titania, Queen of the Fairies. The same Winifred Timburton who – whom – you said meant nothing to you.'

'Lissa,' said Marcus in apparent bewilderment, 'what are you talking about?'

Lissa became almost incoherent. 'Ooh!' she breathed. 'Look at you – as though butter wouldn't melt in your mouth! Of all the despicable...!' Her face crumpled suddenly. 'Oh, Marcus, how could you?'

'For God's sake, Lissa – how could I what?'

'Marcus, stop it! I saw you!'

'Saw me...?'

'I saw you kissing her – if you could call it that. It looked more as though you were nibbling her face off in little chunks.'

Marcus's jaw dropped. He glanced around at the others as though for corroboration that his beloved had taken leave of her senses.

'Kissing Winifred! Lissa, I don't understand any of this!'

By now Lissa looked as though she was about to shoot skyward in a burst of sparks. 'Do not try to cozen me, Marc. You and she stood in the courtyard, and—'

'Courtyard! I was not in the courtyard all evening. And even if I were, kissing Winifred is not on my agenda, and never has been!'

'B-but, I *saw* you! You were standing in the light – it shone on your hair, and you were wearing your cloak from the play.'

Marcus, oblivious to the patently interested spectators clustered about them, placed his hands on Lissa's shoulders and shook her gently. 'Lissa, I don't know what you thought you saw, but I did not kiss Winifred Timburton in the courtyard, nor any place else – ever,' His blue eyes were serious. 'I told you before, my love, she means nothing to me.'

'But ... Oh, Marcus, she is so very beautiful, and she is all the things I am not.'

'What?' Marcus stared at her in blank amazement. 'What has Winifred being beautiful to do with anything? As for her being all the things you are not ...' He grasped her shoulders gently. 'Lissa, I enjoy Winifred's beauty, as I would any work of art, but she is spoiled and shallow and utterly selfish. Moreover, she is not more beautiful than you. You have life and – what is it?' asked in horror as Lissa burst into tears.

'Oh, Marcus, I know very well that I am spoiled and shallow and s-selfish, too. But I do try to be good. Sometimes. And I do love you. That's why when I saw you – or somebody – and Winifred, I—'

'Wait just a moment, Lissa,' interposed Simon before the two oblivious lovers proceeded any further in what promised to be an extremely public and intimate reconciliation. 'Did you say Marc was wearing his cloak?'

Lissa nodded wordlessly.

'His cloak is dark green, is it not?'

This time both Lissa and Marc nodded.

'But, earlier this evening, Marc – after the play – you were wearing one of bright blue. I'm sure it was Jared's, for he commented on the fact that you had absconded with it.'

'Yes,' said Marcus eagerly, 'that's true. I felt rather foolish wandering about accepting the accolades of the masses wearing only that ridiculous tunic. I couldn't find my cloak, so I picked up another, lying on a chair.'

Marcus turned to Lissa, who gazed back at him with an incredulous joy dawning on her delicate features.

'Oh, Marc!' Her eyes fell. 'I have been so foolish.'

'About a number of things,' he replied gently, taking her hands. His head bent to hers, but suddenly bethinking himself, he lifted it immediately and glanced around. 'If you would all excuse us for a moment,' he said, his blue eyes alight with tender laughter, 'Lissa and I have one or two more points to clear up. Placing an arm about her shoulder, he led her to the door.

Lissa blushed rosily as she followed Marcus from the room, her eyes downcast.

Simon expelled a long breath and glanced involuntarily at Jane. Encountering her gaze, it seemed to him that her luminous eyes reflected his pleasure at Marc and Lissa's imminent reconciliation. She sobered almost immediately, however, and shooting a glance at

Gerard and Harry, who sat in bemused conversation at the far end of the room, she moved hesitantly toward him.

'But, what then, of Winifred?' she asked, her voice husky.

'Oh,' said Simon. Lord, he had almost forgotten about Winifred. 'Well – I am assuming she's at Selworth somewhere. God,' he added wearily, 'I wonder who she was kissing. I mean, Lissa surely wasn't imagining the entire episode.'

Jane raised startled eyes to his face. 'You wonder who – do you not care?'

'Of course, I care. The little twit seems bent on ruining herself.'

Jane shook her head in a baffled gesture. 'But, surely it must pain you to know that she was kissing another man.' Jane's voice was strained and she had paled visibly.

'Another man?' What the devil...? he thought, thoroughly puzzled.

'Winifred told me,' Jane whispered. 'About this afternoon....'

His eyes still on her face, Simon cast his thoughts back with an effort. Lord, this afternoon seemed a hundred years ago. Anyway, why were they wasting time talking about Winifred? Jane's nearness was having its usual effect on him. Her upturned mouth, with lips slightly parted seemed an almost irresistible invitation, and an urgent need rose within him to draw her close so that he might press his mouth on hers.

What? he thought dazedly, aware that she was speaking again.

'She told me of your offer.'

'Oh. Yes,' he said stupidly. 'Offer.'

'I am happy for you, of course.' Her voice was a bare whisper now and he bent his head to catch her words.

'Ah, well, it certainly solved my problems,' he said.

Jane uttered a little choking sound. 'Your problems?' A peel of hysterical laughter broke from her. 'I – suppose that is one way of looking at it, although I would think—'

'Look, Jane,' said Simon earnestly, feeling that if he had to stand there much longer without touching her he might simply explode. 'Could we shelve the subject of Winifred for the nonce? Come.' He grasped her arm gently. 'Can we speak privately? There must be another room where we—'

'We have nothing to say to each other,' returned Jane rigidly, drawing away from him.

'But—' he began in puzzlement. The next moment, he swore

softly as he was interrupted by the hurried entrance of Lady Hermione who fairly bristled with importance.

'He's asleep,' she announced breathlessly. 'Where is the landlord's wife? I would like to have more broth ready for him when he wakes.'

Jane and Simon stared at her and then at each other. It was as though the woman had just emerged from a spell put on her at birth by a wicked fairy. Her stony features were softened by a becoming pink flush, and her eyes glowed with a tender light. Even her form seemed suddenly supple and more feminine.

'How – how is Charles?' asked Jane.

'Oh, he seems much better. I expect he will experience some pain in the morning, but – oh, my goodness!' she exclaimed, glancing out the window. 'It is morning already.'

'Why, so it is,' declared Simon, observing the faint outline of the inn yard, just becoming visible in the gray light of dawn. 'I had forgotten how early the sun rises in England in the summer. Do you think Charles will be ready to travel soon?'

'Oh, my no,' replied Lady Hermione. 'Selworth is a good two hours from here' – she shot a malevolent glance at Jane – 'driving at normal speed, and such a long carriage ride would be most deleterious to his condition.'

'But, the doctor said—' interposed Jane, only to be silenced by Lady Hermione's impatient gesture.

'Pahl The man is competent enough in his way, but he is a country practitioner, after all, used to dealing with rustics. He cannot be expected to understand the complexities of Wye's delicate constitution.'

'Of course,' said Simon gravely, remembering Charles drinking half his regiment under the table after a day of campaigning in the rain and mud of a Spanish winter, only to repeat the procedure again the next morning.

'I shall remain here with him until you can send my mother to me. I trust I shall not be wholly compromised,' she concluded with an unmistakable note of relish in her voice as she turned to ascend the stairs once more.

'Charles will have to marry her, now,' muttered Gerard to Harry in a gleeful undertone.

Lissa and Marcus strolled into the room at that point, and as they gazed blissfully on the assemblage, it was more than apparent that two hearts beat again as one. Simon moved forward and, with a grin, flung an arm about each of them.

'God, it's good to see you two actually smiling again,' he said with satisfaction.

After several minutes of expressions of good will and congratulations, Simon disclosed to them the plans for their imminent departure. The lovers drifted from the room then to make their way to the inn yard, followed by Gerard and Harry. Simon, noting that he and Jane were alone in the room, hurried to her side, grasping her arm once more as she stood, apparently poised for a precipitous flight.

Jane stared numbly at Simon. She had paid little attention to the events that had just taken place. Her mind was still whirling at Simon's casual acceptance of the fact that his betrothed had been discovered kissing another man. Even if she was right in her assumption that he was not in love with Winifred, he must expect to be a real husband to her. Surely, he would be faithful to his wife, and would expect the same from her. The chill that had settled in the bottom of her stomach when she had first become apprised of Simon's betrothal churned dismally, for beneath her bewilderment at Simon's cavalier attitude toward his engagement lay a despair that she knew would never be quite dispelled.

She supposed that she would get over Simon eventually – at least to the point where she would no longer feel that part of her was missing when she was not with him, but a permanent pall seemed to hang over her. She had not expected to fall in love, and now that she had, the whole process seemed too painful to be borne. Winifred was her cousin, and she could hardly sever the connection between them, even if it meant having to maintain—

'What?' she asked, aware that Simon had spoken to her.

'I said,' he replied with surprising awkwardness, 'there is something I wish to discuss with you before we return to Selworth.'

He released her arm, slipping his hand down to clasp her fingers in his.

'You already know of my offer to Winifred,' he began.

Dear God, she wondered miserably. Was he about to ask for her assistance in preparing her cousin for her wedding?

'Now that I have pretty much settled that affair, I—' He swallowed. 'I want to talk about us.'

'I beg your pardon?' she asked in blank astonishment. *Settled that affair*? She felt as though her heart had leaped into her throat, making it impossible for her to breathe. 'Us? There *is* no "us", my lord.'

For a moment, Simon said nothing. Then, he lifted a hand and drew his fingertips along the curve of her cheek. A deep trembling started within her.

'I know you and I have had our differences, Jane, but I hope I am not imagining that there was – something else between us. Oh Lord!' he exclaimed impatiently. 'What a stupid thing to say,' He took a deep breath. 'Jane, I do love you so desperately, and I want to believe that—'

'What?' gasped Jane, feeling as though the room had suddenly tilted on its axis.

'I said, I want to believe that—'

'No, before that.'

'Oh. I love you. You mean you didn't know? Everyone else seems to.'

Jane was a sometimes reader of Gothic novels, but she had always been most disdainful of heroines who tended to swoon in times of crisis. Now, however, she thought that for the first time in her life she was about to simply collapse in an unconscious heap on the floor. Indeed, it seemed a consummation devoutly to be wished, for then perhaps she would not feel the pain that swept through her in great, slashing waves. Dear God, he loved her – he said – and he was marrying someone else! To what kind of monster had she lost her heart?

'Jane?' said Simon questioningly. 'Are you all right? You're white as milk. I did not mean to discommode you.' He sighed. 'It appears it's a good thing I left the diplomatic service; I seem to be making a mull out of everything I touch lately. I had hoped – after yesterday, that you felt the same as I.' He raised her fingers to his lips and she trembled slightly at the contact. 'Jane, I – oh, for God's sake, what are you two doing here?' he finished suddenly as the door to the coffee room opened to admit Jared and Diana, expostulating loudly with each other as they entered.

'I only meant, my love,' Diana was saying, 'that we do not wish to be precipitate about this. If Jane— Why there you are, Simon!' She ran forward lightly to throw her arms first about her brother-in-law and then Jane.

'Simon!' exclaimed Jared simultaneously. 'What the devil has been going on? Are you all right? Is Lissa—?'

'Yes,' replied Simon, trying to keep the frustrated impatience out of his voice. 'Everyone is well, except for Charles, of course. It was his blood you saw, but he's fine now.'

Once more the sequence of events leading from Charles's misdeeds of the night before was detailed.

'But what are you two doing here?' asked Simon. 'You're supposed to be deflecting suspicion and maintaining the status quo at Selworth.'

'My bride' – Jared cast a sardonic glance at Diana – 'found herself constitutionally unable to wait quietly at home while momentous goings-on were taking place elsewhere. We shuffled off the manning-the-fort duty to Aunt Amabelle and started off not long after you left.'

'Jared!' interposed Diana indignantly. 'Of all the plumpers! Who was it who paced the floor nonstop until I thought you would wear a path in the carpet, and who finally said, "I'm damned if I'll just sit here with my hands folded!" ' She paused for breath, and her husband promptly silenced her with a quick kiss before she could resume her brief tirade.

'Well,' he said, waving his hand, 'howsoever, here we are.'

'Yes,' said Simon, 'but I don't understand— Good God!' he finished as the coffee room door opened once more followed by the entrance of Lady Wimpole, her ladyship's maid, and Fletcher, Lady Hermione's maid. 'What is this? A gathering of the clans?'

Jared sighed irritably. 'Just as we were ready to start out, Lady Wimpole came up, wondering where Hermione had got to. We tried to put her off, but she sniffed out that something was amiss and insisted on accompanying us.'

'Where is my baby?' demanded Lady Wimpole, clearly on the verge of hysteria. 'I knew we should never have set out from Oxfordshire to this godforsaken hellhole, and now look what has happened!' The others stared at her in some astonishment, for none of them had ever heard the woman raise her voice above a whisper. She whirled on Simon. 'What have you done with my baby, you wicked man?'

Stunned, Simon pointed mutely to the stairs, whereupon Lady Wimpole whirled and hurried upstairs, followed by the thoroughly cowed maids.

Simon looked quietly at Jane and their eyes met in an involuntary sharing of amusement and surprise before Jane hastily dropped her gaze.

'Well!' said Diana after a moment, and the others nodded in dazed agreement.

At this point, Gerard and Harry burst into the room, followed more slowly by Marcus and Lissa.

'What the devil is keeping you?' asked Gerard indignantly. 'We've been waiting out there for— Oh!' He subsided in some confusion on observing the marquess and his wife.

Some minutes later, having put them in possession of the circumstances surrounding this latest arrival, Simon said abruptly, 'Now then, there is no reason for any of us to remain here any longer, so may I suggest we take our departure – before anyone else shows up? I am still anxious about Winifred's whereabouts.' He moved to Jared and spoke in low tones to his brother.

At the sound of her cousin's name on Simon's lips, Jane stiffened. Of course, Winifred would be Simon's primary concern right now – and forever more, for that matter. She glanced at him from beneath her lashes, conscious of the tension that bubbled between them. Despite the inner chill that seemed to have spread over her entire being, she was obliged to fight the instinct to move to his side. It was almost as though they stood alone together in the midst of the press of people and the tumult surrounding them. Would it always be like this? she wondered dully.

She was aroused from her unpleasant reverie as the group began to exit the coffee room toward the outer door of the inn. Gerard and Harry had already left the chamber, and Jane moved after them. Jared intercepted her, however.

'I'm sorry, Jane. There won't be any room for you in Harry's curricle, since Gerard is riding with him. Marc and Lissa are coming with us and that will pretty much fill up our coach, as well. Simon has plenty of room, though,' he concluded with a cheerful wave of his hand.

'Oh, but...!' cried Jane rather wildly. It was too late. She looked around to find that she was once more alone with Simon in the inn's dark, little coffee room.

Twenty-one

'So shall all the couples three
Ever true in loving be.'
—A Midsummer Night's Dream, V, i.

'Jane.' Simon said the word simply and without expression, but she flinched as though he had hurled a stone at her. He moved toward her, and she backed away until she stood against a wall.

He looked at her for a long moment and Jane noted with a sense of deep unease that his eyes had turned to an intense cinnamon, and the gold flecks in his gaze seemed to form a compelling vortex into which she could feel herself slipping despite herself.

'Jane, what is it?' he asked, his eyes filled with what appeared to be honest puzzlement. 'I do not wish to distress you, but I must speak. I told you that I love you, and surely that came as no surprise. My dearest love, last night I held you in my arms, and I could have sworn you felt the same as I. Jane, I want to spend the rest of my life with you.'

At this, the dam of ice that had built up within Jane burst. My God, he wanted her for his mistress! A wave of fury struck her with such force that she shook with it.

'How dare you! I have heard of men like you – without soul or principle, but I – I would never have thought you to be one of them. Nor did I ever expect to listen to such a despicable proposal! Please let me go.'

Simon simply stared at her, white-faced and bewildered. 'Despicable proposal?' he asked finally in a hoarse voice. 'But, I want to marry you, Jane. If you don't like the idea, feel free to tell me, but "despicable?" '

'M-marry me! What about Winifred?' cried Jane.

'Winifred? What's Winifred got to do with anything?'

Now, she was sure she was going mad. 'I do not know what is going on in your mind, my lord – perhaps it is better that way – but I have no more to say to you except to say vary plainly that your attentions are distasteful to me.' Her resolution almost failed her at the expression of pain that flashed in his eyes, and she continued in a rush. 'If I seemed to – to encourage you before, I'm afraid you misinterpreted what was merely confusion and – and embarrassment on my part.'

She stopped, almost panting in the effort it took not to sob out her hurt and humiliation.

Simon stood very still, his gaze shuttered. After an initial sensation that the world had just blown up in his face, he was brought to the sure realization that Jane was not speaking from the heart. Confusion? Embarrassment? No. Those searing kisses had been given freely and with genuine passion. There was something she was not telling him. Why could she not trust him? he thought with a trace of bitterness.

'Jane,' he said, moving toward her. 'What the devil—?' He was brought up short as the entire party to whom he had just waved farewell, trooped back into the inn.

Simon felt an urge to throw his head back and howl his frustration.

'Now what?' he asked in a strangled voice. The next moment, he noted that the group seemed to have swelled in size, even given Jane's unwilling presence in the midst of the multitude. After a moment, he brought himself under control enough to focus on the individual components of the chattering throng and thereupon made a startling discovery.

'Winifred!' he croaked. 'What are you doing here?'

His ward, her transcendent beauty more pronounced than ever, moved through the group to him, the stolid Sir James Beecham close behind her.

'Lord Simon!' she breathed, her eyes sparkling like amethysts in sunlight. 'Please wish me happy.'

Uncomprehending, Simon gaped at her for a long moment as, with a monumental effort, he thrust his hurt to the back of his mind. Then, assuming the most menacing frown at his disposal, he advanced on her. 'What the devil have you been up to, Winifred? I tell you right now, I will no longer tolerate—'

'One moment, my lord.'

Simon glared in astonishment at Sir James, who moved forward to interpose himself between Winifred and her wrathful guardian.

'I am happy to inform you, Lord Simon, that the lady is no longer your responsibility,' said the bulky baronet in his usual, colorless tone of voice.

Simon merely stared in blank stupefaction as Winifred laughed aloud.

'It's true, my lord. The most wonderful thing has happened!' She turned a blinding gaze on Jane. 'Oh Jane, you will never guess!'

'Winifred, what have you done?' asked Jane in a constricted voice.

'Why, I am married!'

Unconsciously, Simon turned to Jane, grasping her hand in his. Together they watched, speechless, as Sir James bent a benevolent glance on Winifred.

'M-married?' echoed Jane.

Winifred thrust forth her left hand, upon which could be seen a sapphire ring the size of a small cabbage. 'Isn't it wonderful?' She cried. 'My dear Sir James proposed last week, and we were married yesterday by special license.'

'Special license?' croaked Simon. He was having a great deal of difficulty absorbing what she was saying, as though she spoke in a foreign language. 'Special license?' he said again, rolling the words about in his head in an effort to make sense of them. He glanced at Sir James – unassuming, unattractive, unwealthy Sir James, and his gaze swiveled back to Winifred. 'But ...'

'Apparently,' said Jared dryly, taking pity on his stricken sibling, 'the vicar married them yesterday afternoon by special license, right before dinner. The reason we could not find Winifred after the play was that they had retired to Sir James's chambers to, er, celebrate their union.'

'So,' put in Marcus excitedly, 'it must have been Sir James, wearing my cloak, who Winifred was kissing in the courtyard.'

'Oh, was that yours?' Sir James was all nonchalance as Winifred laughed unashamedly. 'Sorry about that. I just took the one handiest.'

Lissa sighed contentedly and, tucking her hand in Marcus's, leaned her head on his shoulder.

'Good God!' exclaimed Simon faintly, turning back to the nuptial couple.

'But—' Jane spoke as though plodding through her own cloud of confusion. 'Sir James? That is – what about Lord Simon?'

'It's perfectly all right, Miss Burch,' said Sir James magnanimously. 'Lady Beemish and I anticipated your astonishment. I am not a demonstrative man, thus my growing affection for her was not apparent to anyone, least of all Winifred.'

Simon suppressed an urge to assure Sir James that he felt no surprise whatsoever that he should become smitten with Winifred, It was the fact that Winifred apparently returned his regard that boggled the mind. One would think this bland, unappealing person the last man in the universe to capture her heart.

Jane felt as though the floor had given way under her and she was plummeting into a vast, whirling abyss. Surely Winifred could not have been so wicked as to accept one man's proposal only to go off and marry another. She glanced at Simon in bewilderment, noting that his expression betrayed only surprise touched with amusement.

Winifred spoke again. 'Sir James resides most of the time in London, you know.' Her satisfaction could be clearly discerned in her chiming laughter. 'And he is utterly convinced that I should go on the stage.' She leaned forward as though imparting a confidence. 'Can you imagine my astonishment when dear Sir James told me that he is actually involved in the theater? He has assured me that I shall be the toast of the West End!'

Jared uttered a bark of laughter. 'Not to wrap it in clean linen, Simon. Our friend here is the majority stockholder in the Sheridan Theater, in addition to his other successful endeavors. He is,' he continued with a glance at Simon, 'a very wealthy man.'

'That's why we invited him!' piped up Gerard, who had so far been a silent spectator of this fascinating discourse. 'Harry introduced me to his uncle last year when we were in London, and I knew he would be just the chap to give Winifred a push in the right direction.'

Sir James nodded modestly. 'I believe I can be called plump in the pocket,' he said with a slight smile, 'and I also believe I shall experience no difficulty in making Winifred a success in the theater.'

'Which should swell your pockets to an even more pleasing plumpness,' interjected Jared softly. Sir James turned a penetrating stare on him, but said nothing.

'But,' said Simon suddenly 'how could you possibly get married by special license without the permission of her guardian – that is, me?'

Winifred's blithe laughter rang out again. 'Why, we simply signed your name.'

Once more bereft of speech, Simon goggled at her, and once more Jared stepped into the breach.

'Winifred was able to convince her betrothed,' he said a trifle unsteadily, 'that you would make no objection once the deed was done.'

Sir James coughed. 'Well, my lord, it did seem as though we were providing you a way out of a situation you obviously found disagreeable.'

'Yes,' Winifred chimed in, 'we got the vicar to marry us when he arrived for the party yesterday afternoon.' She laughed musically. 'We had such a time convincing him that we wanted the ceremony to remain a surprise until after the play.'

'But,' said Jane bemusedly, 'what are you doing here?'

Sir James shifted uncomfortably. 'Ah. Well, Lady B. and I decided to leave for London immediately. The little dear was naturally anxious to take up her new life. We came upon some men attempting to drag a chaise from the ditch. The road was blocked, so we decided to stop for breakfast at the nearest village before traveling on. And since there was only one inn hereabouts—'

Simon uttered a strangled sound that might have been laughter. 'But what about Selworth?' he said at last to Winifred. 'I offered to share the profits from its sale with you under the belief that I had failed to receive an offer for your hand, when in actuality—?'

Jane gasped, and as all eyes turned to her, she asked in a constricted tone, 'Offer? Is that what you meant when you told me that Simon had made you an offer, Winifred?'

'Of course,' replied Winifred innocently.

Across the room, Simon shot Jane a speculative glance. A spark of something unreadable flared in his gaze, but he said nothing.

'As to that, my lord,' said Sir James portentously, 'Winifred has told me of her arrangement with you, and it is my decision that it be made null and void. She was a naughty little puss to accept your offer, when I had asked her to be mine some days earlier, thus canceling your obligation to her.'

'But, Jamie-bear,' wailed Winifred, 'I would get thousands of pounds.'

'Jamie-bear?' whispered Simon and Jared in unison.

'You might also get sued,' Sir James said shortly. 'That is,' he said immediately with a conciliatory smile, 'we want to do the right thing, of course.'

'Of course,' murmured Simon.

'What about Charles's five thousand pounds?' asked Gerard abruptly.

'Five thousand pounds?' This time it was Simon and Jane who spoke in unison.

Sir James lifted a questioning brow at his beloved, who hung her head.

'He gave me the money in return for my promise to run away with him,' she muttered.

'When you were already on the verge of being married to the baronet?' interposed Jared incredulously.

'Well, it was a lot of money,' she replied sulkily. She lifted her head suddenly. 'Do I have to give that back, too?' she cried, outraged.

'I'm afraid so, my love,' Sir James said admonishingly. 'It's no good whiddling money out of people who have the means of getting back at you, you know.'

With which piece of sapient advice, he drew his bride from the room, leaving the others to stare at each other in bemusement.

'Well!' breathed Gerard at last. 'If ever any two people deserved each other ...'

Jared, succumbing to the laughter that had been bubbling up in him for some time, fell into a chair and mopped his streaming eyes.

'Well put, my lad,' he gasped. To Simon, he said, 'You're not going to cry "fraud" on the ceremony, are you?'

'Absolutely not,' replied Simon fervently. He turned to gaze at Jane. 'Unless, of course, you have some objection to this extremely bizarre union, my dear cousin Jane?'

'Oh my, no,' said Jane, her voice trembling. She had never felt less capable of coherent speech. Dear Lord, she had made the most inutterable fool of herself. How could she have leaped to such a stupid conclusion, and then to have spoken so to Simon like a veritable fishwife, when she might have known he would never— Oh, God, if only the floor would simply open up and swallow her.

She paused in her self-inflicted diatribe, suddenly aware of odd little bursts of happiness that were sizzling upward through her fog of gloom like small incendiary rockets. Simon was not betrothed to Winifred, and never had been! Moreover, he had said those three wonderful, magical words. He loved her! Or at least he had up to a few minutes ago. Then she had virtually flayed him with her tongue, revealing herself to be not only shatter-brained, but vituperative and intemperate – saying things she did not even mean! Dear God, had she actually said that she found his touch distasteful? She had undoubtedly driven him from her forever, and it was no better than she deserved, she ruminated despairingly.

Diana moved to her husband with a soft rustle of her skirts. 'Dearest,' she said, 'I wonder if I could speak with you – outside.' She shot him a meaningful glance.

'Eh? Oh, of course. And then, perhaps, we might consider some breakfast. I saw the landlady headed toward the kitchen, and if my ears – and my nose – do not deceive me, ham and eggs are underway.' Jared tucked his wife's arm in his own and stepped to the door, grasping Gerard's arm as he did so.

'But I need to talk to Janie,' protested the young man. 'I must make plans for Harry and me to—'

'Later, halfling,' said Jared firmly, tightening his grip.

'But— Oh. Yes. Breakfast.' Gerard moved hastily to join the others, beckoning to Harry to follow. Lissa and Marcus were the last to leave the room, seemingly adrift in their own world and floating several inches off the floor.

'Ah,' breathed Simon as the door closed behind the group. 'Dare I dream that we are actually to be left to ourselves?' He turned to face Jane.

Lord, she was beautiful. Her hair was a tumbled mess and her gown had long since lost any claim to propriety, stained as it was with blood and hanging from her slight body in a mass of wrinkles. But the early morning breeze that fluttered the curtains at the window stirred the silken curls that drifted over her temples, and her eyes were like summer mist. He ached with the need to pull her into his arms.

Jane moved toward him. 'Simon—' she began in a voice that was barely more than a whisper, but, taking her hand in his, he drew her into a small room that opened off the rear of the hall. It appeared to be a writing room, for it was furnished with chairs, a small settee, and a desk with ink and writing paper.

Closing the door behind him with great firmness, he pushed her gently on to the settee and sat beside her. With one finger, he drew a line along the tender, vulnerable line of her jaw.

'It seems,' he said gently, 'that we have been talking at cross purposes.'

'Oh, Simon,' she replied, lifting her eyes to his. 'I don't know what to say. What must you think of me – railing at you that way? I meant none of the awful things I said, and I feel so—'

Simon grasped her fingers in one hand, while with the other, he caressed her cheek once more. 'I take it that Winifred told you I had made her an offer, which you – understandably enough – took to mean an offer of marriage.'

'Yes,' breathed Jane tremulously. 'Diana had told me of your predicament, and I'm afraid I assumed ... Oh, Simon, I feel so stupid!'

'No, my love. To anyone in the English-speaking world, an offer from a gentleman to a lady can only mean one thing. Unless, of course, one is dealing with Winifred. Then, all rules are off. It was a perfectly simple misunderstanding, which I sincerely hope is completely cleared up. That is – regarding my attentions...?'

Jane smiled tremulously, reaching to touch with her fingers the place where Simon's lips had rested a moment before. 'When you kissed me,' – she gasped a little – 'I liked it very much,' she concluded firmly. 'And I wish you'd do it again.'

Her eyes gazing up into his, seemed to gather all the brightness of the sunrise that flooded the room, and with a groan, he gathered her into his arms. Their mouths joined in a shattering, eminently satisfying kiss that left them both shaken with wanting.

'Now then, where were we?' Simon whispered harshly at last. 'Ah, yes, when last heard from, I believe I was in the process of pouring my heart out to you. Being a tenacious sort, I would like to return to that theme so, if you don't mind the repetition – I love you, Jane Burch, and plan to keep on doing so for the rest of my life.' He pressed a soft kiss against the base of her throat before moving once more to the infinite sweetness of her lips.

He drew back a moment later. 'Well?' he asked, his voice ragged.

Jane laughed softly against his mouth. 'Of course, I love you, Simon. I've loved you for so long and so hard that I am positively embarrassed by my feelings for you.' She drew back just a little to look at him. 'But I thought you disliked me excessively.'

'Disliked you?' Simon's voice was blank with astonishment.

'Well, you kept telling me about your ideal wife, a biddable comfortable sort, who certainly did not sound like me.'

'I have no recollection of such a conversation,' said Simon hastily. 'Who would want a biddable, comfortable wife, when he could have an enchanting termagant instead?'

He bent once again to silence the protest forming on her lips and for several long moments the room was silent except for the sound of the breeze that ruffled the curtains, and the small indistinguishable murmurs emanating from the settee. At last, Jane placed her fingertips against Simon's chest, and he drew away very slightly.

'I think,' she said unsteadily, 'that we had better join the others.'

Simon drew a long, shuddering breath. 'I expect you're right. I can't allow you to corrupt my maidenly virtue, you seductive wench. However,' he added as he kissed her fingertips, 'I have by no means exhausted my feelings on this subject. For one thing, we must set a wedding date.'

'Oh.' Jane glanced at him from beneath the thick fringe of her lashes. 'Is this to be a marriage proposal as well as a declaration of your undying devotion?'

'Of course,' returned Simon promptly. 'My military training, you know. Once the rough ground has been covered, it's time to move in the heavy artillery.'

Jane laughed softly and reached to caress Simon's cheek with one, last, feather-soft kiss. She thought she would burst from the happiness that flowed through her in a joyous tide.

They found the others in the coffee room, tucking into the generous repast provided by Mrs Biddle and the two village girls she had called in that morning especially for the occasion. Lady Hermione and her mother had descended to join the group and were seated, engaged in low conversation, a little distance from the others.

'Ah!' said Jared, looking up from his coffee. He grinned at Simon and Jane, observing their clasped hands and blissful smiles.

'Yes, indeed, brother,' Simon said briskly. He knew his happiness must be as obvious as though it were running from him in rivulets. 'You may wish us happy.'

'By Jove!' Jared scrambled to his feet, as did Diana. 'This is good news. Though certainly not unexpected.'

'Jane!' cried Diana, her eyes sparkling with pleasure. 'Simon! I knew it!' She flung an arm about each of them in an exuberant hug.

Lissa and Marcus moved toward them as well, offering congratulations and more hugs. Lady Wimpole offered her felicitations in a twitter of platitudes, and Lady Hermione, remnants of her own happiness still to be perceived in her pebble-bright eyes, offered prim expressions of good will that seemed genuine and unforced. Last of all came Gerard and Harry, hands thrust out. This, however, Jane would not countenance, and she swept her brother and his be-skirted friend into a laughing embrace.

Diana turned to her husband. 'Did I not tell you, my love? Aunt Amabelle was right in sending for us, was she not? Oh!' she stopped guiltily, pressing her fingers to her mouth.

'Ah,' said Simon, laughing. 'I see it all now. "Respite from the duties of motherhood", was it?'

'Of course not,' retorted Jared. 'It was merely another fiendish female plot against an unsuspecting male. Aagh!' he yelped in an exaggerated expression of pain as Diana pinched him. 'Perhaps I phrased that rather badly,' he concluded with a bland smile at his wife.

'I should think so,' she said severely, somewhat ruining her effect by sticking her tongue out at him.

Jared bent to plant a kiss on Jane's forehead, declaring his delight that Simon had showed such acumen in his choice of a bride.

'You will be a most welcome addition to our family, my dear,' he said, smiling broadly. 'I suppose in time you will forgive us for inflicting Simon on you in Diana's wily scheme to claim you as a sister.'

Jane flashed a mischievous smile as she raised her eyes to Jared's. 'Thank you, my lord. I shall try to bear up under the burden you have thrust on me.'

'Here now,' interposed Simon, grasping Jane's hand to pull her to him. 'It's a sad state of affairs when a man's family conspires to turn his beloved against him.'

Diana laughed unrepentantly.

'But,' Simon said, after a moment, 'should we not be on our way? Our guests will be out and about before—'

'I expect so,' agreed Jared.

'Aunt Amabella will be quite beside herself at our news,' caroled Diana, gathering bonnet and shawl to her.

Thus, the group – all but Lady Hermione and her mother, of course – made preparations once more to set out for Selworth.

To Jane's delight, Jared informed them with great solemnity that Gerard and Harry were riding in Harry's curricle, and since Lissa and Marcus would be riding with himself and Diana in their carriage, he very much feared Simon and Jane would have to ride by themselves in Simon's curricle.

Once on the highway, Jane was intensely conscious of Simon's nearness on the seat beside her and, delighting in her new proprietary rights, she snuggled close and pressed an occasional kiss on Simon's ear. The curricle slowed its pace and finally stopped at the side of the road.

In the silence of the golden morning that surrounded them, Simon took Jane into his arms once again. After a few moments, he drew back to gaze at her with satisfaction.

'To quote the bard one last time, "All's well that ends well", don't you think? Winifred is out of our lives, as are Charles and his ghastly fiancée. Marc and Lissa are back together, hopefully for good, this time, and I – I am the happiest man on the planet at this moment.'

He allowed himself to bathe in the magic of her eyes, now the color of sunshine on summer clouds. 'Now that I do not need to sell Selworth, do you think you would rather live here than at Ashwood!'

'Anywhere, as long as it is with you,' sighed Jane. She added after a moment, 'Although, I was wondering if we might not live in London, just for awhile. You see ... Have I ever told you about my sisters, Patience and Jessica?'

'No, you have not,' replied Simon in a tone of deep foreboding. 'And I rather feel I'm going to need fortifying before you do.'

He bent his mouth to hers once more.

Author's Note

A *Midsummer Night's Dream* has always been one of my favorites among Shakespeare's plays. This sprightly tale of magic and mixups seems to me to be particularly suited to a Regency background, thus, Gentle Reader, you found herein the story of a country house production of the play, in which the tribulations of the characters in the book reflect those of the Bard's hapless lovers.

A Midsummer Night's Dream is set mainly in a forest outside Athens, a few days before the wedding of the Duke of Athens to Hippolyta, Queen of the Amazons. In the forest, as the result of a domestic dispute, Oberon, King of the Fairies, casts a spell on his queen, Titania, resulting in Titania's infatuation with a lowly rustic, Bottom, whose head has been magically replaced by that of an ass. Two sets of lovers, part of the duke's court, also find themselves at odds, and in an effort to solve their problems, Oberon dispatches his elfin henchman, Puck, to make all right. Either by chance or by mischief, Puck creates even more problems for the four young people, and comedic chaos ensues. Of course, by the end of the play, all the lovers are happily reunited and the curtain falls to Puck's assurances,

'... this weak and idle theme,
No more yielding than a dream.'

CANCELLED